Jackson's expression was stony. "You don't think much of me, do you?"

Bitterness he'd have no way of understanding colored Cat's answer. Bitterness and piled-up, long-buried resentment. "You've been gone a long ti̶me.̶ ̶I don't ̶think of you at all."

Apparently Jackso̶n̶ ̶...̶ ̶her hostility.

Cat's feelings, alwa̶y̶s̶ ̶...̶ ̶was concerned, softene̶d̶ ̶...̶ ̶what had happened wasn't his fault, or at the very least, it had been as much her doing as his. Now, forced by circumstances, he had to return to a lifestyle and a town he hated.

Cat couldn't be a part of making him stay. She couldn't tell him the truth about her daughter, now or ever. The pain of not telling replaced the fear, and a chill settled in her chest, spreading icy hurt to every part of her body.

Dear Reader,

Have you ever made the wrong decision for the right reason? Or the right decision for the wrong reason? If so, you have a lot in common with Wild Cat Darnell. She's a hardworking single mother with a secret, and Jackson Gray is about to discover the truth.

When Jackson comes back to Engerville, North Dakota, he intends to stay just long enough to help his father get back on his feet after a farming accident. Then Jackson sees Cat again and he knows leaving is going to be hard. After he meets Cat's little girl, leaving gets a whole lot harder.

I visited several small towns in North Dakota to set the scene for this book. My fictional town of Engerville is about fifty miles north of Fargo. The land is fertile and grows a bountiful crop for the hardworking farmers of that area, but the harsh winters make it a tough way to earn a living.

My respect for these hardy descendants of Norwegian, German and Swedish pioneers knows no bounds. I visited a small-town museum and listened to two elderly ladies of the historical society describe how the pioneers walked barefoot across Minnesota to get to North Dakota—there were no cobblers and no way for pioneers to replace their shoes. Picture a covered wagon pulled by oxen, lumbering slowly across an untracked prairie. Father sits in the driver's seat. Behind the wagon a young woman picks her way through brambles and gopher holes, barefoot. All the way to the Goose River in North Dakota, where the Indians told the settlers they'd find good farmland.

Cat and Jackson are descendants of those pioneers, and they're just as strong, just as brave and every bit as stubborn. I hope you enjoy reading about them.

I love to hear from readers. You can contact me at the following e-mail address: Jade@jadetaylor.com.

Sincerely,

Jade Taylor

Wild Cat and the Marine

Jade Taylor

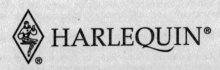

HARLEQUIN®

TORONTO • NEW YORK • LONDON
AMSTERDAM • PARIS • SYDNEY • HAMBURG
STOCKHOLM • ATHENS • TOKYO • MILAN • MADRID
PRAGUE • WARSAW • BUDAPEST • AUCKLAND

ISBN 0-373-71156-5

WILD CAT AND THE MARINE

Dedicated to my parents, Robert C. and Idell Beam Groves, for all they gave me, and especially for raising me with a love for books.

For the friends and family who supported my dream:

My siblings, Roberts, Jr., Albert, Roy, Sarah, Bertha, Tommy, David and Harry. We were a rowdy bunch of kids who grew up knowing how much we loved each other. We still do.

Bill, Sheri and Holly Ann Groves. You have my heart.

My critique partner, Alisa Clifford, for all she taught me; my friends at Midwest Fiction Writers, especially Pamela Bauer, Stacy Verdick Case and Rosemary Heim; LaVyrle Spencer for her wonderful books, for inspiring me to write and for telling me about RWA; my editors, Beverley Sotolov, who liked my story and bought it, and Johanna Raisanen, for making it better.

My friends at American Financial Printing for December 10, 2001 and for many other things less dramatic, but just as meaningful.

Jane Lindstrom for calling me up one day and saying, "Let's write a book."

PROLOGUE

BEFORE SIX-YEAR-OLD Catherine Darnell went to sleep, she said a prayer. Squinching her eyes shut, she swiped tangled black hair away from her face and pressed thin, scratched hands together under her chin. She recited the appeal she made nearly every night. ''Please God, don't let us move somewhere new tonight. I really want to stay here so Bobby and Arlene Sanders can be my friends forever. Don't let Daddy get mad at his boss again. Please, please, God, make Mommy come back and live with me and Daddy. Amen.''

God didn't answer that prayer, either. Two nights later, her father woke her in the middle of the night, kissed her once and carried her out to their rusty brown Ford Maverick. He laid her on the back seat along with two battered suitcases, sheets, blankets and the chipped ceramic figure of a rearing black horse he'd given her two months ago. Daddy put her mother's jade necklace around her neck and whispered something about being sorry, then got into the driver's seat.

Catherine watched as her father used a leather string to tie his straight black hair into a ragged ponytail. He pitched his cigarette out the window, tossed the road map onto the seat beside him and slammed the old car into gear. The wheels tossed gravel from the worn rear tires as he gunned the car out of the driveway and left the shabby little rented house on Roosevelt Street, her mother and all things familiar behind.

CHAPTER ONE

HEAD DOWN, Catherine Darnell trudged the worn path from the barn to her home. Halfway to her destination, she lifted her gaze from the uneven ground. The low-slung, one-story ranch house blended into the North Dakota prairie as if it had sprouted from the furrowed earth. Nothing about the dull siding, weathered gray where the white paint had peeled away, set it apart from the sameness of the surrounding farm land. It was as ordinary and unassuming as the plowed rows drifting off into the distance behind it.

The spring air reenergized her and her steps quickened. For all the faults the old house had—and those faults were beyond counting—it still welcomed her at the end of a long day with the comfort only a home could give. Her home. The thought warmed Cat, despite the chill breeze finding its way through her loose-knit sweater.

A strong wind sprang up and whipped the clothes on the line in the yard into a frenzied dance. She'd forgotten about the clothes. Evening dew hadn't fallen yet, so they'd still be dry. Every bone in her body ached with the weariness of all the chores she'd rushed through that day. For a few minutes, she'd thought her work almost finished. Taking the clothes from the line and folding them, then bringing them inside to iron or put away meant at least another hour. Finally, supper for Joey. For herself, coffee and a sandwich would have sufficed, but her daughter deserved—no, needed—a good hot meal. At eight, Joey was small for her age.

Cat smiled, fatigue forgotten, as she pictured Joey stepping out of the shower and tugging on faded pink pajamas. She hoped the picture was accurate. Joey was a dreamer, forever forgetting her chores and, instead, picking up a horse magazine and mooning over some tall Kentucky-bred stallion, or turning on the television and becoming deeply engrossed in a Disney movie.

After grabbing a laundry basket from the porch, she hurriedly unpinned the shirts and sheets and towels and jeans and underwear from the clothesline. It took longer than it should have; the cold made her fingers clumsy. After the last piece had been placed in the basket, she caught it up and hurried to the kitchen door.

The wind sucked at the worn old door as she opened it and slammed it hard behind her. A grunt of annoyance accompanied the accusing glare she cast toward the drafty entranceway. The basket handles bit into the blisters that had popped up on her palms while she shoveled manure and wheatstraw from the barn stalls. She winced and shifted her grip. Her hands should have hardened to the work by now, but they hadn't.

As Cat entered the living room, Joey looked up from her seat on the floor in front of the TV, then scrambled to her feet. "I'll help you carry the basket, Mom."

At least she was in her pajamas. Cat grinned ruefully at her offspring. "Never mind, Teddy Bear. Why don't you set the table for dinner while I put away these clothes. I'll reheat the stew from lunch. That won't take long."

"Okay." Joey sat down on the floor and turned her

attention back to the television, dismissing her mother with a completeness Cat couldn't help admiring.

"Now, please," she insisted. It was always tough to put a sharp edge in her voice with Joey. Well, not always, but mostly. Joey was a good kid, but on a bad day she ranked right up there with those cartoon Simpsons. The ones she wasn't supposed to watch. The ones Cat gave in and let her watch once in a great while and regretted immediately. She shook her head at the sight of Joey trying to stand up an inch at a time, keeping an unwavering gaze glued to the TV screen. She carried the basket of clothes into her bedroom.

Dropping the basket on the bed, she glanced at the answering machine. The red indicator light blinked twice slowly, then paused and blinked twice again. Two messages. She wasn't expecting any calls. It was probably Tommy Karl wanting Joey. Those two were always up to something.

She pressed the button to play the messages. A cool, official-sounding voice began to speak.

"Catherine? Greg here. Greg Lundstrom from Engerville State Bank. We need to get together and talk about the mortgage on your farm. There are two quarterly payments overdue now and, frankly, I'm very troubled. Call me as soon as possible, will you? Thanks."

A cold chill settled on Cat as nausea hit her stomach. She backed up to the bed, still staring at the phone in disbelief. Her legs gave way and she collapsed on Aunt Johanna's colorful handmade wedding ring quilt.

Her hands shook. She clasped them together in an unsuccessful effort to stop the trembling, then untwined her fingers to reach for the jade necklace at her throat. Nervously, she clutched the beads. The spring payment had come due last week, but she'd been sure she could get an extension. In the confusion and grief of burying her father two months ago, she hadn't even thought about the January payment. Why hadn't her father taken care of it?

He hadn't said a word to her about being short of cash when he bought RugRat, the newest addition to their small herd of horses. But then, he wouldn't. It was like him to joyfully hand over the last bit of their cash for a pricey colt they couldn't afford.

Now, she had to make up two payments. How could she do that? There'd been no horse ready to sell since the previous fall. It was high odds whether she could get RugRat ready by October and not a chance before then. Her jewelry business, more hobby than a means of support, brought in a bit, but not nearly enough.

Cat's hands clenched so tightly her short, ragged nails dug into the new blisters. She'd neglected the horses' training schedule badly. Too much to do just keeping them fed, groomed, their stalls clean and the vet bills paid. The horses were beautiful and she loved them as much as Joey did, but her father's way with them had skipped her and gone directly to her daughter. It was too bad Joey was only eight. If she'd been older, maybe she could have taken over the training.

Cat stood up, stiffening her legs in grim determination. Dammit, she wouldn't take refuge in foolish wishes. There had to be a way out, and she'd find it. This broken-down, beat-up, almost useless ranch was their home, the only real home she'd ever known, and no way in hell would she let the bank take it.

She pushed the play button to listen to the second message. Cassidy Gray's usually cheerful voice was somber.

"Pop's been hurt awfully bad, Cat. I knew you'd want

to know. I'm at the hospital with him, now. I'm going to call Jackson to see if he can come home. I'll call again as soon as I know more about Pop's condition. Bye.''

If finding out she needed to make two payments to the bank had sent her reeling, then the news of her nearest neighbor's injuries and his son's probable return was the knockout punch. She sagged back onto the bed, her legs betraying her again. Her heart raced in frantic beats. Jackson back in Engerville? The thought sent excitement coursing through her body, warming her with sudden speed. A second later, the brief burst of joy faded and a nightmare wave of dread overwhelmed her. Somehow, she had to avoid Jackson. Stay as far away from him as was humanly possible. It was her only chance.

CORPORAL JUAN SANCHEZ LOOKED up as Jackson Gray entered the company office. ''Hey, Jackson, it's about time you got here. You've had three phone calls in the past hour. New babe?''

Jackson rubbed his eyes. They burned as if cinders had worked their way under the lids. ''Give me a break, Sanchez. I didn't get back to barracks last night.''

''It's not me you should worry about, Red. Captain's been asking for you. You're late.''

''Five minutes, for crying out loud! What's the problem?'' He watched Juan toss a handful of papers into the ''out'' bin.

''Not my problem, Jack. Yours. Captain Ricky is ready to chop you into little, bitty pieces and have you for lunch. What'd you do?'' Sanchez practically salivated with curiosity.

Jackson glared at the company clerk. ''Why don't you tell the Captain I'm here, Juan? If he wants to see me that bad, then he's not going to appreciate your holding up the show.''

"Okay, no problem, but I wanted to talk to you about our trucking deal with Marty. He needs us to make up our mind whether or not we're with him.''

"Sure we are. We already decided that. We'll both have our release by September.''

"Yeah, well, the word up the line is that headquarters is going to offer up to three months early release to anybody whose discharge date is between April and October. I guess they recruited too many guys. Whaddaya think?''

"It would be a chance to get a head start finding a place to stay in Seattle. We'll talk about it later.''

"Sergeant Gray?'' The curt voice belonged to a lanky male in sharply creased khakis, who stepped through the hallway door into the room. The officer threw an irritated frown in Sanchez's direction, then glared at Jackson. "I'm glad you could make it. Come with me to my office, please.''

Without his even thinking about it, Jackson's body stiffened into a near-attention pose. "Yes sir, Captain Richards.''

Sanchez hurriedly bent to his filing, his tan cheeks highlighted with pink. Jackson repressed the urge to snicker at his friend's sudden industry and quickly followed the company commander down the short hallway, wondering what he'd done to attract the captain's attention.

The captain walked around his desk and sat down in the chair. He shuffled some papers, looking preoccupied, then glanced up at Jackson who maintained a rigid pose.

"At ease, Sergeant.''

Jackson snapped smartly into parade rest, his feet

slightly apart, his hands behind his back, one nesting the other. He stared straight ahead at a position on the pale green wall just over the Captain's head.

"I'm sorry to be giving you bad news, Sergeant," Richards picked up a pencil and twirled it between his dark fingers as he continued, "but that's in my job description."

Jackson's heart leapt to his throat. This wasn't what he'd prepared himself for. Bad news to a soldier only meant one thing—trouble at home. He shot a quick glance at Captain Richards's somber face. A frown marred the lean features.

"Your father has been badly injured."

Jackson struggled with a surge of dismay. "Sir?"

"Your sister called for you early this morning."

For one dizzying moment, the office spun. Jackson fought for control. The spinning stopped with a jerk that left him shaken. The Captain waited for his reply. "Is he dead?" Force of habit made him add, "Sir."

"No! No. He's hurt, but your sister says he's holding his own."

Jackson's heart banged hard against the chest wall surrounding it. His voice sounded raspy as he asked, "May I leave, Captain? I'd like to call her and find out what's happening."

"Sit down, Sergeant. You don't look too steady. Take the near chair. Relax a moment. Your sister is calling this number sometime in the next ten minutes."

Jackson sat on the edge of the straight-backed wooden chair, reluctant to lean back and relax. Sitting in the Captain's presence made him uneasy, even if it had been his suggestion—order. "Thank you, Captain."

"You're a tough man to locate, Gray. I've had the

duty sergeant at the barracks up half the night waiting for you to come in.''

"I'm sorry, sir.'' His reply was automatic, his thoughts in turmoil, barely aware of what he said.

Richards growled his reply. "No need to be. You're a good-looking pup. You're entitled to spend your nights screwing around if you choose to. It's your time.''

"Sir, I wasn't screw— I wasn't out messing around.''

The Captain looked disbelieving.

Jackson's body wanted to twitch under the man's metal gaze. He didn't have to explain. Let the Captain think what he wanted to. In fairness, though, Richards had reason to think as he did and his commanding officer didn't have to let him wait for Cassidy's call in his office.

Jackson was suddenly relieved that his explanation for being gone all night was legitimate, even if it had started as a bored impulse. "Sir, I'm sure you've heard about the forest fires north of Richmond?''

Richards nodded. "It's been very dry.''

"I spent the night with volunteers digging a fire line to protect Cottage Grove, one of the suburbs lying in the fire's path.''

Captain Richards was obviously skeptical. "Very good of you, Gray. Why didn't you say so?''

Jackson barely managed to keep his voice even. "As you said, Captain. It was my free time.'' If one of the guys hadn't suggested the trip… If he hadn't jumped at the chance to leave the red-brick barracks, he might have spent the evening at the NCO club and had the kind of night the captain suspected.

"Yes, but—'' The phone rang. Richards picked up the receiver. "Captain Richards here. Yes, Mrs. Alexander, he's with me now…. Of course… Not at all.'' He handed the receiver to Jackson, then stood. "Take your time, Sergeant. I'm going to walk over to Colonel Blackstone's office."

"Thank you, sir."

The captain hesitated a moment. "I hope things work out okay."

"Yes, sir. Thank you, sir."

The door closed with a quiet click. Jackson looked at the receiver in his hand as if it were a grenade with the pin already pulled. If he didn't hear the words, then it wouldn't be true, at least for him. As long as he avoided raising the phone to his ear, he could put off finding out his father had died in the night while he was off helping strangers.

A sudden ache wrapped around his heart. He couldn't avoid the truth that easily. He put the phone to his ear. "I'm here."

"Jackson?"

His sister's familiar voice triggered a strong wave of homesickness, a longing for her sweet pixie face and, unexpectedly, a nostalgic picture of the farm he hated. "Yeah, Cass. How is he?"

"Jackson, where've you been? I woke up your captain three times last night. This morning, I mean."

"Hell, Cass, what does it matter where I was?" He clutched the receiver so tightly his knuckles turned white. "Sorry. Just tell me. Is Pop dead?"

"Not yet... I mean, no! No. He's doing okay, the doctor said."

"Okay? What does that mean, exactly? How badly is he hurt? What happened?" He stood and paced as far from the desk as the phone cord allowed.

"He's pretty bad, Jackson. He's banged up something

terrible, but the doctor said he'd live, unless the internal bleeding started again.''

''Cass, what happened to him?''

''He bought a new bull from Bertha Gillis. A big, black mean bastard! Pop went out to the barn to feed him and opened his stall door to check something. We aren't sure what. Anyway, the bull knocked him down and stomped on him. Good thing he'd been dehorned. If he hadn't been, Pop would be dead.''

''Oh, damn! Was he alone?''

''Buddy Sutherland was with him. You remember Buddy, don't you?''

He thought hard for a moment, then the name joined a face. ''Yeah. Little guy. Works odd jobs, or used to. Kinda drifts from one farm to the next.''

''He's been helping Pop since January. Anyway, he managed to distract the bull and get him off Pop, then Blue drove the bull into another stall. Would you believe the same dog that let Mom's calico cat run him out of the house could take on a young bull that way? Thank goodness he was there! Then Buddy slammed the door shut and called for help.''

''You said 'banged up.' What do you mean?''

''Three ribs are broken. His shoulder is dislocated. Doctor Lind said his kidneys were bruised and a piece of his liver broke off. His knee. Other stuff, too. Can you come home?''

His brain couldn't take it all in. The image of his tall, work-hardened father lying in a hospital bed hit him hard. Pop could die. ''Oh, Lord.''

''Can you come?''

Her question didn't make sense. ''Come home? Cass, I can't. You know that.''

''Because of the Marines? Or do you mean that

blowup you two had when you left home? For crying out loud, Jackson, that's ancient history! Pop needs you, now."

An awful ache in his chest made breathing difficult. "Not me. He wouldn't want me there."

"Jackson, he might be dying."

"He wouldn't want me, even then." Jackson's tightened fist threatened to crush the phone.

"You don't know that."

"Has he asked for me?" He threw the challenge out, not knowing if he wanted to hear the answer.

A reluctant silence filled the space before she spoke. "I've only talked to him a little bit. He's pretty foggy with the painkillers and all. I know he wants to see you, Jackson. You're still his son and he's still your father."

Bitterness prodded the old pain. "I'll never step foot in Engerville again. You may not remember, Cass, but I do. He told me if I left, I wouldn't be welcome back. If he wanted me, maybe... Aw, hell, it's ridiculous to discuss it. I'm not coming home, Cass. I can't."

"Even if Pop is dying? You still won't forgive him?"

The accusation hurt. It wasn't true. Couldn't be. His answer grated against the bitter memories. "You have that backward. He'll never forgive me...and I'm not sure I want him to, so drop it. I'm sorry, Cass. I can't come home."

"No matter how much he needs you?"

The anger in her voice shamed him. He and Cass had always been close. His hurt forced an answer he didn't want to give, yet couldn't hold back. "Yeah. No matter how much he needs me."

"In that case, I'd better hang up. They're going to do some X rays and I want to be there to see what they find. I'm sorry for you, Jackson. Sorry you can't forgive and forget, but our father is the one I'm worried about right now.''

''You'll call me if anything changes?'' There was no reply. She'd already hung up. Jackson loosened his white-fisted grip on the phone and replaced the receiver.

Engerville, North Dakota, so many miles—a lifetime—away, but the memories were here in the room with him. His big, red-haired father working beside him in the fields. The tiny high school where he'd led the basketball team to the state championship when no school as small as theirs had ever won it. And Catherine, the girl he'd taken to the senior prom. Her image came to mind with such sharpness it might have been yesterday: tall, skinny, shy, too serious. Green eyes, high cheekbones, a tendency to hide her thoughts behind a sweeping curtain of black hair and, of course, the most vivid portrait of her—moonlight pouring through the windshield of Pop's old truck, washing all the color from her face, making her emerald eyes gleam with an intensity he'd not known she was capable of.

Jackson shook his head, angry at himself for being tempted. No, he wasn't going back. He'd never go back. He waited until he had the lump in his throat under control before he left the Captain's office.

''I COULD DELIVER THAT FEED out to your place on Saturday, Cat,'' Marvin Nordstrom pointed out as he heaved the last bag of feed onto the truck bed.

''I should have called you last week, Marvin. The feed bin is nearly empty. I'd better take it myself.''

Marvin looked dubious. His brief glance traveled up and down her slender figure. ''How will you get it unloaded?''

''I'll manage.'' Cat didn't have the muscles to be a

rancher. She knew it and so did Marvin. The place needed a man to run it, but Cat didn't have a man and certainly didn't want one. She'd take care of it by herself, as she always had.

"If you have a problem, call. I'll have Rafe stop by when he makes his rounds Saturday and unload it for you."

Turning a grateful smile on the store owner, she said, "Thanks, Marvin. I'll let you know."

"Don'tcha go lifting those heavy bags by yourself," he insisted. "Just yell if you need help. See ya." The overweight feed store owner backed away, then turned to go into his store.

Cat lifted the tailgate and banged it closed. The metal had taken a beating over the years and needed to be forced into place. The squeal of air brakes startled her. She looked up. Across the street, a dusty Greyhound bus rolled to a halt. She watched as the driver left his seat and, a moment later, returned to it. The bus pulled away from the curb and continued down the street, revealing a lone figure standing beside a drab green duffel.

Her memory of him kept trying to fit over the reality. A tall man with short red hair and wide shoulders returned her stare, not the slim eighteen-year-old boy with a dazzling, wicked smile. That smile had enthralled her the first time she met him. Now, she saw the adult version as he recognized her. Its power hadn't diminished with time.

CHAPTER TWO

"HEY," HE CALLED. "Cat? Wild Cat Darnell?" The tall Marine grabbed his duffel and loped across the street toward her, narrowly dodging a white Chevy tooling down the street much faster than was safe.

Her breath caught in her throat, just as it had the first time she'd met him. "Wel— Welcome home, Jackson."

He grinned at her, dropped his duffel, then gave her a bear hug. "It sure is you! I thought so, but I could hardly believe my eyes. You haven't changed a bit."

Oh, but I have, Jackson. I have. Cat tried to breathe and couldn't. He held her too tight. His arms were steel bands pressing her against a rock-hard chest. For the first time in years, a pool of heat centered in her breasts and trickled down her stomach. His embrace felt warm and familiar and, at the same time, dangerous. How had she forgotten, even for a minute the secret he must never guess? She tried to get away. He must have felt her movement. His grip loosened and, nose still jammed against his khaki shirt, she drew in warm, male-scented air. Her legs turned to water. Jackson chose that moment to release her and she stumbled.

He caught her again. "Easy there! I didn't mean to knock you off your feet."

For a single dizzying second, she ached to remain in his arms. Reason returned. She couldn't.

Cat stepped away from the closeness of Jackson Gray.

It was difficult to appear casual as she asked the first question that came to mind. "Is someone meeting you?"

He hesitated, then shook his head. "Nobody knows I'm coming. I didn't call." He glanced away, his fair cheeks a pinker shade than usual.

Embarrassed, she guessed.

"Not sure of my welcome, you know," he muttered to the sidewalk.

Sympathy washed over her. "Cass called me the day after the accident. She hoped you'd choose to come home." She took a deep breath, willed the butterflies in her stomach to quiet their frantic clamor, and reluctantly decided there was no help for it. "I'll give you a lift out to the farm."

He brightened. "That's good of you, Wild Cat. Thanks."

"Nobody calls me Wild Cat anymore," she observed, as calmly as if his use of her old nickname hadn't stirred a hundred heart-stopping memories.

He laughed. The same careless laugh that used to make her heart bump against her chest. And still did.

"Well, I've never stopped thinking of you as 'Wild Cat Darnell.' There was a time when you'd try anything. Nothing was too outrageous. Remember that Halloween we hoisted the coach's old Volkswagen up to the roof of the school? And draped it with crepe paper in the school colors? It rained all night and the paper broke. Colors ran over the car until it looked like it had been painted with pieces of confetti." Jackson chuckled as he stared down at her, warm regard in his eyes.

Remembering, Cat thought. Well, damned if she'd give him any sign that she remembered, too. She made an attempt at airy indifference. "I've grown up, Jackson. Didn't you?"

"What's the fun in growing up? Next thing you'll be asking me if I've decided to return to farming." A snide smile spread across his angular face.

Same old Jackson, she thought. *I've changed. He hasn't.* Despite the rush of heat his smile caused, she took a firm grip on her emotions. "No. I won't. I already know the answer. Let's go. I've got chores to do at the ranch."

"Right. That's one thing that never changes."

He followed her around to the driver's side and held the door for her. One large hand hovered next to her elbow as if he would help her climb into the truck. Hurriedly, she rushed to get in by herself, knowing she'd react to his touch the same way cattle did to an electric prod.

He must have changed a little bit, though. The old Jackson had been too carefree to think about opening a door for a woman unless his father had an eagle eye on him. She watched as Jackson loped around the truck, threw his duffel carelessly into the back and climbed into the cab with her. For a big man, he was graceful—lean-hipped, wide-shouldered, and too sexy. And totally unaware of his breathtaking attraction.

Cat drew in a deep, calming breath. She'd been lonely too long. He endangered her peace of mind and she needed to stay far away from him.

As he closed the door, he said, "Thanks for the lift, Cat…Catherine."

The cab, roomy when only she and Joey were in it, became tiny as he laid one arm along the seat back, dangerously close to her shoulder. She retreated into censure. "Since when would a neighbor *not* offer a ride?"

Jackson busied himself with fastening his seat belt.

"It's been a long time, Cat. You know that. Cut me a little slack." He glanced out the window, then back at her and changed the subject. "Tell me what's changed since I left. Cass tries, but she doesn't remember our group of kids. Fill me in on what's happened to the Dragons of Engerville High."

His mention of the school's team name brought memories of their high school years back with a hard focus on Jackson, the prince, and the girl who was Engerville's blond princess. A bitter stir of jealousy replaced the heat his nearness caused. Of course, he wanted to know about Rebeka. Mutinous anger shot through her. Well, he could damn well find out from someone else. "Remember Roy Thoreson?"

He shot her a sideways look of unexplained disgruntlement. "Sure. Your boyfriend for a while in our senior year. Editor of the school newspaper." He hesitated, then grudgingly added, "And pretty darn good for a kid."

Cat downshifted at a red light and looked quickly at the man beside her. He'd matured physically in a powerful, shockingly attractive way. His beard-darkened cheeks had fascinating shadows and angles her hand itched to explore, but above the sensual lips were a pair of cold blue eyes that belonged to a man she no longer knew.

How could this man's eyes flash intimate warmth one moment and look right through her the next? Jackson might be two men now. A little bit of the one she remembered and the rest of him a stranger. She returned her gaze to the road ahead, determined to resist this new Jackson. "Roy's a reporter for the *Traill County Tribune,* now. The *Express* offered him a job in Fargo, but he turned it down."

Jackson's eyebrows shot up. "He actually turned down a newspaper job in Fargo to stay in this nowhere town? Is he still hanging around you or does he have another reason?"

"Some of us like living here, Jackson," Cat reminded him.

Jackson's cheeks reddened and he looked out the window. "Sorry. I have no business bad-mouthing Engerville," he said.

He turned back to her, his engaging smile in place again.

"You know something? I'm so nervous about what Pop is going to say when he sees me that I really wasn't thinking. I didn't intend to be rude." His lips twisted in rueful self-derision. "Why did you stay, Cat? You told me you'd be leaving, too, in the fall."

She glanced at him and couldn't help smiling at the stranger beside her. Despite the foreign air about him, he was still the boy she'd spent her high school years tagging along behind. Still the boy who hated the sameness of life in a farming community. Still the only male in Traill County who made her heart beat faster. With a straight face, she said, "No big mystery. I stay for the night life."

He snorted with laughter. "Are you talking about the tavern or the diner? I'm serious. Tell me."

Of course, she couldn't tell him the truth, though for a split second, that's what she wanted to do. His laughter brought back so many memories. Cat resisted the crazy impulse and shrugged. "I meant to. Things happen."

"I guess so, but you sure sounded like you wanted to leave as bad as I did. What happened to you?"

Cat wondered if she had the nerve to admit she only pretended a desire to leave Engerville because that's what he wanted. Truly, he was the only person who could have convinced her to leave the home she loved, but that was years in the past. He no longer had that power. She was indifferent to him. Touching the jade necklace around her throat as if it were a charm, she felt her stomach contract with tension.

Five minutes alone with him and she ached to tell him. Hurriedly, she diverted his attention with the one bit of news certain to interest him. "Did you know Rebeka and her husband are looking for a summer home in Engerville?"

"Really?"

Cat expected more interest, or at least a smidgen of surprise, from him. "They have a winter home in Virginia," she added. That last bit of information startled him. He hadn't known he'd been living in the same state with Rebeka. Unwanted satisfaction warmed her. How far was Quantico from Richmond?

His expression revealing nothing, Jackson shrugged, his broad shoulders straining the fabric of his jacket. "Very convenient. Mild winters and a cool summer home. Most people can't afford two homes."

The truck drifted to the right a bit as she glanced at him. Cat corrected the truck's path and decided she'd better keep her attention on the road, for more reasons than avoiding a traffic accident. "Burt and Rebeka can. Everybody knows how wealthy they are."

"Does anybody care?"

His tone of voice said more than the words did. Cat hurried to fill the awkward space. "Without Burt's money, our farm would have gone under six years ago." She hadn't intended to tell him, but his attitude irked her. Of course he cared that the girl he'd been crazy about in high school had ditched him for a rich man's son, as Jackson had characterized him on that long-ago prom night. Cat liked Burt, though, and Jackson's attitude couldn't change her mind.

She might have liked Rebeka more, if the teen queen hadn't claimed Jackson as her private property from elementary school all the way through high school. Until the last three months of their senior year, the two had appeared to be joined at the hip.

Jackson looked curious. "Did he loan your dad money or something?"

"Not exactly. He bought a very expensive colt from us. Burt sells horses, hunters mostly, in Virginia and he liked the looks of the colt well enough to pay a darn good price for it."

"But your father inherited that property. How could he need money that bad?" He frowned, swiping his hand across his forehead where beads of sweat had formed. "Sorry, Cat. That's none of my business. I shouldn't have asked."

"I don't mind. The farm had a major mortgage on it when Aunt Johanna died, so it wasn't free and clear when Dad inherited it. Then Gary Jansen needed help and Dad cosigned a note when his wife was in the hospital with cancer. After she died, Gary gave up. The bank took over his farm and he couldn't pay us back."

Jackson looked disapproving. "That's too bad, Cat. Your dad shouldn't have cosigned for him. Not if he had to put the farm up for security."

His selfishness disturbed Cat. If this was the real Jackson, then she'd wasted a lot of years wanting him. Her tone more caustic than she intended it to be, she said, "It may not have been the practical thing to do, but my father wasn't famous for practicality, you know."

Jackson protested, "I didn't mean that the way it

sounded. Just that he shouldn't have risked the farm. I've helped friends before."

An unbidden chuckle escaped from Cat. "I can imagine what a footloose, carefree guy like you considers 'helping a friend.' With a ten-spot for the bar?"

Jackson's expression became stony. "You don't think much of me, do you?"

Bitterness that he'd have no way of understanding colored her answer. Bitterness and piled-up, long-buried resentment. "You've been gone a long time, Jackson. I don't think of you at all."

It had been her choice not to tell him, but the resentment didn't disappear. Apparently, Jackson didn't know how to answer her hostility. He stared out the window, watching an endless field of corn stalks slide past the truck. The sharp line of his jaw stood out against the sun-splashed window. No flicker of regret showed in his face.

Another mile to his father's farm. Cat's feelings, always inconsistent where this man was concerned, softened in sympathy. What had happened wasn't his fault, or at the very least, it was as much her doing as his. Now, forced by circumstances beyond his control, he had to return to a lifestyle and a town he hated. Nine years hadn't changed the way Jackson Gray felt about sugar beets, hogs, cows and Engerville, North Dakota.

Cat couldn't be a part of making him stay. She couldn't tell him, now or ever. The pain of not telling replaced the fear of telling. A chill settled in her chest, spreading icy hurt to every part of her body.

WHEN THE TRUCK ROLLED to a stop in his father's front yard, Jackson hesitated before opening the door. Cat's attitude puzzled him. He'd felt a rush of joy when he'd seen her across the street, like a missing part of him had suddenly been found.

He'd been stunned by the changes in her. Skinny teenager had morphed into a delightfully curved woman. Gawky adolescence left so far behind it was like looking at a different person. Different, yet the same. She still had the world's most stubborn chin. She definitely had the same gemstone eyes, but the green was deeper now. The same wide mouth, though the lower lip had a pouty fullness that hadn't been there in high school. Or if it had been, he didn't remember it. Jackson was sure he'd have remembered.

Cat still wore the jade necklace her mother had given her before she left and she still clutched the necklace when emotion got the better of her. Cat had always hoped that her parent's separation wasn't final. It was too bad her mother's accidental drowning years ago had destroyed any chance of reconciliation.

The jade beads, as green as her eyes, curved around her slender throat. The pendant, an uneven circle, lay in the vee of her shirt opening, though now her skin gleamed a darker shade against the soft denim. Her breasts made his hands itch. He reacted like a pimply teenager all over again. That part was exactly the same. He shifted uncomfortably on the hard bench seat.

The companionable catching up on hometown news and old friends hadn't happened as he'd thought it would. Still, he and Rebeka, along with Roy Thoreson and Cat, had been closer than best friends, so whatever caused her glacial manner couldn't be his doing.

"I'll stop by in a few days," he offered, just to be polite. "I'd like to talk to you and catch up on everything. I've missed all the people I knew." He paused, then continued. "I never hated anybody here, just slopping the hogs, plowing the fields, planting ten million potatoes and picking corn worms.''

She nodded, her gaze focused on something he couldn't see.

''Is that okay?'' he prompted.

Jackson studied her as she took too long to reply. Her eyes flashed green fire. Her tawny complexion reflected hours in the sun. Her blue denim shirt, though faded and obviously old, set off her straight black hair as well as the finest silk might. The color of her hair had changed, too, he realized. It used to be inky black, falling down her back. Now it seemed a shade lighter, with more texture and fullness. She wore it in a single plait, with dusky strands falling loose around her face. Her lower lip, full and sexy, disappeared for a second beneath strong white teeth. Desire shook him.

''Of course it's okay.'' Cat glanced at him, her face reflecting nothing.

He struggled to remember what he'd asked. She'd taken so long over her answer that he'd lost his concentration. Why had she hesitated? ''It's been a while. I'm not butting in, am I?''

The provocative lips widened in a delicious, pensive smile, though her answer still sounded reluctant. ''Not at all. I'll show you RugRat.''

''RugRat?'' He tried to shift his gaze and couldn't. Had she always been this incredibly desirable? Was that why she haunted his dreams?

Enthusiasm brightened her mood. ''He's our three-year-old thoroughbred-quarterhorse cross. One of six we're working with now, but Dad thought Ruggie could pay for the ranch all by himself. He's a rogue, and I'm not having much luck reforming him. Even so, I think I can get a decent price for him from Burt. He'll be worth more, if I can get him calmed a bit.''

"I'll look forward to seeing your devil horse." Hoping to see that grin again, he smiled to show he was kidding. She stared straight ahead. "Okay, then. I'll be seeing you."

Jackson watched her pull the truck out of the driveway and onto the gravel road. Why did Cat seem glad to see him one minute and angry the next? He waved, but she didn't look back.

Behind him the house waited like a dark cloud ready to descend on him. He could put it off no longer. He swung around to face old memories.

The shabby farmhouse, two stories high, surrounded by weathered barns and outbuildings, hid behind a huge maple tree. The wild roses his mother had planted covered the back side of the barn.

The acrid smell of manure and wheatstraw rode the cool breeze. Off to the right, new corn plants broke through dark soil. The sugar beets would be in the far field this year. He pictured his father atop the green and yellow tractor, the muffled roar of its engine shattering the quiet. Though he dreaded seeing him, the remembered picture brought him a sense of security he hadn't felt since he'd left Engerville. A cot in the barracks wasn't much of a home, certainly not one that could replace this familiar farmhouse.

A broken rope dangled from the barn's loft door. He and Cassidy had swung from it and then jumped to land in a pile of hay below. It could have been the same rope or another just like the one they'd used. Wooden rocking chairs and a porch swing with peeling white paint still sat on the front veranda where they'd gathered in the

late evenings to listen to Pop playing his guitar and singing country songs.

It was still the place he'd escaped from. No matter
how nostalgic he felt on seeing it again, the wide fields
still marched in furrowed rows to the horizon, interrupted only by tall pine windbreaks. Faintly, he heard
the high-pitched squeal of a hog coming from the distant
barn. If he closed his eyes, he'd be able to smell the
stink from here. He shuddered. There was nothing he
hated more than pigs.

Jackson swung his gaze back to the house. Would he
be welcome? Or would Pop stare at him coldly, wishing
he'd stayed away as Jackson had vowed he would when
he left his home that June morning. A moment of cow-
ardice pierced him to the backbone. He thought about
slinking away. Just heading to the road and loping back
toward town. He might get a ride, after all, and it wasn't
so far, if he didn't. Within a few hours he could be back
on a Greyhound bus heading to Seattle, where the rest
of his life awaited him with a new, exciting career.

The moment of indecision faded as he realized he
couldn't leave. His father needed him, whether the stubborn old man wanted to acknowledge that fact or not.
Too late, anyway. The front door opened and Cassidy
stuck her head out and shouted in delight.

"Jackson! You came! I knew you would. Oh, I'm so
glad to see you!" Then she launched herself off the
porch straight into his arms.

Cassidy held on to him as if it had been centuries
since they'd seen each other. It had only been a bit over
a year. She'd invited him to Minneapolis to meet her
new husband and to see his very new nephew. It had
been a lot longer since he'd seen Pop. In nine years,
he'd only come back once and that occasion had been

his mother's funeral. He'd arrived in town one day and left the next, hardly exchanging more than a cool hello with his grief-stricken father.

"So how's the old man?" he asked, finally setting Cass down. Her short height had given him an unfair advantage with her from the start. Now she looked up at him, a happy smile lighting her whole face.

"He's so much better, Jackson. Maybe I shouldn't have asked you to come home, but, darn it, it's way past time for you two to make up."

He gave her a freezing stare, which didn't seem to bother her at all. "I'm certainly glad he's recovered, but if this is your idea of a joke, getting me to come home on false pretenses... I can damn well tell you I don't find it a bit funny."

Cass snorted. "Oh, cool it! I told you the exact truth. Pop is doing better, but he's far from well. Very far. He's out of danger and the doctor is happy with his progress, but the truth is, he's still a long way from being back on his feet."

"Then what the hell are you trying to tell me? Is he hurt bad or not? Dammit, I'd like a straight answer."

"Don't cuss at me, Jackson! I'm a mother, you know. Show a little respect!"

He laughed. Her bright red hair and defiant stance couldn't enhance her five feet, four inches much. Grabbing her by the shoulders, he pointed her toward the door. "Inside, Cass. And while you're leading the way, spit out a few answers about how Pop is going to treat me when we get there."

Twisting around, she glared back at him. "He'll chew you up and spit out the pieces, Marine! For heaven's sake, Jackson, what can he do to you? He's practically chained to his bed." She softened a tad. "He'll be glad to see you. Don't worry."

Easy for her to say. He and Pop had almost come to blows the morning he'd left, the day after the senior prom. He tried not to think about the cruel, callow things he'd said to Pop. Tried not to remember Pop's reasoned, soft-spoken advice and the way he hadn't lost his temper at all until Jackson had yelled at him. Jackson tried not to think about anything as he followed Cass inside his boyhood home.

The rooms were cool and shadowed, a welcome change from the heat outside. Through the doorway into the kitchen, he saw an older woman, her back to him. Bertha Jean Gillis stood stiff and straight in a blue housedress and a large white apron, her Swedish blond hair plaited and wrapped in a coronet. She turned at their approach. An unusual sight to see the woman the whole town had nicknamed "Crabby" smiling at him, even if it was a brief wintry token of a smile not intended as a personal welcome.

"I'm glad to see you, young man, and not one second too soon, either." Her faded gray eyes snapped with concern.

Before he could reply, she spoke again. "Will woke up a few minutes ago. Go on in and say hello."

For a single moment, time stood still. The faded kitchen linoleum butted against the worn cranberry carpet he stood on. The hardwood floor in the hall needed waxing. Then, time restarted. Two doors down the short hallway, the stern, older man waited.

Jackson strode toward Pop's room, trying to walk like a Marine, proud and confident, but feeling more like a little boy about to get his hiney tanned. He tapped on the open door. Tentatively, he spoke. "Hi, Pop."

"Is that you, boy?" the reply came back. "You've grown a foot, seems like. Cass said you'd come, but I guess I didn't believe it."

Jackson's heart jerked to his mouth. The worn-out old man lying in the bed his mother had died in looked as if he, too, were ready to cross over. Jackson tried to say something, but no words came out.

The old man spoke again, his voice stronger. "I'm not dead yet, so quit looking at me that way. That damn black bull Bertie sold me just beat up on me some, out of pure hell, I guess."

"I've missed you, Pop," Jackson said, and wondered why it had taken so long to get over his anger.

The appallingly weak voice pleaded, "Son, I've waited a long time. Are you going to come over here and hug your old man or not?"

Jackson stumbled toward the bed on weak legs, his heart beating so loud it sounded like the bass drum in a parade.

CHAPTER THREE

THAT NIGHT, Jackson donned a pair of pajama shorts and stretched out on the same bed he'd slept in as a boy. It must have shrunk, because his feet touched the tailboard. He turned off the bedside lamp and lay still for a few minutes, then restlessly sprang from the bed. At the window, he pushed aside the blue linen curtains. A few miles away, he could see the distant glow of lights from Catherine Darnell's home.

In the wintertime, those lights cast a yellow cone against rolling drifts of snow. Now the night swallowed them, so they were just small reminders that this wasn't the only farm in Traill County, that he wasn't really alone, that if he climbed out the window and started walking toward the lights, at the end of his journey he'd see a well-remembered face.

He wouldn't do that, of course. He couldn't. Stopping by to see Cat, as he'd told her he would, simply wasn't in the cards. Logic dictated that he stay away from her.

Cat Darnell hadn't been very friendly, anyway. She must be married, though he'd noticed she didn't wear a ring. Not to Roy Thoreson, or she would have said so when they talked about him. He'd have to find a way to ask Pop. Casually, of course.

He turned away from the window. No, hell, he couldn't do that. He didn't need the complications she would bring and as he remembered the pink fullness of her lower lip, he knew there'd be complications. He'd do what he came to do and then get the hell out of Engerville. Christmas and maybe a week in the summer, he could come back and see Pop. Jackson thought he wouldn't mind coming back on visits that much, now that he and Pop had come to terms.

He lay on the bed again, thinking. Inevitably, his mind returned to that long-ago prom night. The memory came back to him as if it had happened yesterday. Cat in his arms, her face lit by a bright spring moon, the rose corsage she wore crushed beneath the lapels of his formal sport coat.

He groaned, his body stiff and hurting, not from the protracted bus trip, but because, on that long-ago night, Cat's shy smile had soothed the hurt Rebeka caused. And Cat was the first girl he'd ever made love to.

CAT LOOKED IN ON Joey. Her daughter had fallen asleep almost immediately. She lay on her side, knees tucked up against her tummy like a small baby. Her hair all tangled and curled, swirled over the pillow and half covered her face. Cat wanted to go in and touch her, tuck the covers more securely around her, but Joey slept light. Cat blew a kiss toward her and pulled the door shut, taking care that its closing made no sound.

She turned on the TV, but tonight Jackson filled her mind. She ignored the flickering light and thought about prom night and Jackson leaving town the next day, how her father reacted when she told him she was pregnant, and being in the hospital all alone. Her father had refused to come with her. Shame, she knew, though an unmarried mother was no great novelty, even in Engerville.

She remembered her first drug-hazy look at the infant

she'd brought into the world, her relief that the baby's hair was as black as her own and her disappointment that it wasn't the same beautiful red as Jackson's. She remembered wondering if he would know, by some kind of mental empathy, that he had a child.

Restless, she went to the door, looked back at Joey's room for a second, then stepped outside. A clear moon shone down. Aunt Johanna's lilacs scented the night. Cat missed her aunt. She missed her father, too, but he'd been a strict parent, often reminding her that her wild mother had run away from husband and child. Only Aunt Johanna had bothered to show Cat that love motivated her discipline.

From the barn, a questioning whicker came from one of the horses. Probably Ruggie, she thought. The troublesome colt was always alert.

The bank wasn't happy about waiting until September for their money. They might even foreclose, though Greg Lundstrom had said he'd see what he could do. Where would she go then? Maybe if the yearling colt her father bought a year ago hadn't had the bad luck to step in a gopher hole and break his leg, they'd have a horse ready to sell now. One whose price would make the mortgage payment for a year and take this load of worry off her shoulders.

Dad's funeral expenses ate up most of the remaining emergency money in his account. There hadn't been much to begin with, since her father seldom planned ahead. After Aunt Johanna died, she'd taken on the job of balancing the farm's books and worked out a budget, which her father followed only sporadically.

Jackson. He was home again, a bare couple of miles away, and how was she supposed to handle that? If she'd thought she was over her infatuation with him, one glimpse of the Marine had knocked that thought "hind end over tea kettle" as her father used to say. How come she'd never wanted anybody else, anyway? Why had her attention settled so securely on one skinny redheaded boy that nearly fifteen years after meeting him she still ached with unrequited love? Unrequited? That was like saying the sky was blue. Jackson didn't care about anybody but himself.

He'd grown up spoiled by being the eldest child, the handsome boy, the star athlete. Only his kindness kept him from being labeled a royal jerk, instead of Engerville's crown prince. A prince who ran away from the throne, not because he didn't care for the soft seat, but just to see other kingdoms.

Cat crossed her arms in front of her white T-shirt. Why *did* she care about him? It couldn't be just his looks. Even if a glimpse of his red hair did melt her legs so she could barely stand up. No, it was more than his physical looks, more than the stir of sensual longings.

It was the softness behind his tough exterior. The way he'd included her in his gang at school, so she'd never had one day of strangeness after she and her father moved to Engerville. It was that time she'd been caught shooting a rubber band at him in study hall and gotten detention. He'd immediately confessed his own involvement and shared the detention with her, grinning behind his notebook, winking lazily when the teacher turned her back, so what had been intended as punishment turned into a favorite memory.

Behind her Cat heard the door close. Whirling around, her musing interrupted, she saw Joey emerge from the house, her white pajamas easily visible in the moonlight. Her unplanned daughter.

"Mom? Where were you? I woke up and you weren't there."

"Sorry, Teddy Bear. I came outside for a breath of fresh air. Why'd you wake up?"

Joey rubbed her eyes and yawned, her pink mouth sweet and small, even when stretched wide. "I don't know. I think I had a bad dream."

Cat reached out and tousled Joey's dark hair, allowing her hand to slide down her daughter's cheek in a soft caress. "Were you scared?"

"No-o-o, I don't think so. It was just a funny dream."

"Want to tell me about it?" Her daughter's petulant shrug was Jackson. The winsome glance out the corner of her eyes to see what effect it had on her mother had been borrowed from an expert at capturing his audience's interest.

"Nah...I don't remember. Will you come in now? I want to go back to sleep, but I can't sleep if you're out here."

The sweet pleading was her daughter's own contribution, Cat thought. She smiled. "You're still my baby girl, aren't you?"

"I'm not a baby anymore, but I like it when you're in the house with me."

"That's okay, sweetie. I like it when I know where you are, too."

Joey's head tilted sideways as she looked up. "Would you ever leave me, Mom?"

Cat was shocked. "No! Whatever caused you to think such a terrible thing? Did you dream that?"

Narrow shoulders shrugged again. "Not exactly, but kinda. Do you love me?" Her innocent voice begged reassurance.

"Teddy Bear, we belong together. I'm your mommy

and you're my darling girl. We'll always be together. Except," she paused dramatically, "when you run off to marry Tommy Karl."

Joey giggled. "That won't be for a long time. Tommy said we have to be sixteen. That's almost forever."

"Right, darling." Cat tried to smile and found it an effort. The first eight years of Joey's life had passed so fast. Would the next eight go as swiftly? And when her daughter did get old enough to fall in love and marry, would Cat be alone again? This time for the rest of her life?

VERY EARLY THE NEXT MORNING, Cass came into Jackson's bedroom and woke him from a tantalizing dream. It vanished from his memory the moment he opened his eyes and saw his sister's elfin smile above him. "Early, isn't it?" he mumbled, seeing no light at all behind the blinds he'd closed over the bedroom window.

She knelt beside his cot. "I'm getting an early start. I can't wait to see the baby. And Sam. Now that you're here, I feel okay about leaving Pop."

Jackson grinned sleepily as he swung his legs over the side of the bed, ignored the clothes in his duffel and followed Cass into the living room. Grabbing her suitcase away from her, he threw his free arm around her shoulders. "Let's fly, chickadee."

"I'll get the door for you, since you're stretching those Marine muscles for me."

A few minutes later, standing beside the car, her suitcase safely stowed in the trunk, Cass gave him a last tight hug. "Try not to argue with Pop, Jackson. Okay?"

"Who? Me?"

"Duh-h-h! Who else? Seriously, Jackson. Do it for me, will you? Agree with him."

"On everything?"

"Would it hurt so much?"

"Okay, okay. I promise."

"I love you, Jackson."

"Me, too, runt."

"You're supposed to say you love me back."

"I did."

She sighed. "You'll never change, will you? Think about it, Jackson. Think about loving somebody else more than you do yourself. Think about admitting it when you do. You might even find out you like it."

She started the car and waved as she left, tossing a last phrase at him. "I'll call."

A swell of discontent washed over Jackson along with the dust Cass's car kicked up in its wake. He wasn't a selfish idiot thinking only of himself. His sister should know that. He still wasn't sure from what direction Cat Darnell was coming. He could've sworn she'd been glad to see him at first, but then she'd turned colder than a winter blizzard. Who could understand women? He tightened his hands into fists as he launched his body toward the porch. He had too much to do to waste time wondering what either woman wanted to tell him.

EVERY NIGHT SINCE Jackson Gray had returned to town, Cat went to sleep remembering the solid feel of Jackson's chest beneath her cheek. Every morning, she rose from bed a little quicker than usual, always glancing out the window toward Will Gray's farm. Every day drove her depression a little deeper. Her hostility had forced him away. Her open anger kept him at a distance. She'd not seen him for years and now, when he was home, she'd made sure he wouldn't come around.

She'd missed him every single day since he'd left Engerville, but if he came around now, he could discover the truth about Joey. She had to keep that from happening at any cost. If that meant not seeing the only man she'd ever loved, then so be it. Nothing mattered more than Joey and keeping the ranch for her.

Two weeks after she'd given Jackson a lift to his father's farm, she stood watching Joey canter Moonshot, a strawberry roan filly, around the paddock. Wearing her daily uniform of jeans, T-shirt and riding helmet, she sat in the old English hunting saddle as if she'd been born in it, despite it being too large for her.

Joey brought the filly to an easy stop beside her mother. "Can I jump her, Mom? Just some little baby jumps? Please?"

Cat shook her head. "In a week or two, we'll start her. Not yet. She's a green girl, just like you. We don't want to spoil her."

"Oh, Mom, she's so good. I know she'll like jumping! Please?"

Cat frowned. Her daughter saw the look and knew she'd pushed too hard.

"Never mind. Next week will be okay, won't it, Moonshot?" She rubbed the filly's neck and gave her mother a sly look.

The filly snorted and tossed her head.

Cat laughed. "I caught that sneaky little try. *Maybe* next week, but not for certain. It depends."

"Sure…sure. I know you'll let us. You know, too, don't you, girl?" Joey leaned forward and pulled a hank of hair straight, flipping it back over the filly's neck so it lay on the same side with the rest of the coarse mane.

"I'd place a small bet that says you will, too," a husky voice near Cat's ear agreed.

Cat jumped, so startled she knocked her coffee cup

off the rail. Moonshot shied as the cup rolled near her and sprang sideways in a series of hopping jumps.

"Oops," Jackson said. "I'm sorry, kid! Hang on!"

Joey gripped tighter with her knees, while going easy on the reins, and gently brought her mount back to a standstill.

"Are you okay, Joey?" Cat asked.

"Yes, Mom. Moonshot didn't mean it. She was just playing."

Cat glanced at the man beside her, her gaze skipping away before he could know how hungry she was for the sight of him. He wore faded jeans and a white T-shirt that contrasted sharply with the sun-reddened skin on his upper arms. A tinge of pink darkened his cheeks above the sandpaper shadow of freshly scraped beard. His hair gleamed in the morning sun.

Her stomach tightened with fierce desire. Damn him, anyway, for sneaking up on her before she had a chance to get her defenses in order. She looked at Joey, not at him. "Where did you come from?" she asked. "I didn't hear a car."

He looked guilty. "I walked over from the farm. I had a sudden impulse to talk to somebody besides Buddy and Pop. You don't mind, do you?"

"Mind?" She struggled to speak, to sound normal, to cover up her shakiness, despite the rapid beat of her heart and the watery lack of strength in her legs. "Oh, no. Of course not, but if you insist on sneaking up like that, get ready to catch me." Cat placed one shaky hand on the second rail of the fence and hastily combed back stray strands of hair with the other.

Jackson's lopsided grin showed no remorse. "Sorry. Next time I'll sing out. Is that pretty little girl yours?"

Unprepared for this first reference to Joey, she said,

"Y-yes. My daughter, Johanna. Everybody calls her Joey."

"Hi, Joey!" Jackson said, pitching his greeting in the direction of the girl.

She waved, but didn't reply, ducking her head in sudden shyness.

Cat watched Jackson with complete attention, determined not to miss the slightest nuance of expression. Would he know immediately? And God help her, how would she explain? Despite his cheerful greeting to her daughter, different emotions flashed across his face. What did he think of Joey, and how could he *not* know?

"Is your husband around? Introduce me. I'd like to meet the guy who tamed Wild Cat Darnell."

Relief ran through her. He hadn't guessed. Cat hesitated a moment before she realized only the truth would do. The truth up to a point. "Uh, no, I mean…that is, I'm not married."

"Mmh. Well, um, that's too bad, I mean, actually, I'm kinda glad."

Cat's awareness of his every emotion didn't miss his sudden cheer. The relaxing of facial muscles, the unguarded upturn of lips told her he'd meant his words. Her own heart lightened. "Glad?"

He hesitated before answering. His broad palm rubbed the weathered rail. "Well, yes. I was hoping you'd take me around town and maybe look up some of our old crowd with me." His grin straightened itself out as another thought occurred to him. "Unless you have a boyfriend or…significant other who might object.… Do you?"

Cat resolved to get a grip on her volatile emotions. His question meant nothing, though just for a moment she saw something else in his face. He wanted a tour guide, not a girlfriend. He'd never wanted her except that one, single time. She pretended amusement. Her cheek muscles twitched in a beginning smile. "I'm a rancher, Jackson. I'm way too busy for the dating game."

He cajoled. "You must have somebody, but probably not any of the guys I knew."

"Why do you say that?"

"I can't think of a guy in our class who'd be dumb enough to let two such beautiful women out of his sight."

Joey giggled and covered her mouth with one hand, the other still holding carefully to Moonshot's reins.

Jackson intended his remark to provoke Joey's shy giggle, not her own speculation, Cat thought. She shot a look of reproach at Joey, glad she had that diversion. "Walk your horse, Joey. Moonshot is too warm to let her stand around."

"Yes, Mom," Joey answered, suddenly contrite. She touched the filly with her heels and the young mare stepped away.

Cat's gaze followed her daughter. Joey sat straight, her slender body in the correct riding position as if by instinct.

"She's a good rider," Jackson remarked.

"I was just thinking that."

Jackson's voice softened. "I know."

Cat raised an eyebrow. "You knew what I was thinking?"

Jackson grinned. "Your pride is obvious, Cat. And warranted. She *is* a good rider."

He stood too close to her. It made thinking difficult. She stooped down, retrieved her cracked coffee cup and looked at it ruefully before speaking. "Jackson, you know how to warm a mother's heart, but this was my first cup of coffee and my caffeine addiction needs feeding. Would you like a cup?''

"Will she be okay?'' He nodded toward Joey.

"Moonshot is the gentlest of our horses. She has a wonderfully sweet nature and is the one Joey loves best. They'll be okay.'' Why get a silly warm spot in her stomach just because he showed concern for Joey? Cat knew she teetered on the edge of disclosing her secret and it scared her. She called out to her daughter, "Joey, we're going to get some coffee. Put Moonshot in the barn when you're through walking her. Okay?''

Her little girl, in a sweet, clear voice, answered, "Sure, Mom. I'll curry her before I put her away. Tommy Karl is coming over later, so I might not have time this afternoon.''

"Good idea, honey. See you later.''

"Who's Tommy Karl?''

"You remember Luke Anderson, don't you?''

"Rebeka's older brother? Of course.''

Of course, he remembered. "His wife left their boy with him when she took off a couple of years ago. Tommy Karl is Joey's best friend.''

Jackson nodded. "That's a shame. It can't be easy raising a kid alone. You're in the same boat, aren't you?''

For a second, Cat knew this would be the perfect moment to tell him. Again, she realized she couldn't. Fear of his reaction kept her silent. Forcing a smile, she said, "Joey is a gift. Nothing tough about raising her! How's Cass managing with her baby? I saw her in town a couple of weeks ago, but didn't have a chance to talk to her.''

Jackson looked at her. He couldn't possibly guess the

truth about Joey, and the sun would rise in the west before she'd tell him and force him to stay when he wanted to go.

IN THE KITCHEN, Cat watched as Jackson sat at the table, his long legs sprawled out in front of him. When she filled his cup, she had to stand close to him. It was sheer torture to look down at his hair without reaching toward those soft, beginning curls. Desire caught her unaware. Desperately, she fought to keep her attraction from showing. She chose the chair at the far end of the table.

Jackson studied her, his blue eyes steady and true. Which he was not, she reminded herself.

"Roy's a reporter. Rebeka is living in Virginia. Who else is still around?"

Me, Jackson. I'm still here. "Let's see…Sally, Roy's youngest sister, married Allen Grinager, the preacher. You wouldn't know him, though. He came here after Pastor Skadeland died. Heather and Holly Halvorson married the Solberg boys, Sammy and Paul. Let me think a moment. Who else in our crowd are you curious about?"

"It seems the whole town married somebody. Are you the only one who didn't?"

It took effort to prevent a surge of pink from reaching her cheeks. She even chuckled, though it didn't sound much like amusement to her ears. "Oh, I had an offer or two, but somehow it just hasn't happened."

"The guys around here must be on the slow side. Don't you want to get married?"

"Someday, I suppose. Not right now." Jackson practiced his charm on whatever woman was handy. He meant no harm, but her heartbeat speeded up, despite her determination not to let him affect her. "Oh, I forgot to mention Shirley. She went to New York to be an actress. I heard she got a part in a real Broadway play.''

''Really? Shirley McGill in New York? Good for her. She loved acting and her singing was special, too.''

''I remember.'' I didn't forget anything about you, she wanted to say, surprised at the strength of her yearning. Jackson stared back at her as if he had no interest in Shirley McGill, as if the one he wanted sat across from him. Did she read too much into the glint in his eyes, the languid smile, the way his long fingers drummed on the kitchen table as if it took great effort to remain still?

Finally, she heard the screen door slam. Not a moment too soon, either. She needed a distraction to calm her long-denied emotions.

Joey came over to her and assumed a position just behind her left shoulder, one hand holding on to the chair her mother sat in. Cat smiled proudly at her. ''Sit down, honey. I'll get you a glass of milk.''

Joey cast a shy glance at Jackson. ''That's okay. I'm not thirsty.''

Cat flicked a quick glance at Joey. While her wide eyes betrayed nervousness, and not fear, it was obvious that she didn't plan on straying far from her mother. Cat looked at Jackson. His open face showed a keen interest in her sprite. ''Jackson is Cass Gray's brother, Joey. You remember Cass, don't you? She's married now to a policeman and lives in Minneapolis.''

''Uh-huh. She's got red hair, too.''

''The curse of the Grays,'' Jackson quipped.

''I like red hair,'' Joey responded. ''I wish I had red hair.''

Jackson turned his charm on the child. ''Your hair is beautiful, Joey. Almost the same color as Cat's, but maybe a shade lighter.''

"It's okay." Joey edged closer to her mother.

Cat took a deep breath, her nose wrinkling. "It might be a good idea for you to take a shower, Joey. You smell like a horse."

Joey giggled. "I know. I always do and you always say that."

Jackson stood up. "I'll be going, then. Pop will be wondering if I went AWOL. It's been great talking to you, Cat."

She had a sudden urge to keep him there, to say something that would prevent his leaving, but no words came. She nodded, a tightness in her throat stopping any statement she might have made.

"Nice to meet you, Joey. You're a crackerjack rider."

"Thank you," Joey responded politely, then grinned at her mother. Though used to being told she was a good rider, hearing those words from a stranger excited her.

"I'll see you again before I leave, Cat. Thanks for the coffee."

Cat stood and walked with him to the door. A drumbeat of regret pounded at her. She wanted to hold him, to stop him, and at the same time, she wanted him to go quickly before he destroyed the small world she'd built without him.

He hesitated at the door, turned, leaned casually down and touched her cheek with his lips. "Bye, then."

And he was gone. Again.

CHAPTER FOUR

JACKSON WROTE THREE LETTERS that night, including a note to Juan telling him about the ranch and a little about Cat Darnell. That surprised him, since he hadn't planned on even thinking about her, or her midnight hair, or the leggy siren's body that lied about having a child who must be...what? Six or seven years old. Where was the kid's father?

Hadn't Cat given him a thought after he left Engerville? Not that he'd expected her to carry a torch. After all, love hadn't been involved in their one night of reckless teenage passion. Still...still, he remembered. Didn't she?

It must have been the letter that caused him to dream about her. The dream began before sleep did.

The moon shining through the truck's windshield made the night misty, brushing Cat's face with dewy gold. She wasn't beautiful, Jackson decided. Cat didn't have Rebeka Anderson's even-featured beauty. Rebeka was the girl he'd wanted to take to the prom, not Cat.

Her green eyes were mesmerizing. He wouldn't mind kissing her, even if she wasn't Rebeka. He surely wouldn't mind one little bit.

He draped an awkward arm around her shoulders, then asked a clumsy, too-direct question. "You don't have to be home right away, do you?"

Her clear gaze turned to him. "Not right away. Why?"

"I thought maybe we'd drive down to Needlepoint Rock." He paused, suddenly diffident. The rumbling of the truck wheels on the gravel road nearly drowned out his words. "And count the stars...or something." Okay, he'd said it. Nobody went to Needlepoint Rock to star-gaze. The Rock was a well-known make-out spot. If she said no; then he'd take her home and say good-night. If she said yes, maybe she wanted something to remember prom night by as much as he did.

The sound she made was a breathy soft whisper, as if she'd sucked in air too quickly. He almost missed her answer.

"There's no reason why Rebeka and Roy should have all the fun." She stroked back a long dark strand that had drifted away from the rest of her hair.

Sometimes, it seemed as if she used that thick hair to hide her face when she didn't want people to know what she felt. He'd noticed that in school. He glanced side-ways. She looked down so he couldn't see her expression. "Goose River is pretty at night when the moon is full."

Jackson let his fingertips dangle over her shoulder and very lightly brush the soft skin at the top of her dress.

Turning right at Elmer Anderson's farm, Jackson drove down the arrow-straight dirt road to Needlepoint Rock near the band of pine trees along the riverbank. He tried to ignore how his fingertips were getting a little too familiar with Cat's breasts. It was impossible to ig-nore the pebble-hard tip that rose to meet his exploring hand.

Her breath quickened as he parked the truck beneath

the shadowed overhanging branches of a towering pine standing sentinel beside the rock.

"Jackson?"

"I won't hurt you, Cat. Any time you want me to stop, just say so."

"I'm not afraid, Jackson. Are you?"

"A little, I guess."

Her answer was a silky-smooth arm wrapped around his neck, resting there for a moment, then tugging him closer. He heard her whisper words so soft he had to strain to hear her.

"I dare you."

His nervous laugh sounded scared even to him, but he returned her embrace and let the heat claim him. He had her panties off inside of two minutes, afraid the whole time that she'd change her mind and half-afraid she wouldn't.

Clean, crisp air with a springtime chill to it and the pungent scent of pine trees aroused from their winter's sleep. The damp smell of Goose River swollen with spring rains and rushing between its banks with a noise like a faraway freight train. The heady perfume of Cat's rose corsage. All became a permanent part of his memory.

He'd been so wrong. She was beautiful.

Three times that night he awoke and lay in the narrow bed remembering. Twice he got up and looked out his bedroom window toward the Darnell farm. It seemed incredible that he was back in Engerville. Impossible that he'd had the same dream nearly every night he'd been here. Unbelievable that he couldn't figure out why. The third time he awoke, he knew the answer but, like

fog fleeing before a sudden breeze, the answer was gone
with his return to awareness.

JACKSON REMOVED THE CLAMP and tugged the fuel line
loose. He peered into one end of the line. Pointing it
toward the ground, he took his finger off the opening. A
few drops of fuel trickled out, then nothing. "Must be
junked up," Jackson muttered under his breath.

"Have you checked the fuel filter?" Will Gray asked.

Jackson turned around. His father stood behind him,
leaning heavily on a polished walnut cane. A twinge of
concern zapped through him. His father shouldn't even
be out of the house, let alone limping around the farm.
Jackson grunted his annoyance. Just try telling him that.
The old man was stubborn to a fault. "Pop, go back to
the house. You aren't well enough to be running around
this dirty old shed telling me how to fix the tractor."

"I just asked if you checked the filter. What are you
so grouchy about?"

Jackson modulated his growl. "Sorry. I didn't sleep
much last night."

Will nodded, looked all-knowing, and said, "I heard
you tossing and turning half the night. Musta been those
pork chops. I told you to stay with the beef stew Bertie
fixed before she left."

"Pop, never mind me. What are you doing out here?
If you fell on this junk—" Jackson looked around the
shed, gesturing toward the many pieces of old farm
equipment that hung on the walls and spilled over to the
floor, leaving only narrow aisles to navigate through
"—you'd be hurt for sure. Probably get lockjaw."

"Don't you think I've had about all the bad luck one
man is due? At least for this summer." Will flung out
his left arm in a gesture that included the whole farm.

"Yeah, yeah. Go back to the house, will you?" Jackson turned back to the engine, his mind already spinning

past a dozen solutions for its reluctance to fire. This chore was one he enjoyed. No shovels involved, anyway.

"I have to start back to work sometime. I can't sit around that house another day without going crazy." Will limped to his other side and peered over his shoulder.

Jackson stared at his father and tried not to show the concern he felt every time he noticed how much weight his father had lost, how much gray blunted the copper in his hair and how hard his father sought to regain his strength. Pop ought to sell this damn back-breaking, pancake-flat piece of godforsaken prairie and try raising a little hell for a change, instead of sugar beets. Maybe he'd quit looking around every corner as if he expected Jackson's mother to be there. Jackson gave a dry snort of annoyance. "Then why don't you take the other tractor and plow the south forty, if you're feeling so blasted good?"

"You sure are grouchy! When I was a kid like you, I could go a week without sleep and never show it." The older man stepped back, more weight on his good leg than his bad, so he looked off-balance with the movement.

Jackson picked up a greasy rag and wiped his hands with it, swiped his shirt sleeve across his face, then turned to his father. They were inches apart. His father looked ready to flinch at harsh words. He was past that. In a quiet, even voice, he protested, "Pop, I'm not sixteen anymore. Look at me. I'm not a kid."

His father, unshaken by his gritty announcement, replied softly, "Time sure flies, doesn't it? I've got eyes in my head, son. You're an inch taller than me, but I can't help thinking of you as my boy. Wait 'til you have kids of your own, then you'll know what I mean."

Jackson sighed in resignation. "Okay, I'll wait. Now, you go on back to the house like a good Pop, so I can figure out why this hunk of junk won't run."

Will leaned closer to the tractor, peering into the tangle of wires and hose. "Did you check the carburetor?"

Jackson straightened and took a deep breath. "I was just going to do that when you came in. Be a sport, Pop. If you fall in here, you could be hurt really bad."

Faded blue eyes looked skeptical. "You're honestly worried about me, not just irritated that I'm in here bugging you?"

Jackson gave up. He laughed and patted his father's cheek. "Yes, Pop, I am honestly worried about you."

Will nodded. He turned to go. "I'll get out of your hair then."

Being hurtful to his father was something he did as a teenager. Despite his exasperation at his father's need to tell him how to do a job, he had no intention of walking that road again. Jackson touched his father's shoulder. "Not out of my hair, Pop. Out of danger. Tell you what I'll do. I'll fix you a place to sit over there by the door. The sun ought to feel good for a while, before it gets too hot, and if you're over there, I won't worry about you falling. We can talk while I'm working. Maybe you can help me figure out which part is screwy on this old heap."

Will Gray nodded, his face brighter, a bare smile tilting his lips. His lean angular body straightened as he patted Jackson's hand where it rested on his shoulder. Reluctantly, he agreed. "My knee is starting to hurt some."

JACKSON HADN'T INTENDED walking over to Cat's place that evening. Tired and irritable from the previous night's lack of sleep, he wanted only his bed, but Bertie came over to keep Pop company. He didn't have the patience to sit around the living room with them discussing how much he'd grown or how he seemed exactly the same as when he was sixteen, even though time had really flown.

He knew a mysterious force tugged him toward the Darnell farm, but thinking about why it existed made the skin on the back of his neck prickle with unease. He preferred to believe Bertie and Pop caused him to flee his home.

He kicked at the dusty road. Hell, it was a good two miles over to Cat's. An early night was what he needed, not a half hour's tramp along this graveled excuse for a road. Across a wide, untended field, he saw smoke drifting from the chimney of her house. An image of Cat's straight, black hair whipping out behind her filled his mind. Her high cheekbones gave her green eyes a suggestion of mystery and hinted at a secret only she knew.

Damn. She was just the girl he left behind in a town too dull for words, too dry for spit and not worth remembering for all the sugar beets in Traill County. He absolutely knew that, but he left the road and struck off across the field.

Coming up on Little Dog Creek, he heard rustling sounds near a sparse grove of boxelder trees. He stopped. The sun had almost vanished beneath the flat horizon. There weren't any bears or moose around here and not much else that might be dangerous. The light was still good and would be for another hour or so, but maybe this wasn't such a bright idea, for a different reason than the anonymous rustling noise in the weeds.

He thought about turning back. Jackson came to a halt

near a patch of thistles just waiting to glom onto his jeans. Hanging around Cat Darnell was plain foolish. If he didn't watch out, he'd find himself caught in her silky, sable hair as surely as a fox in a steel-jawed trap. That old fox would sure as hell have to quit his roaming, if he got caught.

He'd always loved the crisp feel of striding into a place more exciting than the one he'd left behind. Cat was just a friend, after all, though one he'd made love to, a long time ago. He'd step around that trap. They could still be friends without him yielding to a hell-sent temptation to weave his fingers through the dusky strands of her midnight hair and kiss that soft, sweet spot near her cat-green eyes.

Jackson tramped resolutely forward. Thirty yards from the creek, a low coughing stopped him in his tracks. Then almost in his face, six deer leaped to their feet and bounded away, their white tails lifted like flags behind them.

The beautiful animals had startled him. He skirted their bedding area and jumped the creek at a spot where it narrowed to only a couple of feet wide. Resisting Cat's considerable temptations would test his determination to leave Engerville, but there'd be no real contest. He'd already decided the ending.

CAT, EYEING HER BEAD BOX on the dining room table, resigned herself to washing the dishes first. Joey swept the kitchen in lazy, unambitious strokes of the straw broom, drawing out the task far past the time when she should have finished it. Her attention caught by something, Joey went over to the window. The broom lay forgotten on the floor as she gazed out. Suddenly, Joey's back stiffened.

"Mom, that guy is outside."

A beat of apprehension clutched Cat. Who would visit this late in the evening? Careful to keep her alarm from showing, she asked, "What guy, Joey?"

"The one with red hair. I forget." She turned to glance at her mother, bright curiosity lighting her face. "What's his name?"

The apprehension vanished with a suddenness that left Cat weak. "Jackson. It must be Jackson Gray."

"Yeah, that's the one. I like him. Why's he coming to see us?"

Jackson's knock sounded at the back door.

Cat pushed back sweat-dampened strands of hair from her face and hurriedly dried her hands on her apron and tossed it on the counter near the sink. She'd like to have a little warning of his visits. Enough to greet him in something pretty, instead of one of her father's old T-shirts and her own well-worn, faded jeans. She stroked the compact braid she kept her hair in. Neat, yes, and not pulled tight away from her face, but left loose, before it formed the thick rope dangling halfway down her back, tied with a length of red leather from her bead supplies. With her deep tan, it gave her an exotic look. She smiled wryly. Well, maybe just interesting, not really exotic. She glanced down at her body. She'd worked too hard over the years to put on extra weight. Her concern for Jackson's opinion troubled her, but she had no time to examine what it meant. "Let him in, Teddy Bear."

Joey hesitated, then darted toward the door. As if she didn't know whether to be eager or afraid, Cat thought, in complete sympathy with her daughter.

The tall, red-haired man smiled unsurely at her. Despite his size and the inevitable intimidation caused by her guilty secret, his deference put her in charge and her nervousness vanished. Her property, her home...her daughter, she reminded herself. "Jackson, what a nice surprise. Come in."

"Are you sure you don't mind, Cat? I should have called, but all I could think of was escaping from the farm. I had an irresistible urge to get away from Pop and Bertie's discussions of my wayward youth."

"You weren't so bad. Is that the real reason you came by?"

His mouth stretched into the delicious smile she loved. He looked suddenly shy. "Bertie came by to visit and I saw at dinner they were warming up my bones for a good chewing. You know how parents like to remind you of every stupid thing you ever did, before you grew up? Yeah, well, they were making notes, so they wouldn't forget anything."

A sympathetic giggle escaped from Cat. Joey, half hidden behind the door, peeped out at the two of them and Cat sobered. "Honestly, Jackson, the way you talk, you'd think you were abused as a child!"

"What do you call shoveling sh—manure all day long?"

Cat glanced at Joey again, silently warning Jackson to watch his language, but her own mirth bubbled over. "Not *all* day?"

"It seemed like it. Never mind. I see you're still in the bead business. Were you planning on making jewelry this evening? I didn't mean to interrupt you."

"You're not. You're welcome anytime. The beads can wait." She brushed off his question with a casual wave at the plastic box packed with beading materials. A moment ago, she'd been eager to get through her chores and let the bright beads fall through her fingers as she chose the perfect size and color for a new necklace. Now, with Jackson here, she pushed them aside as if they meant nothing.

Jackson grinned. "Pop and I have about as much in common as the Army and the Navy. I haven't decided who's going to win the battle and it will be weeks yet, before I can leave. Coming over here to talk to you might keep me sane."

It hurt to know how badly he wanted to go, but she should have been prepared for his eagerness to leave. "Is farm work getting you down that much?"

His face settled into a disgruntled frown. "I'm not a farmer, Cat. My plants don't grow, my hens don't lay, my pigs don't get fat. Even my tractor doesn't run. I'm not cut out for this stuff. Pop knows it. He's walking pretty good now and he follows me around worse than Blue does, always trying to tell me how to do it better."

A wave of sympathy enveloped her. How terrible to have to do what you hated most in life. No wonder his eyes looked shadowed as if he hadn't slept well for weeks. "Let me get you a glass of iced tea and we'll go sit on the front porch. Joey, would you get a cloth to wipe the chairs? With the wind blowing all day, those chairs will have an inch of dust on them."

"You're a good friend, Cat. Hey, Joey, remind me to tell you about the deer I saw on my way over this evening."

Joey snagged a dish cloth from the sink and paused at the refrigerator. "Cool! Were there any babies?"

"One, I think. They were moving so fast, I didn't see much."

Joey nodded, then opened the refrigerator and asked, without turning around, "Mom, can I have a can of Coke?"

"Make it milk, Joey. You know I don't like you to drink pop this close to bedtime."

"Aw, Mom! I had milk at dinner. How about Sprite?"

"Well, there's no caffeine in it. Just this once, then," she warned. "It's not going to become a habit, young lady."

"Sure, sure." Joey came from behind the refrigerator door, soda in hand, a broad smile dimpling her cheeks, and sauntered toward the living room.

Jackson whispered, his voice low so Joey couldn't hear him. "Sounds like she has you pegged as a soft touch."

Cat grunted, then the beginnings of a frown shaped her mouth. "She might think so, but never for long."

One corner of his mouth tipped up in a mocking question. "Are you sure you don't beat her?"

Cat twisted away from the casual smile that gripped her like a pair of handcuffs. She reached for glasses from the cabinet and then looked over her shoulder at Jackson. The moment became suddenly tense and still. The rest of the world disappeared. Heat enveloped her in one shattering, electric instant. Hastily, she turned back to the cabinet shelf and pretended great interest in the array of mismatched glasses. "Never on Thursdays! Joey's perfectly safe one day a week."

"Yeah, right."

Cat put the glasses on the table. Carefully.

His devilish smile broke out full force as he moved closer. His voice got lower. "If you knew what I dreamed last night..."

"What?" She straightened and faced him.

The smile faded and his cheeks took on a characteristic ruddy blush. "Oh, I couldn't tell."

The blush, against cheeks stubbled with the day's

beard growth, intrigued her. She fumbled ice cubes into the glasses and poured tea over them. She forced a lightness she didn't feel into her voice. ''Why not? You have my full attention now!''

''As Cassidy said, you have to have a little respect for mothers. I don't want to embarrass you.'' Jackson ducked as Cat tossed a towel in his direction.

She grimaced. ''I don't think you can embarrass mothers.''

''Been through too much?''

''You might say that.'' Memories surged over her. The fear, the embarrassment, the long months of wishing she wasn't alone. Loneliness bothered her most. Being alone, when she ached to have this man beside her.

Jackson's voice came low and soft and edged with anger. ''Who was he? Who was the jerk who left you in the lurch?''

Cat went pale. How could she tell him what he'd left behind? This man hated being in any place long enough to watch a crop mature, never mind the time it took to raise a child. She took refuge in annoyance, spitting back her reply. ''That, Marine, is none of your business! Come on, you have your iced tea. Let's join Joey on the front porch.''

Jackson came closer to her, his bulk overshadowing her own slender frame. ''Wild Cat, you know I'm not just curious, don't you? It isn't like that with me.''

Jackson's voice came as soft as a whisper, enticing her to confide. For his sake, and her own, she had to keep her secret. ''Joey's waiting,'' she replied, her voice quiet and cold.

After that, she kept the conversation away from the personal. She was also careful to keep Joey by her side.

With her child listening intently to his every word, Jackson couldn't pursue his interest.

At nine-thirty, he stood up. "Time to go home. There's always another stall needing to be shoveled at Gray's Way."

She relaxed. The danger of her secret being spilled no longer threatened. "And I'll bet you do a heck of a good job, too."

"I can shovel, uh, manure with the best of them. Ladies, I bid you a good night."

Joey giggled.

Jackson swooped on her and held her high over his head. She shrieked in delight. "And you, my fair princess," he said, "you have to go to bed, too. How about a good-night kiss for Uncle Jackson?"

Joey shook her head in denial. "You're not my uncle!"

"No," Jackson teased, "I'm not. I'm your handsome prince come to carry you away from the dragon lady over there. Would you like that?"

"Mommy's not a dragon!" Joey screamed, wiggling with glee.

"No! Did I say she was a dragon? No, no! I meant she was a dragon*fly!*" Jackson proceeded to tickle Joey so industriously that she hardly breathed as the giggles pealed out of her.

Cat watched them together. Why hadn't he guessed? Except for the hair color, they were so alike. Both full of scheming mischievousness. Both of them so dear to her. For a second, Cat wondered what it would be like if this scene was the norm. If every night Jackson picked his daughter up and hugged her, tickled her and kissed her, tucked her into bed and then turned that charming smile on her, what dreams could they weave together?

At that moment, he put Joey down and turned to her and Cat wondered if he'd guessed her thoughts.

"I don't suppose you'll give me a good-night kiss either, huh?"

Oh, she shouldn't, but she couldn't help it. Just this once, she thought. Just this once! "You haven't asked yet."

"I usually take." He came over to her and touched her cheek gently, his action belying his words.

Cat tipped her head up to look into his eyes. The brilliant blue dazzled her, framed as they were in rich, dark lashes. She got lost in their depths.

Jackson leaned down and touched his lips briefly to hers, then stepped back hurriedly, as if her touch burned him. He turned to Joey and said teasingly, "See, Joey, even your mother can be nice when she tries."

Joey giggled, but retreated toward the door, as if afraid Jackson would try to kiss her, too. He didn't. He waved over his shoulder as he jumped off the edge of the porch, not bothering with the steps only a few feet away.

"I'll see you ladies in a day or two. Good night." He loped toward the road, then broke into a sprint.

Running, Cat thought. Running away. Joey came over to stand next to her and the two of them watched as Jackson disappeared into gathering night.

CHAPTER FIVE

WILL PEERED OUT the kitchen window as his tall son left the gravel road and started walking across the field toward Catherine Darnell's place. He shook his head and went over to the coffeepot and filled two cups, then carried them back into the living room with the awkward limping gait the knee injury forced on him.

He handed one to Bertie and sat down next to her on the sofa. But not too close. Carefully easing his injured leg onto the patchwork ottoman, he shook his head again. "Looks like Jackson is going over to see Catherine."

"I wondered when he might. Jackson's been working so hard he hasn't had time to visit his old friends."

"He's a good boy, mostly."

"Now, Will Gray, why can't you say one nice thing about your son without watering it down?"

"I love him right enough. It's just that he worries me no end. I'm afraid he's fixing to mess up his life."

"I can't see how visiting an old school friend could do that." She lifted her coffee cup and eyed Will over the steaming brew.

Will looked back at her and for a moment forgot what he'd intended to answer. He set his coffee cup down on the end table. It gave him time to think. Then he turned back to her. "Don't you?"

"Catherine Darnell is the finest woman in Engerville.

There's any number of things she could have done after she had her girl, but what she did was settle down and raise her the right way. I admire that. A woman isn't a mother because she has a baby. She's a mother when she takes care of it. Same thing I've always said about men.''

"I agree. One hundred percent."

"Then why are you worried about him seeing Catherine?''

"Just seeing her won't hurt anything, I guess."

"Well, then?''

"I don't have to ask you not to repeat this. I know you won't. I've always wondered if that little girl is my granddaughter.''

"Wasn't Jackson going with Rebeka back then?''

"He took Catherine to the prom. Both of them busted up with their steadies about two weeks before the prom. The opportunity was there, but I can't see Jackson not owning up to it. If Joey was his, he would take care of her, at least. I raised him not to lie, cheat or steal, and if he's guilty here, then he's done all three.''

"'If' is a big word. Opportunity doesn't mean he's the culprit.''

A sudden rush of emotion choked Will. He took another sip of coffee and the hot liquid helped him speak. "Believe it or not, but I'd give anything if that child was my granddaughter. I fell in love with her when she was a baby and first started going to church with me and Helen. She's the cutest little thing and she reminds me of Helen in some ways.''

Bertie smiled, reached over and patted Will's hand. "You still miss her, don't you?''

Will nodded.

JACKSON HEARD VOICES as he approached Gray's Way. Stepping off the road, he moved to the shadows underneath a tall tree. Will stood in the yard, his walnut cane beneath his hand as he said good-night to Bertie Gillis.

"Awfully good of you to come by again," he said.

Despite the heat of the day, the night air chilled bare arms. Bertie tugged her shawl closer about her shoulders, and tilted her blond head toward the older man. "I please myself, you know. I bear some of the responsibility for your injuries, and besides, if I didn't enjoy cooking for you and Jackson, I certainly wouldn't do it."

"You bear no blame for giving me the chance to buy a young bull at a good price. I should have been more careful. I appreciate your coming by, though. More than the cooking, even, is the talk."

"Now that is one thing I know how to do."

Will laughed.

Bertie smiled and looked toward the tree that sheltered Jackson.

Jackson knew she couldn't see him. The night obscured his presence too well, so why did uneasiness crawl up his spine as if he leaned against an ant's nest, instead of a sturdy maple tree?

Bertie turned back to face Will. "Well, I'd better be leaving. Tomorrow's my sewing circle night, but I'll come by the day after. If you'd like?"

"I haven't enjoyed such wonderful cooking since Helen died. Not to mention the company. With Cassidy gone and Jackson just here for a little while, I get lonely."

Bertie nodded shortly and turned away from her companion. "Well, then. 'Bye, Will."

From behind the tree, Jackson watched and listened.

There was no mistaking the hungry look on his father's face. His stomach went hollow, as if he hadn't eaten in weeks. His father and Bertie? Surely not.

Jackson watched his father hold the car door for Bertie, then stand there alone, frowning as he watched the taillights until they curved around a bend in the road and vanished. He turned to go back into the house.

Pine needles rustled under Jackson's feet. The sound from the shadows startled his father.

"Who's there?"

Jackson winced. Pop's hearing was as good as ever. "Just me, Pop."

"Jackson?"

"Yes. It's me."

"Why are you lurking in the dark? Trying to scare a man to death?"

"Aw, Pop, I was just giving you a chance to kiss your girlfriend good-night."

Pop's voice rose. "Mind your manners, boy! I can still tan your hide."

"So what's wrong with a good-night kiss?"

Will looked sharply at him. "How long were you standing there?"

Jackson countered his look with a long, cool stare of his own. "Long enough."

"You still planning on leaving?"

"After you're better."

"If that's the case, then maybe you ought to stay away from the Darnell place."

Jackson knew what Pop hinted at. He couldn't admit it to his father. "Cat's a friend, that's all."

His father snapped, "Then act like a friend and stay away from her. She's already been hurt once."

Jackson stiffened. "Don't you think I'm a little old to be giving orders to?"

"It's not orders, son. It's advice. Do Cat a favor and take it."

Will climbed the porch steps slowly. He paused on the third riser and looked down at Jackson, his angular features hard. "She's been hurt before. I don't want my blood to be a part of hurting her again."

Jackson's quick temper edged his voice with anger. "Maybe you should practice what you preach, old man!"

"Who're you calling an old man? I've got half a mind to see if a little North Dakota dust on your backside would teach you some manners!"

For a long moment Jackson stared up at his father coldly. He didn't look fragile, and the hard set to his jaw announced his feelings in no uncertain tones, but his hand clutched the walnut cane. Jackson shook his head as if to clear it, and shot a weak smile in Pop's direction. "If you think it might, I'd be willing to roll around a bit and see how much dust I can gather."

His father's keen gaze relaxed and a thin smile tipped his lips. He nodded. "You probably would. Forget it. What did you mean by telling me to practice what I preach?"

"It doesn't take a farmer to see you and Bertie are two peas in the same pod."

"Nonsense! She's being a good neighbor." He turned, climbed the last step and limped across the porch to the door.

Jackson called out to the stiff back, "Well, you try kissing her good-night next time she's over and see how neighborly she gets!"

His father looked back, indignation pulling down his

rusty brows and making his face go all angles and planes. "You think because you've been away in the Marines you can come home and try to tell your old man the facts of life? I've known Bertie since the day she was born."

"I suppose you'd remember?"

"Sweetest woman in the county, despite the village idiots who named her 'Crabby,' and one of the nicest, too." He paused. "I was almost ten years old. Of course, I remember. Now you get yourself in bed, and leave me to tend my own chickens. You'll need to be up by four-thirty to meet the Greyhound bus carrying the new fuel pump for that tractor you broke this morning."

"I broke? You're kidding, aren't you?"

"Not more than a smidgen. Come on, now. Let's go in."

"Might as well. You're as good at changing the subject as anyone I've ever met. If a guy is going to get a stepmother, then I think he ought to be told about it."

His father's anger faded as he stared over Jackson's head into the shadowed farmyard. A vagrant breeze stirred the leaves of the trees, so they rustled softly. "It's not been four years since your mother died. Even if I wanted to, and Bertie was willing, it wouldn't seem right."

Jackson quit his teasing. It wasn't funny anymore. He offered a token of peace. "I wouldn't mind. Cassidy would be okay with it, too."

"Go to bed, boy, and quit trying to marry off your father."

Jackson laughed and climbed the steps two at a time. Before he went inside, he looked toward Cat's place. He couldn't see any lights. She might have gone to bed. The instant image the thought provoked made him uneasy.

He had no business picturing Cat in bed and himself beside her. Maybe the danger was real.

"OH, MOMMY! They're beautiful!"

"Pick one to keep, Joey. You worked as hard as I did."

Joey pondered the gleaming necklaces they had made after Jackson left. Outside, the wind rose and Cat heard it keening against the pine siding of the house. The weather always seemed just on the verge of breaking in.

Joey's small hand hovered over the neatly laid rows of rhodinium, crystal, jade and jasper. She reached for a necklace of fire-cut crystal as boldly red as rubies, yet its value only a few dollars. Picking it up, she held it to her neck and bent forward to use the table mirror to check its effect, her shoulder-length hair swinging forward as she did so. Then she laid it back down.

"Pick one, Teddy Bear."

Joey took the crystal necklace and slipped it over her head. It lay in a blaze of red against her yellow T-shirt.

"Not exactly a match," Cat said.

"What's a match?" Joey asked.

"When things go together. You know, like bees and flowers, like you and your best buddy, Tommy Karl."
Like me and a certain redhead.

"Like me and you. Right, Mom?"

"Yes, honey, like you and me." Cat hugged Joey and kissed her cheek. Joey smelled like the strawberry ice cream she'd had for dessert and something else. Cat sniffed again. Horse. The faint odor of horse clung to her daughter despite her shower before dinner and the fresh jeans and T-shirt. Cat laughed. "Exactly like you and me." She rubbed her cheek against Joey's hair. In full sun, her daughter's walnut hair would show a bit of auburn. A tiny bit, but enough to remind Cat of fire.

After shoving the bead box against the wall near the lamp, Cat picked up her high school yearbook. The book fell open, as it always did, at the picture of a boy holding a strip of newspaper covered with dripping flour glue. He stood in a threatening posture over a teenage girl up to her elbows in a tub of the same glue.

"That's you, Mom," Joey announced.

"Yes, darling, that's me."

Joey read the caption, "Wild Cat Darnell tries to avoid becoming a perm—what's that word, Mom?"

"Permanent, honey."

"'Perm-a-munt part of the snowman project the senior art class is making for the Christmas dance,'" she finished triumphantly, then looked up at her mother. "Mom, are you crying?"

"No, I'm not crying. I have something in my eye."

"Oh." Joey looked dubious. "I'm sorry."

"It's not your fault." Cat swiped at her eyes. "There. All better, now."

"Who's the boy, Mommy? How come his name isn't here, too?"

Cat stared at the slender teenager. In the picture, his hair blazed as fiercely as the necklace of ruby crystals hanging around Joey's neck. She didn't intend to answer with the truth, but the words slipped out. "That's Jackson Gray, Joey."

"I like him. I was really high when he held me over his head, wasn't I?"

"Wonderfully high." Cat turned her head away from her daughter.

"I wish he was my daddy, don't you? He's lots of fun."

Cat braced herself, pushed away the pain and observed calmly, "Last week, you wanted Luke Anderson for your daddy."

Joey considered. "Yeah, but then Tommy Karl would be my brother and I couldn't marry him when I grow up. I think Jackson would be better."

Cat's chest tightened. She stood. "Time for bed, Joey. I let you stay up too late tonight. It's past ten o'clock."

"Mommy, why didn't my daddy love me?"

The squeezing sensation in Cat's chest hurt. She drew in a deep breath of air. "He would have, if he'd known you, but he had to go away."

"I don't love him, either." Her small voice was petulant.

"You'll understand better, when you're older. Go brush your teeth and put on your pajamas."

Obediently, Joey got up and went to the bathroom. Now Joey knew the boy in the picture was Jackson, but the words had slipped out before Cat thought. She hoped Joey didn't mention her desire for a father to him. Jackson Gray might worm his way into her daughter's heart, the way he had done with hers.

Cat stood in the middle of the living room, thinking about Jackson and Joey together. It couldn't happen. Joey must forget. Cat shook her head. Joey *would* forget. Maybe as soon as the next day.

It would never be that easy for her.

IN THE LAST HOUR BEFORE DAWN, Jackson crept out of the house to avoid waking his father. He let Pop's Ford roll down the driveway as far as it would, so the noise of the engine starting wouldn't disturb him. He turned on to the gravel road. Instead of taking the left turn toward town, some inexplicable urge caused him to turn right toward Cat's place.

He parked a hundred and fifty feet from the house, left the motor running, and sat for several moments, staring at its dim outline. Thinking about Cat was fast becoming a risky occupation, one he indulged in too often. Behind the outline of a window, he saw a flickering light. Cat must have left it on through the night. Was she nervous about being alone here, with just the child for company? He wouldn't mind keeping her company. The dangerous thought jarred him from his reverie.

He put the truck in gear and started to turn around. An uneasy memory caused him to hit the brakes. He'd looked at Cat's house last night before going inside. There'd been no lights on then. For a tense moment, he watched the flickering.

Fire! He drove toward the house as the light flared brighter. He threw the truck into park, switched off the engine, jerked open the door and jumped out. Racing toward the house, a terrible moment of déjà vu enveloped him, as he remembered the searing heat of the forest fire outside Richmond and the burnt body of a firefighter trapped by a sudden shift in the wind's direction. *God, no! Don't let me be too late!*

Jackson vaulted the rail fence in front of the house instead of pausing to open the gate. He stopped in front of the window where the flickering light blazed out of control. So quickly it had become a threatening thing instead of what he'd presumed was the reassurance a woman alone might need.

He stood for a second, wrapped in indecision, his thoughts jumping from one alternative to the next. The light leapt in the window closest to the front door. If that were the only way, he'd go through flames to save Cat and Joey, but the sickening memory of the dead fire-fighter made his guts churn. There had to be another way to get in. He ran around the side of the house to where the bedrooms were.

The window ledge was nearly five feet from the ground. That made rescue harder. He needed to get inside, and quickly, before the fire spread out of control. He rapped sharply on the window framing, hoping this was Cat's bedroom and not Joey's. The child would be frightened out of her wits by an unexpected noise outside her window. Jackson called out, "Cat, wake up!"

No answer.

He rapped again. A surge of nausea choked him. "Cat, dammit, wake up!"

The window slid up, and Cat stood there above him, coughing, the puzzled look on her face quickly turning to alarm. "Jackson, what's wrong? There's smoke in here! The house is on fire, isn't it?" Realization dawned. "I've got to get Joey."

"No!" he yelled. He had to shout to penetrate her confusion. "I'll get her. You come out this window. Now, Cat!"

"Joey!" she said, starting to turn away.

He swung his fist through the screen, ignored the ripping of wire against the back of his hand, the knife-sharp pain, the swift welling of blood in the furrows, then grabbed the edges with both hands and tore the storm window from its frame.

"Cat, dammit, come out now! I'll get Joey."

She looked back at him, then came over to the window. "I'll get Joey first."

He grabbed her arm and urged her toward him. "Cat, you can't do that! The smoke could knock you out—"

"Stop yelling. You'll wake her up." The absurdity of her reply hit her.

She tried to get away from him again. He wrapped both strong arms around her and forcibly dragged her through the window.

For a brief, almost unnoticed second, he cherished his teenage love, her warmth, her safety, then Jackson set her on her feet and looked around desperately for something to stand on. It was not so dark now, but still hard to see. Nothing...no...wait. There'd been an old sawhorse in the front yard, near the porch, last night. "Get the garden hose and bring it around front," he yelled to Cat.

Sprinting to the front of the house, he almost tripped over the sawhorse. He grabbed it and ran back to where Cat still stood. "The garden hose, Cat," he said, trying not to shout. She looked as if she were in shock, her face ghost white in the early morning light.

"Not 'till Joey's safe! I don't care about the damn house!"

"We might need the hose to reach her, Cat! If the fire is too hot to get close enough.... Calm down, Catherine, I know what I'm doing. I'll get her out. Please don't put yourself back in danger. I can't save both of you at the same time." His words ran together in his haste to make her understand. He could see nothing penetrated her panic, not thought, not reason, not the urgent need to act. He said the only words she could hear. "Okay, okay. I'll get her."

He ran to the window past Cat's bedroom. Rapping on the frame drew no response. Neither did repeated shouts. "Joey! Answer me! Joey!" No sound came from the house, not even the crackling of the fire. Beside him,

Cat trembled, chanting her daughter's name like a litany, her voice rising with each repetition.

Desperate, Jackson lifted the sawhorse and swung it at the window. He hoped Joey wasn't near it. No time to waste. Fire killed, but so did smoke. An image of the little girl's lifeless body formed in his brain, sending panicky messages to limbs already shaky with foreboding.

The legs of the sawhorse smashed through screen and glass, shattering the dawn air with an explosion of noise. Jackson grabbed the edge of the screen and ripped the storm window free. He started to climb on the sawhorse, then realized that one leg had broken off. "Shit!" he swore. Propping it against the side of the house, he used it as a takeoff point, jumping to propel his body onto the windowsill. Carefully, he reached through the broken shards of glass, inside and upwards. Bracing all his weight with one arm on the sill, he unlatched the window lock, then pushed the frame up.

"Jackson, please!" Cat's urgent words catapulted him through the window and onto the bedroom floor where he landed in splinters of broken glass. Wisps of smoky blue haze filled the room, swirling with the sudden breeze from the window. Jackson's chest spasmed and he coughed. The room seemed too warm. His forearms stung from deep scratches and cuts. Rivulets of blood tracked down his hand and left a half-finished palm print on the carpet.

He looked toward the bed. Empty. His heart sank. Damn! Had she left her bed and entered the living room? He had to find her for Cat's sake and— He stopped thinking as an overpowering smell filled his nostrils with the stink of something plastic melting. He coughed again and forced his burning lungs to take only small shallow breaths.

Where the hell was she? "Joey?"

He started toward the hall, then stopped, remembering something he'd heard once. Kids hid from fire, not knowing it would find them anyway. He dropped to his knees and peered under the bed. There was enough light now to show that no one hid in the smoky shadows beneath it.

He stood, coughing, holding the tail of his shirt to his face. Looking around, fear made his heart pound like crazy. Not fear of the fire, though he was afraid, but fear he would fail. Outside, Cat waited for him to bring her child to her. Cat's lovely smile would be stilled forever if he didn't come out that window with Joey unhurt. He couldn't bear never seeing her smile again. Jackson's lips tightened in a thin, hard line. If necessary, he'd put the fire out with his hands. Anything for Cat. Anything. God, don't let that little girl die!

It was all the prayer he had time for. He spotted the closet, its door slightly ajar, and hurtled toward it. Slamming the door open, he dropped to his knees. Joey huddled against hanging clothes, her knees tucked up to her chest, arms wrapped tightly around them. She looked at him with frightened, wide green eyes, exactly like her mother's.

His heart leapt with joy. "Thank you, God," he whispered. Keeping his voice calm, he held out his arms and said, "Come on, Joey. I'll take you to your mother."

Just for a second, she looked as if she didn't know him. Then recognition dawned. Trustingly, she nodded and reached out to him. Just as before, when she'd allowed him to toss her high in the air, she gave up fear for the safety of his arms.

With her small body held close to his chest, her face buried in the security of his neck, her own arms wrapped tightly around him, he stood. She smelled of lilac dusting powder and smoke. The lilac powder smelled like little girl and the smoke smelled like danger. The combination caused relief and dismay to sweep over him. A different outcome might have been only minutes away.

"Where's Mommy?" the small voice whispered in his ear.

"Waiting for us," he answered, then hurried to the window. Cat stood on the broken sawhorse, clinging to the edge of the windowsill, looking as if she intended to climb into the room with them. At the sight of her daughter safe in Jackson's grasp, her expression changed to overwhelming relief.

Jackson's broad grin mitigated his sharp order. "Get back on the ground before you fall, Cat. I'll hand her to you."

Obediently, Cat jumped back to the ground, then reached up, eagerly waiting.

Jackson had to pry Joey's arms from around his neck. She was surprisingly strong for such a waif of a child. He put her gently into Cat's waiting hands, then climbed out and dropped to the ground beside them.

Cat held Joey in a viselike grip, rocking back and forth, kissing her daughter repeatedly on the face and arms, making funny choking sounds as she did so. A long moment later, she took a deep breath and relaxed her hold. Her runaway emotions in check, she said in an almost-calm voice, "It's okay, honey. You're safe now. Jackson saved you. You're okay."

Jackson hated to interrupt the reunion, but there was no other way. The fire would quickly spread to the rest of the house. "The hose, Cat," he reminded.

Cat looked up at him and nodded, still clutching her daughter. He reached for Joey and she came readily. Reluctantly, Cat let go of the little girl. ''I'll put her in my truck where she'll be safe, Cat,'' Jackson said. ''Get the garden hose.''

Cat turned to go. She looked back once, her lovely eyes huge, her face stark white, then she ran.

CHAPTER SIX

JACKSON CARRIED Joey to his truck, enjoying the warm weight in his arms more than he would have thought possible. He was intensely glad he'd decided to drive past Cat's home before continuing his errand, no matter what reason had prompted him to turn right instead of left.

He deposited Joey on the front seat of the truck and admonished her severely to stay there and not touch anything. He started to leave, but her frightened look touched some place inside of him that tightened up in response. He reached across her to where he'd left his jacket, picked it up and carefully draped it around the child's thin, shivering shoulders.

"It's okay now," he whispered, touching her cheek. He smiled his most reassuring I'm-a-Marine-and-nothing-will-ever-hurt-you-when-I'm-around grin, waited a moment for the fear to leave her eyes, then returned to the broken window and climbed back in.

He groped his way through the thickening smoke to the kitchen door and unlocked it. Cat wrestled with the weight of a metal bucket and a hundred feet of awkward garden hose, trailing its length behind her from the spigot near the garage. He took the hose from her and pulled it toward the living room as she ran to the kitchen sink and filled the bucket.

Although smoke polluted the entire house, the fire appeared to be confined to one corner of the living room where flames licked eagerly at the drywall. Wielding the garden hose, Jackson played the barely adequate stream of water back and forth across the hungry blaze. Cat, choking and coughing from the thick smoke, frantically tossed buckets of water on smoldering embers.

Finally, Jackson grabbed her arm as she started to throw another bucket of water into the corner. "That's enough, Cat. The fire's out. You don't want to fight a flood, too, do you?"

"It's out? Are you sure?" She looked around, seeming only now to see how much the fire and smoke had damaged the room. Her soot-darkened face paled beneath the shadow of ashes and smoke.

"I can see the sky through the roof. It's burned through."

Her forlorn voice brought an ache to his throat that had nothing to do with the smoke. "Go get Joey out of the truck. You two wait on the front lawn. I'll open up some windows and clear the smoke out of here. No point in all of us breathing this stuff."

As if suddenly awakened, Cat turned to him. "Oh, Jackson, what if you hadn't passed by at the right moment? We'd both have—"

Jackson wanted to reach out to her, but his father's words came back to him. He couldn't give Cat the wrong impression and still call himself an honorable man. With no intention of staying in Engerville, tasting Cat's sweet lips was out of the question. He turned away, unable to face the light in her eyes without wanting to feel her against him. His voice ragged, he ordered, "Go get Joey before she decides to start the truck and drive it into town. The keys are still in the ignition and she is your daughter, you know."

After he opened every window and door, the smoke began to clear. Jackson's raw throat burned as if he'd swallowed some of the fire. Ignoring the pain, he worked at clearing debris. The sofa, one arm consumed by the fire down to its wood frame, had created most of the smoke, he realized. The twisted burned wires of the lamp's electrical cord gave him a clue as to how the fire might have started. Jackson wrestled the water-soaked sofa out the front door, then dragged it into the yard.

"When can we come in to help?" she asked.

What damage the fire had done was nothing compared to the dirty mess the smoke had made of every room in the small farmhouse. It would shock her and scare Joey. He hesitated. "In a little bit. I want to clear out the worst of the garbage first. Can't have Joey deciding that stuff would be great to play in, can we?"

Cat studied his strong, purposeful air of command. This side of him definitely wasn't the old Jackson. Had the Marines made a man out of the rebellious youth she'd fallen in love with? Did the love she held for the youth carry over to this stranger?

She'd been on her own a long time. Maybe Jackson was too used to giving orders and she was too used to acting on her own. Probably the two of them wouldn't have much in common now. She glanced down at the warm weight burrowed into her side. They had Joey, but Jackson didn't know. She felt the sharp stab of guilt sweep over her.

Although Jackson had no idea that Joey was his, he'd risked his life for her as casually as if it meant nothing. Maybe all the change in Jackson was on the surface. Down deep, he might be the same reckless teenager who'd joined her in the committing of youthful folly. If he'd really become the thoughtful, considerate, brave man he seemed, how would he react to her having kept his daughter from him?

Cat shuddered as she pictured Jackson's anger. Beside her, Joey twisted free of her arm and looked up at her. "Mommy, are you still afraid?"

"We're safe now, honey, and that's all that matters. Thanks to Jackson."

"I like him. He found me in the closet and picked me up. He's so big."

Cat's throat tightened at the remembered image of Jackson leaning out of the window, Joey safe in his arms, to hand her a miracle. "He's about the biggest guy I know," she agreed.

"I think he's bigger than Tommy Karl's dad, don't you?"

Cat smiled. "Maybe a little taller," she admitted.

"I like him," Joey said, firmly repeating her previous statement.

And there was another danger, Cat thought. Jackson would be leaving in a few weeks. Would her daughter's fragile heart be broken?

"Teddy Bear, Jackson won't be around forever. It's okay to like him, but don't go thinking he'll be here a long time. He's leaving as soon as his father is well."

Joey considered. "How long will that be?"

"A few weeks, maybe a month or two. Certainly not more than that."

"That's a long time. Maybe he'll like living on a farm and he'll decide to stay."

A childish dream began to appear in her daughter's words. Cat needed to destroy that dream to protect Joey. Anger at the injustice of life rose in her. Harshly, she said, "Jackson doesn't like farms, Joey. That's why he left Engerville. He's not going to stay, so quit thinking he will.''

Joey huddled into Cat's side. Her voice quavered. "Are you sure, Mom? He smiles a lot. I don't think he's sad.''

"Jackson is happy because he knows he doesn't have to stick around. I'm sorry, Joey, but you think every nice guy who comes along would make a good daddy. I want you to realize Jackson won't be here for long so you don't get your hopes up. He's leaving and that's the end of this discussion.'' Cat looked up as Jackson walked across the lawn toward them, his face covered with smoke and soot, a splash of gray ash down one lean cheek. There didn't appear to be much hope for Joey…and none for herself.

Jackson held out a hand and pulled Cat to her feet. Joey rose with her.

"I'm going to drive home and tell Pop what happened. I'll be back in an hour or so to help you clean up, but first I want to go in with you while you look around.''

"You've done enough already. I'll call my insurance agent and then finish the cleaning. You don't have to help.''

"I wouldn't dream of allowing you to fight this mess alone. You're going to need a couple of the wall studs replaced, and part of the floor is burned pretty bad. I'm not sure how much of the ceiling is gone, but it didn't burn all the way through the roof, except in that one spot. I can cover it with heavy plastic. Most of the damage is due to smoke and that'll wash up with soap and water…and maybe a coat of paint.''

Cat nodded. "Really, I can take care of it. You've

saved our lives at the risk of your own. That's quite enough for one day, don't you think?"

Jackson laughed, then reached out and flicked Joey's cheek with one finger. "I can't imagine anyone hesitating for a second if they knew this little girl needed help. And the fire wasn't that bad, so I was never in danger."

"Don't make light of it, Jackson."

"For pete's sake, Cat, don't say any more. I only did what anyone else would do. Let's go take a look at the damage."

The reason Jackson wanted to be with her when she got her first clear look at the water-drenched, fire-blackened living room was quickly apparent. Cat sucked in a deep breath. Jackson's arm snaked around her and pulled her into his chest.

"Hey, Wild Cat…what'd I tell you? This isn't nearly as bad as it looks."

Cat choked back a sob. "Yes, it is, too…. Damn! I sound like Joey. I'm sorry. It's just…oh, never mind."

"Don't cry, Cat," he whispered. "Please. I'll help you, I promise. So will Joey. Won't you, Short Stuff?"

Joey looked ready to cry too, but she nodded. Her pink lips trembled.

"I'm going to go now, but I'll be back. Just take it easy, will you? Don't go mopping and scrubbing until I'm here to help." He left them standing at the door.

Cat watched him go, feeling half sick at the damage the fire had done. The home she'd worked so hard to make had nearly gone up in smoke. She'd be weeks, maybe months, repairing the damage and even then, it wouldn't be the same. The fire made her realize her vulnerability in a way the bank's threat to foreclose hadn't been able to achieve. Jackson's going made her know the aching emptiness inside her would never disappear.

"We're getting to be experts, Joey," she whispered.

"Expert at what, Mommy?"

At watching Jackson Gray leave, she thought, but she didn't say the words aloud.

It was hard to decide what to do first. Cat ran her hand over the wall and it came away black. She went into the kitchen and washed her hands at the sink. Everything she touched was covered in soot. Even the handle of the faucet. She heard the sound of an engine and glanced out the window over the sink. Luke's truck.

Luke looked like he'd just come from the fields. His denim jacket was dusty and his jeans had a dirt smear on the left leg. He came around to the kitchen door, the way he always did.

She opened the door and he came in, looked around for just a second, then said, "What the— Cat, did you burn something on the stove, or what? It smells terrible in here."

She told him what had happened, about the fire and how Jackson saved them both. There was no mistaking his concern.

"Oh, Cat, I'm so sorry this happened to you. Damn, you shouldn't be living here all alone, anyway."

"Luke, being alone didn't cause the fire. If six other people had been here, it still would have happened. And Jackson would have had a very busy morning trying to save eight people instead of just two."

Luke frowned. "That's not exactly what I meant. I wish you'd taken me up on my offer. It's still open, you know."

"To marry you? Luke, don't be silly. You don't love me and marrying somebody to get a mother for Tommy Karl would end up making you miserable. Tommy Karl will be okay. You're doing a good job with him."

His voice softened. "I didn't just need a mother for Tommy."

Cat shook her head. "I know. I get lonely, too, but we both know that friendship, even a great friendship, is not the same as love."

He nodded. "Well, as a friend, the least I can do is offer to help clean up. I've got to pick up Tommy Karl in town and we could swing by here on our way back."

"No," Cat said firmly. "Jackson's coming back and I know how much you have to do at home. We'll be okay."

Luke sighed. "I guess you're right, but are you sure you should let Jackson come back? I'd hate to see him hurt you again."

"I'm not a starry-eyed teenager anymore. Jackson can't hurt me unless I let him. And I don't intend to do that."

"What was that old saying about 'good intentions'?"

After he left, Cat thought about his question. She didn't just have good intentions. She had resolution and nothing could sway that. Not even Jackson Gray.

JACKSON TOLD HIS FATHER about the fire, watching the different emotions race across the older man's face. Fear and concern for his son and for Cat and her daughter. "Cat's pretty shook up. She looked sick when the smoke cleared out and she could see how bad it was. I'm going to clean up, put a bandage on these scratches and then go back and help her. Okay?"

"I'll call Buddy and ask him to come out here. He can use the work."

"You're sure you don't mind?"

"That's what neighbors are for, besides it's the least you can do."

Jackson lifted a brow. "The least I can do? What does that mean?"

Will stared up at the ceiling as if debating a reply, then shook his head. "Nothing. Not a thing. You're sure they're both okay?"

Jackson nodded.

"Good. Go on, then."

As Jackson stood in the shower, he thought about his conversation with his father. Pop's fear for Cat and Joey's safety seemed a bit excessive, even with them being the older man's closest neighbor. Ah, well, his father had a soft heart.

Smoke and soot slid down Jackson's body along with blackened, translucent soap bubbles. Afterward, he applied cortisone ointment to the deep scratches on his hand. He'd lost a fair amount of hide on Cat's behalf. And Joey's. He thought about the fear he'd seen in the little girl's eyes, and the sudden change as she recognized him. Something melted in him. Something warm and sweet to replace the lump of resentment coming home had put there. Who was the horse's ass who'd had the lack of human feeling to walk away from her?

If he ever got married, he'd not mind having a bit of sweetness like Joey to give him a reason to come home every night. Her mother would make the deal even better. He shied away from the thought. Cat loved her dilapidated, broken-down horse farm. She'd never give it up, even if it burned to the ground. She'd live in the barn while she rebuilt, as surely as his father would. Right now, she was probably cleaning up the ashes and debris.

A ball of bittersweet anger formed under his ribs. No way was he going to stay in Engerville. No way was Cat going to leave. No way for the three of them to become a family. Quit thinking, he ordered himself. Quit thinking about the impossible.

A MOP IN ONE HAND and a pail of water in the other, Cat studied the devastation the fire had caused to her home and how little progress she'd made in the last hour. She swiped at her eyes and turned away from Joey. If this accident had destroyed her security, what would it do to Joey? She didn't want her daughter to realize how shaken she was at the mess fire could make of their home in a very few minutes.

The doorbell rang, jarring her from her misery. She looked through the front window. Jackson stood outside. Six feet, two inches of heroic rescuer. He looked the part, she thought. His hair still curled damply red from his shower. A white T-shirt stretched its seams across his broad chest and snug-fitting Marine fatigue pants hugged his narrow hips. Cat quickly finger-combed her hair. Joey bumped against Cat's side as she hurried to see who waited on the other side of the door.

"It's Jackson, Mom. Can I let him in?"

Cat glanced at the eager look on her daughter's face. Probably mirrored her own, she realized. This hero-worship of Jackson Gray had to stop, on both their parts, no matter how much he deserved it. "I'll let him in. Get the cleaning rags from the closet for me, would you? We're going to have to wash down all the walls to get rid of the smoke smell."

Joey nodded, but instead of running to the closet, she stood still beside her mother. Cat frowned. "Oh, well. You can say hello first. Giving in to you is getting to be a habit, young lady. Remind me to be firm next time."

Joey's smile lit her whole face. "Thanks, Mom. I'll remind you."

"I bet you will, Teddy Bear." Cat laughed and moved to the door.

She opened it and did her best not to dwell on the way the morning sun through the trellis painted his face with bright bands, highlighting his copper hair.

"Hi, Cat. Joey."

Cat held the door wider. "Come on in. We're just starting on the floor and walls. You really don't have to help, Jackson. I wouldn't ask anybody to do this messy job."

"You didn't ask. I volunteered. Remember?"

Cat nodded. "So you did. I thought the Marines taught a guy to keep his mouth shut when the call went out for volunteers."

Jackson eased past her to stare at the damage. "I'm a slow learner. Where do you want to start?"

Cat felt his passing like a warm breeze. It heated her blood and made her heart beat faster. Old memories kept intruding lately. Old memories she'd tried to forget. "Want a cup of coffee?"

He shook his head. "I'd rather make a start first. I had a cup at the farm. That'll do me for a while."

"Your father didn't mind your coming over?"

Again, Jackson shook his head. Fleeting irritation skated across his face. "I'm over twenty-one, Cat. I don't have to ask if I can go see a friend anymore."

Cat shrugged. "I just meant there might be chores waiting at home. Lord knows, there's always something to be done here."

"Pop called Buddy and he's coming over. I'm sure there'll still be work for me to do when I get home, though. That's just the way it is."

Cat gave in. "Well, then, let's get started. What would

you prefer to do, clean the walls or scoop up burned stuff?''

Jackson stood with his arms crossed, surveying the large smoky-smelling room. He nodded as if making up his mind. ''I'll start with the burned stuff. Have you got a large bucket? I thought I'd cut the corner off the carpet, where it's burned so bad. Do you think the rest of it can be cleaned?''

''I'm afraid not. That carpet saw its best day long before the fire. With the smoke and water damage, we might as well take it all out. I wish I could live with this mess, but that hole in the wall has to be repaired, and those floorboards need to be replaced. The roof will need some new shingles on that corner, too.'' She sighed. ''No, it has to be fixed.''

Jackson's eyebrows shot up. ''Why would you want to live with it? It's a total mess.''

Cat looked around for Joey. Her daughter lingered near the door, staring in obvious fascination at their visitor. ''Joey, go out to the barn and get that plastic bucket I left in the tack room. Jackson can use that to put trash in.''

Joey twisted like a worm on a hook. ''Aw, Mom. I want to stay here with you guys.''

''What was that you were going to remind me about?'' Joey hardly ever argued with her before Jackson came on the scene. Cat had no intentions of letting her start, even if she did agree with her daughter that every man in Engerville faded into the background next to Jackson Gray.

''Sure, sure. I'll go get the bucket. 'Bye, Jackson. I'll be back in a minute.''

Jackson stared hard at Cat until Joey left the house, then he asked, bluntly, ''Why, Cat?''

Cat matched his bluntness with the naked truth, though she would have preferred not to tell him. She would manage. She didn't want his pity. "I'm behind on the mortgage payments, Jackson. I'd rather use the insurance money for that than get new carpet."

Jackson walked farther into the living room. He looked around at the damage. "You know what, Cat? I'm a pretty fair carpenter. Pop taught me how a long time ago when he did carpenter work to pay the bills and the farm was just work. Farming didn't pay for anything...not in the beginning. I'll bet I could repair this wall and the floor. Even the ceiling. The joists aren't burned, just scorched. Only a couple feet of the roofing will have to be replaced."

Jackson's heart overpowered his common sense, she thought. He'd been that way in school, too. She refused his too-generous offer. "It's a huge job, Jackson. Far too big for a guy who has to go home and clean stalls afterward." She softened her refusal with a brief smile. "I couldn't ask you."

"Didn't we already talk about volunteering? Pop has all the tools and the work involved is not that bad. It might take me a week or two, working a few hours at a time, but I could do it."

Cat shook her head, moved around him to stand a step or two in front, and surveyed the damage. "Why should you? Really, Jackson, helping a neighbor is nice of you, but I think this is off the scale. There's too much to do and your father needs you at the farm."

Jackson grinned at her. His entrancing smile taking charge of her, her heart and the situation. "Let me worry about Pop. Do you want me to do it or not? It's up to you, Cat."

She'd dreamed about his smile for years. Hesitating, she said, "I shouldn't."

He came over to her and placed one hand on each shoulder, so close his body heat caused unwanted desire to tremble on the edge of happening.

"There are a lot of things I've done that I shouldn't have. For most of those things, I'm only sorry a little bit. If you let your life be ruled by what you should or shouldn't do, then I'll know you're not Wild Cat Darnell anymore. Are you Wild Cat or Catherine?"

He stood too close. It made thinking hard and talking almost impossible, but remembering was easy. "That's not fair-r-r, Jackson."

As if he felt the same things she did, he leaned down and touched her cheek with his lips, so briefly she couldn't call it a kiss, yet it sent a lightning surge of wanting through her.

He stepped back and lowered his hands, quickly, as if he too felt the electricity between them. His whispered words echoed off the smoky walls. "I don't recall making any claims about being fair."

Cat held her stomach with one hand, trying to still the turmoil inside her. "What's in it for you? I can't pay you."

Jackson ran an impatient hand through his hair, failing to disturb the short curls. "What does it matter? I don't know."

Cat thought he sounded exactly like Joey when she asked her daughter to explain something she did on impulse.

"You must know, Jackson," Cat prompted, as she did when she tried to get a reason out of Joey. She didn't know what she wanted to hear from the tall Marine, but she knew she shouldn't accept his offer.

Jackson shrugged, as if her questions were irrelevant. "The whole point is I don't need the money, Cat. What's in it for me is knowing I'm helping an old friend. We used to be good friends. It's reason enough. Does that satisfy you?"

"That's all?"

He grinned the old wicked smile. "Unless you can think of another way to pay me."

Her heart lurched, then righted itself. To say Jackson Gray teased was like saying snow was cold and spring followed winter. His sense of humor knew no bounds. She retorted, "If I didn't know you were kidding, I'd smack you!"

Just for a moment, he hesitated, then looked past her. "Right. That's settled then. Let's get to work."

She could have sworn he meant to say something else.

"Here's Joey with the bucket I need. Thanks, Short Stuff. Want to help me? You can pick up the smaller pieces."

Joey turned to her mother.

She couldn't deny her daughter a bit of closeness with Jackson. Her past decisions had cost Joey enough. Let her have these moments, this bit of time. Cat smiled, feeling the hot sting of tears behind the smile. "I give up. Whatever Jackson says."

Jackson clapped a big hand on Joey's shoulder in a gentle fashion. "That's the way I like a woman to talk. Your mother is finally getting the message."

"Don't listen to him, Joey. You're not that big, Marine. This cat can still scratch."

"I wondered about that," he said, then quickly backed away, throwing up his hands as if to protect himself from her claws.

Even Joey giggled as they set to work.

An hour later, the insurance agent showed up. He looked over the damage, then sat in the kitchen with Cat for twenty minutes. Joey and Jackson continued to clean up the mess. They'd removed all the debris and were working on cutting the carpet into small enough pieces to haul out. Jackson studied the floor. Beneath the worn carpet lay a well-preserved hardwood surface. With a little work, some stain and wax, it would be much better looking than the old carpet. Maybe even better than new carpet. How much, he wondered, did Cat need for the mortgage, and would she accept a loan from him? Not stubborn, independent Catherine Darnell. Well, he could fix this part of her problem.

After the insurance agent left, Cat stepped into the living room, a distracted frown and weary eyes seeking him out. She looked as if a two-ton boulder weighed down her shoulders.

Transfixed by her shadowed eyes, he found it hard to speak. When he did, his voice had the deep suggestion of a growl. "Isn't he going to do right by you, Cat?"

"Yes. He will. As much as he can." Cat scanned the living room assessing the full extent of the damage. She sighed. "He was very generous, Jackson. Really. They'll pay for the fire damage to the walls and ceiling. A percentage of the cost of a sofa and carpet. Nothing for my beading materials."

Jackson couldn't remember ever seeing her eyes so dark with disappointment. His heart felt as if a hand were squeezing it, but he had to say something. Anything. "I'll help, Cat."

"Paul said he'd get a carpenter out here to estimate the damage, but that I could go ahead and get materials from the lumberyard. We can have them send the bill directly to him. He said if I wanted to take care of it myself, they'd pay the full estimate of whatever the carpenter said it would cost. It won't be enough for the mortgage payment after the supplies are deducted, but the bank will be happy to get it, even if it isn't the full payment.'' She tried to smile.

''You're thinking about the downside. Remember, I'm going to do the work. We'll see how cheap we can get by. You might be surprised at how much is left over.''

''Joey is safe. So am I, thanks to you. That's all that really matters. I'll be able to sleep tonight.''

I won't, he thought. ''Good,'' he said.

CHAPTER SEVEN

BUDDY SHOWED UP at the farm a bare two hours after Jackson left. Blue rushed out to greet him with a volley of excited barks. Will nudged the dog behind him and welcomed his helper. "There's a ton of things that need taking care of, Buddy, and I have a feeling Jackson's going to be tied up helping Catherine for a while. Can you work for me the next couple of weeks?"

"The Johnsons asked me to work for them all summer. A man needs steady work, Will. I'd do it, if I could. You know that." The short man shifted his weight and avoided looking into Will's eyes. "I'll help out today, though."

Will took a deep breath. "How about if I guarantee you a job 'till Christmas, and maybe afterwards, if things work out the way they should."

Buddy shrugged and spat a brown stream of tobacco juice off to the left. Blue, who had been edging closer, sniffed at the aromatic spot and hurriedly backed off.

"Don't seem to me like you need a full-time helper with Jackson here. Pity the boy don't like farming. He's a damn hard worker."

"I told you I'd guarantee a paycheck until Christmas. That oughta be all you need to know. Not being sharp with you, you understand. Just that I know what I want and how much help I'll need getting it."

The little man shrugged. "Don't matter none to me.

I guess the Johnsons can get Albert Peterka to help them, living next door the way he does. As long as you pay me, I can stand around and watch beets grow as good as anybody else.''

"You don't need to worry about running out of work. I'll see to that. First thing I need you to do is run into town and pick up those tractor parts. Jackson doesn't have a brain in his head when he gets distracted. He's completely forgotten about it.''

Buddy spat another brown glob of juice. "I reckon all kids is that way.''

"I suppose he had good cause this time.''

Later, Will grinned in deep satisfaction as Buddy drove his rusty pickup out of the yard and on to the gravel road. Maybe now he'd find out if that little girl of Cat's also happens to be his granddaughter. Joey sure looked a lot like Helen. She had the same heart-shaped face and dimpled smile that Cassidy inherited.

Will's throat tightened as he stood in the yard thinking about the good years with his wife. The too few years. Well, things were better now. He'd made up with Jackson, his strength was coming back and, without ever meaning to forget his wife, he enjoyed the time he spent with Bertie. Things were working out just fine.

WORKING SIDE BY SIDE with Jackson excited Cat. Despite his attraction for her, she hadn't thought that would be a problem, but every time his arm brushed hers, a ripple of desire raced through her. Every time he smiled at her, the warm, inner glow of happiness became almost unbearable. When he joked with Joey and then winked at her, she felt the impact in the pit of her stomach.

Finally, she could stand the closeness no longer.

"Let's break for lunch, guys. I'll fix something and we can rest a bit."

"So how much rest will you get if you cook for us, then have to clean up the kitchen?"

Cat pushed away his remark with a wave of her hand. "Oh, I don't mind."

Jackson's brow lifted a half inch. "I do," he said, firmly. "I've got a much better idea. Let's run into town and order some lumber, so that will be ready for me when we finish washing everything down. We can grab a bite to eat there. Okay with you?"

Cat glanced at Joey. She'd been a stalwart helper to Jackson, obediently carrying out his every command. "You're right. We're all tired, and we should be. We've been up since dawn. Joey and I will take a quick shower and change clothes. You can wash up in the kitchen, if you don't mind."

His grin stretched wide. "Right on, but first, I'll take some measurements to get an idea of what we'll need from the lumberyard. You two go on and clean up."

Cat's heart lifted. "Come on, Joey. Let's play hooky."

"Hooky? What's that?"

Jackson leaned down and patted her cheek. "That's when you skip out on work, kiddo. You'll learn to like it. I'm trying to teach your mom, too."

A tug of misgivings pulled at Cat's heart. Would Jackson always want to play? Would he never settle down? Determinedly, she put the thought out of her mind. It wasn't playing hooky when you worked your behind off for hours, then decided to take a break. She motioned for Joey to follow her.

For once, Joey didn't linger in the shower. Neither did Cat. Twenty minutes later, they came into the living room. Jackson sat in the sheet-covered easy chair, his head back and his eyes closed. A soft buzz issued from slightly parted lips.

Joey giggled. "He's asleep, Mom, and he's snoring!" Her high, clear voice rose on the last word.

Cat couldn't take her eyes off Jackson's lean face. In quiet repose, his rust-red brows accented the smooth line of his forehead. His cheekbones were high, his face un-lined, his nose strong and beneath it, sharply sculptured lips. Her hand rose and it took her only a second to realize why. She wanted to touch his lips, to trace their outline, to feel her lips on his. An empty, disappointed ache filled her heart.

"Can I wake him, Mom? Can I?"

Glad to have the moment interrupted, Cat nodded.

Joey tiptoed over to the chair, her hands holding in the giggles that threatened to erupt. She tiptoed to the side of the chair, close to Jackson's face. Then, her small hand reached out to the eye closest to her. Carefully, she pulled the lid up, until the eyeball inside stared back at her. "Wake up, Jackson," she ordered sternly.

A long arm snaked out quickly and grabbed her. Jackson opened both eyes and grinned at his tormentor. "Gotcha! I'll teach you to wake up a man who's getting a little hard-earned rest."

He proceeded to tickle Joey, who giggled and wiggled until Cat ordered him to stop. "If you two don't quit horsing around, we'll be having dinner in town, not lunch."

"You do have a point, Cat. Joey, shall we please your mother by acting like grown-ups for a change?"

Joey shook her head. "I'm just a kid."

"Me, too, but tell you what, we're both in for a spank-ing if we don't do what Mommy says."

Joey shook her head. "Mommy never spanks me. Never."

"No? Well, you're lucky, but she might spank me." He turned his gaze toward Cat. "Would you spank me, Wild Cat? No? Even if I asked you to?" Jackson affected an evil leer.

His wicked grin turned her legs to water.

AT THE LUMBERYARD, the aromatic scent of uncured pine and sawdust filled the air. Jackson rubbed his hands across lumber with the air of a connoisseur. He selected smooth, straight boards to repair the outside wall, several sheets of plywood for the inside, and paneling to cover the plywood. Picking up a few pieces of tongue-and-groove hardwood flooring, he explained to Cat his plans for the floor. She nodded and remarked only that it seemed like quite a bit of work to her.

Jackson scooped Joey up and perched her on his broad shoulder. "Work? Not a bit. I'm going to supervise and Joey will handle the hard stuff."

Joey's excited laughter ran through Cat like a knife. The two of them took to each other as if they belonged together. She'd kept them apart. What would Jackson say if he learned the truth? What would Joey say? Cat made an effort to smile at their horseplay. Until she decided how to handle this, she couldn't tell them. She'd have to pray that neither of the two people she loved discovered her lies. An empty, fearful ache wrapped around her heart.

Later, when they entered the restaurant, Joey immediately claimed a booth near the windows looking out at the traffic on Main Street and announced loudly, "I want to sit beside Jackson, Mom. Okay? Can I? Can I sit with you, Jackson?"

Dubious, Cat asked, "What do you think, Jackson? Joey's table manners are still in the training stage. Eating that close to her can be dangerous."

"I'm a Marine, remember? We love danger. Come on, Short Stuff." Jackson gestured to Joey to scoot across the bench seat to the window.

Cat conceded what had already been decided. "Joey, remember your manners. And do try not to spill anything on Jackson."

"Mom!" Joey protested. "I'm not a little kid, you know."

"Right," Cat commented dryly.

Joey ordered her favorite meal, hamburger with french fries and double ketchup. Jackson and Cat opted for the luncheon special, broiled walleye pike, fried potatoes and a house salad. While they waited for their food, Cat did her best not to stare at Jackson. Every day they spent in each other's company made him more irresistible and there existed an insidious compulsion to look at Jackson, then at Joey and compare the two. No matter how much she tried not to, when the three of them were together, Cat had to hold herself in check to avoid giving away her secret. Once again, she reminded herself that this togetherness had to stop.

Jackson noticed her preoccupied state. "You're not still worried about the money?" He propped one long arm on the bench seat behind Joey and leaned back to study her with deceptively lazy, blue eyes.

Cat jumped on the subject, anxious to divert her own mind. "I haven't added the pennies yet, but if things work out with the materials the way you think, and the money comes through the way Paul promised, then I might have a little left over for the bank. Then if I get a good price for RugRat, I can catch up on the mortgage payments. That's a lot of 'mights' and 'maybes' mixed together with an 'if' or two, but you know what I mean." Nervously, she smiled at him.

Jackson wasn't fooled. He rested an elbow on the table, put his hand under his chin and turned a steady curious stare on her. "Then why the serious look? We're supposed to be relaxing."

As always, his gaze unsettled her. "I was thinking…about something."

"Care to share?" He sat back in the booth, as if he was prepared to wait all day for her answer.

Cat searched for a way to refuse, or a white lie to explain it away, then found a diversion. "Joey, quit fiddling with the salt shaker."

"I wasn't, Mom," Joey denied. "I was just looking at it."

"Cat?" Jackson prompted, apparently unwilling to let her escape so easily.

She looked out the window at the meager traffic, then back at Jackson. What would he say if she admitted the truth of her thoughts? One glance at his lean face, the cerulean eyes that could turn winter cold in an instant, and the fearsomely strong shoulders convinced her of the folly of such a thought. "It's nothing."

Jackson leaned closer to her. "You know what you remind me of, when you swing that long hair in front of your face?"

Deliberately, Cat pushed her hair back. "No," she said. "What?"

"High school. I could always tell when you were upset about something. You'd let your hair swing forward and conceal as much of your face as you could."

"I didn't know anyone noticed."

Jackson sat back again, his face thoughtful. "I did. I

used to watch you a lot. You were never the daredevil you pretended to be.''

Cat shook her head and grinned ruefully. ''You watched me? Nah. I think not. You were all tied up in what Rebeka was doing.''

Jackson went still. ''Not so much that I didn't notice you.''

A cynical laugh bubbled in her throat. ''As Joey would say, 'yeah, right!' You never noticed any other girl while Rebeka was around, Jackson.''

He remained serious. ''That's what you *think*. It isn't what you know.''

Cat's heart thudded with the intensity of his gaze on her. ''If you're trying to say you had a moment's thought for me before Rebeka ran out on you, well forget it. I'm not buying.''

He shrugged. ''I noticed you as a friend, the same way you saw me. Was there more? Maybe not. Not before Rebeka and I parted ways, but after, well, I don't think a day's passed since the senior prom that I haven't thought of you.''

''Oh, come on! I'm not wearing my wading boots, you know.''

Jackson conceded a smile, but remained adamant. ''True, though.''

''Jackson, this isn't going anywhere. Why bring it up?''

Once again his shoulders tightened in a faint shrug. ''Lighten up a little. I'm just talking about the past, Cat. I know there's no future that's going to see us together. You're too stuck on your farm and the Goose River will dry up before I make Engerville my home.''

Cat looked at Joey, then gave Jackson a warning look. ''I don't think all that is something we should discuss with Joey around. She's only eight." The last part slipped out. Cat could have bitten her tongue, but it was too late.

"Eight?" Jackson's brows shot up. "I figured six or seven."

Triggered by the sound of her name, Joey, who'd been gaping at the other customers, now swung her attention back to Jackson and Cat. "I'm a big kid now, Jackson. I'm in third grade already."

The hard look of suspicion vanished from Jackson's face to be replaced by a bland expression that would fool only a child. "Is that right, Short Stuff? Are you kidding me?"

"No, I really am. Aren't I, Mom?" She looked at her mother for verification.

Cat twisted uneasily, then smiled gratefully as the waitress brought their food to the table. She pretended not to see the question in Jackson's eyes. "Oh, good. I'm starved. Your hamburger looks delicious, Joey."

THE REST OF THEIR LUNCH passed in a blur for Jackson. The questions racing through his mind had him in a state very close to shock. He kept wondering if what he thought could possibly be true, or if he were so far off the mark that Cat would never forgive him if he asked her. It seemed impossible. Could Joey be the result of that one night of lovemaking in the shadows of Needlepoint Rock?

He managed to carry on a meaningless conversation through the rest of the meal and during the ride home. Jackson turned the truck into the yard and let it coast to the barn. "I'll unload this stuff and stack it in an empty stall, Cat. Wouldn't want it to get wet, not that it looks like it might rain or anything.'' Keeping his voice neutral, he tried not to give away his thoughts.

"I'll help you, Jackson," Joey volunteered eagerly.

"No," Cat ordered. "You come to the house with me."

"Why, Cat?" Jackson challenged. "Is there some reason she shouldn't stay and help me?" Could she explain her objection in some way that would remove the questions in his mind?

Cat retreated, her face as pale as Jackson thought his own might be. She muttered in a subdued voice, "I didn't want her to bother you."

No doubt existed in his mind that she hid something. "Joey's no bother," he said shortly.

Cat nodded and left the two of them standing beside the truck, her straight, stiff figure refusing him any answers. Jackson set his jaw in a hard line to keep from calling her back. He wanted to know, but fear stopped the actual question. He looked down at the child standing as near to him as she could reasonably get. His heart contracted. Her green eyes were so like her mother's.

For a moment, Jackson couldn't speak, then he found a rough growl to replace his lost voice. "Okay, Short Stuff, it's you and me." He ruffled her feathery dark hair and forced a casual smile. "Let's get this lumber into the barn, but don't you try to lift any of the heavy pieces. You can carry the nails and the wood glue."

Joey's evident delight warmed him.

"Okay, but I'm really strong. I could carry some of the sticks."

"Boards, honey."

"Boards," she agreed.

"Yes, I know you could, but then what would I do? Do you want my fragile male psyche to be humiliated by letting a girl do my work? Don't answer that. You probably don't know what 'fragile' means.''

She craned her head back to look up at him. ''I know what a 'psyche' is.''

Joey smiled a wide smile that dimpled her cheeks. So familiar, but from where? Not Cat's secret smile, but more open. It made Jackson's heart pound heavily. ''Mmh,'' he said, lifting a stack of boards to his shoulder. ''Stay in front of me, Joey, so I can see you. I don't want to bash you on the head with these big sticks I'm carrying.''

She kept turning back to watch him, ''Tommy Karl's got a psyche. Mom said.''

''She did, huh? Why'd she say that?'' Jackson balanced the lumber on his shoulder, then pulled the barn door open. ''Prop the door with that brick, Joey.''

Joey scurried to do his bidding, all the while watching him, instead of her objective, a broken red brick lying abandoned next to the barn wall. ''Mommy said Tommy Karl had a male psyche and that's why he didn't want to play Barbie dolls with me. I asked him to show it to me, but he wouldn't. Boys are dumb.'' She tucked the brick in front of the barn door and stood staring up at him to see how he'd react to her provocative statement.

Jackson stood to one side so she could enter the barn. ''Does that include me?''

Joey looked unsure. ''Do you like to play Barbie dolls?''

Jackson felt as if he were walking through minefields. If he said the wrong thing, it might turn Joey against him. At the same time, a conversation about Barbie dolls seemed ridiculous in the extreme. He compromised. ''Well, I haven't done it much lately.''

Joey stood in the shadowed barn, caught in a wide

band of light coming from the overhead window. Her eyes glistened with happiness. "We could play with my dolls after we finish unloading the truck. I have seven Barbie dolls. And one Ken doll. You can play with the Ken doll, if you want to."

He pictured himself sitting on the floor, dressing Barbie dolls with Joey beside him. For some reason, it didn't seem nearly as outrageous as it should. What would Juan say if he saw his pal playing with dolls? "Maybe another time, Short Stuff. I have to get home pretty soon. How'd you get so many?"

Someone had painted a series of squares on the barn floor. Each had a number inside it. Joey stood on one foot and hopped to the next square. She teetered for a moment, then put her other foot down on an adjoining square. She looked back at Jackson. "Mostly for Christmas and my birthday. Sometimes, I get clothes."

Jackson tried to sound casual. He wasn't at all sure he succeeded. "Oh. When's your birthday?"

"February third," Joey replied, then frowned. "Did you really think I was six years old? I'm lots older than that." She lifted her chin a tad higher.

Jackson didn't hear anything after the date she gave. A roaring filled his ears as he mentally counted backward nine months. He looked down at the upturned face staring intently at him. Now he saw what he must have been blind to miss before. She had the same pixie face as his sister. The same twinkle in her eyes that Cass had turned on him a thousand times as they were growing up.

Joey's hair was lighter than Cat's and her eyes a lighter green, but still her mother's eyes, not the same light blue all his family had. No. It couldn't be true. His heart froze. There must have been someone else after him.

The aching thought drove depression deep and straight into his heart. Cat would have told him if Joey belonged to him. He saw things that weren't there. Blindly, he went back to the truck and gathered up the rest of the lumber, Joey running by his side, chattering away about her Barbie dolls and how they all had different color hair and different clothes.

ALL THE WAY BACK to Gray's Way, Jackson berated himself for a fool. He might've been the first guy to make love to Cat Darnell, but he sure as hell wasn't the last. Not once in nine years had she tried to get in touch with him. Wouldn't she have done that if he were Joey's father? Hell, all she had to do was walk across the field and she'd be at Gray's Way. Pop would have told her how to get in touch with him. Dammit, if Pop had known, he'd have come after Jackson himself, shotgun in one hand and horsewhip in the other. Jackson gave a slight shudder at the very idea. Will Gray was a strong man and his son respected him. Even after years of independence, he still wouldn't want to cross him.

When he walked into the kitchen, he saw his father standing close to the sink, leaning against it to rest his bad knee as he washed dishes. He looked up when Jackson came into the room.

"Back so soon?"

His father's acerbic tone might not have been intended to offend, Jackson thought. He decided to ignore it. "We cleaned up most of the mess, then went to town to get some lumber." Jackson wasn't sure exactly why he didn't tell Pop about having lunch with Cat and Joey.

His father turned back to the sink. "Buddy took the

tractor out to the west field. He's going to till the new corn plants and knock down some of the weeds. Looks like that new weed-killer Charles recommended isn't worth much.''

"I'll go down and help him.''

His father laid the plate he'd just washed in the empty sink and turned to rake his son with a keen gaze before turning back to the dishes. "He'll be pretty near done with that, by now. You look worn out, anyway. Why don't you take it easy this afternoon?''

"I'm not tired,'' Jackson answered, even as the tight muscles in his neck reminded him of how many hours he'd spent washing soot and smoke off the walls at Cat's place.

"I never used to get tired when I called on my sweetie, either,'' Pop said, glancing over his shoulder at his son.

A sudden heat filled Jackson, a raw anger that his father could accuse him of what he'd so carefully avoided. "Aw, crap, Pop! Cat's just a friend. I've told you that.''

Will nodded. "I think maybe you did.''

"We are friends. Only friends.'' Even to his own ears, his words sounded more defensive than they should be. And louder.

"I think maybe I heard you the first time.''

Jackson nodded in silent apology. He stuttered, though the question came out before he could stop it. "Pop, do you know…uh, who Cat's boyfriend is? Was?''

His father put the dish he was holding back in the sink. He wiped his hands on a towel he'd looped through his belt, then turned to face his with a surprised look. "Now?''

Jackson's cheeks warmed under his father's pointed

glare. "No, before. I mean…the kid, her daughter, Joey."

"Are you asking *me* who Joey's father is?"

Jackson shrugged. "Well, not like that. I just thought you might have heard."

Will Gray snorted and turned back to the sink. He addressed his answer to the soap suds in the dish pan. "You know how I feel about gossip."

"This isn't gossip, exactly," Jackson blurted.

"Oh?"

The single, sarcastic word hung like a wall between them. Jackson jammed his hands into his back pockets and widened his stance. He shouldn't feel so defensive about wanting to know. He stared hard at his father's back, willing him to supply the answer to the question that taunted him. "Pop, I have my reasons for asking."

His father didn't turn around. "Seems to me if you have any questions along that line, you ought to ask Cat."

Jackson straightened, the old resentment rising full force in him. "Can't you for once listen to me? I need to know!"

His father turned and looked him up and down in a measuring way. "Then be a man and ask Catherine Darnell who fathered that little girl. Don't come home whining to me about what you 'need to know.' If you had a brain in your head, you'd realize how I'd feel about the whole mess."

Jackson walked over to the kitchen table and sat down. He swiped at the dots of moisture on his forehead. "I didn't say I was involved."

His father snorted. "You didn't say you weren't, either."

The sound of a car pulling into the yard made them

both stop and look up. His father broke the tense silence. "I'd say Bertie's found time to stop by after her trip to the library. You keep your mouth shut around her, hear?"

"You mean you don't want her thinking about whether or not I'm messing around with Cat, don't you?"

Will's voice rose to the same level as Jackson's. "That's exactly what I mean."

Jackson's anger faded, though his frustration remained. His father was right. Somehow, it seemed he always was. His reply was almost a whisper. "Okay, Pop."

CHAPTER EIGHT

WILL GRAY BOWED HIS HEAD for a moment, disturbed by his son's bitter words. "Wish he'd listen once in a while, instead of talking so much. What more can I do? I told him to ask Cat, if he wanted to know."

"Ask Cat what?" Bertie peeked into the kitchen. "Something happen that I didn't hear about?"

Will hastily composed himself and turned away from the sink. "Now how likely is that?"

Bertie Gillis eyed him curiously. "I heard you mumbling. I don't want to be put in the position of defending you."

"As if you would," he retorted. Bertie's dry chuckle fell pleasantly on his ears.

"I've been known to, a time or two, anyway."

A lifted brow refuted her statement. "Like when?"

"Like the time you ran that boy off and him just graduated. From the sound of things when I came up to the door, you two don't get along any better now than you used to. Are you fixing to send him on his way again?"

Her answer surprised him and aroused an anger buried so deep he'd forgotten it was there. "I think that'd be my business, Bertie."

A scoffing noise issued from her as she went to the refrigerator. She helped herself to a can of Coke. "I've been coming over here for near three months now, cooking your supper, and listening to you complain about

Jackson. Don't you think we're a bit past the argument about whose business it is?''

Will gave up. "Probably. Well, I think Jackson's starting to count on his fingers about when Cat's little kitten first opened her eyes.''

Bertie came over to the sink and stood very close to him, her face compassionate. "About time, wouldn't you say?''

Will didn't answer, but he sneaked another glance at Bertie.

"Engerville's small. There weren't many young men around, if you recall.''

Will tried not to stare at her, but he wasn't used to being this close. She was one pretty woman. He wondered why she'd never married. The village couldn't be that full of idiots. She'd be a real catch for some lucky man. He forced his thoughts back to his troublesome son. "If there's two, there's always a doubt.''

She lifted one corner of a mouth still soft and warm-looking. "So who else were you thinking it might be?''

Will had trouble focusing on her words. Who might it be? He exhaled sharply and a disturbing thought about what it might be like to kiss this sometimes aggravating woman shocked him back to his senses. "Nobody in particular. But I sure wish I knew why Cat never told whoever it was.''

Bertie patted his cheek, almost as if he were a child himself. "Do you know she never told him?''

Will moved a half step back, uncomfortable with the gesture. "He wouldn't be wondering if she had,'' he pointed out.

"Well, you were bound to say something sensible if you kept talking.'' As if she knew his discomfort, she went over to the kitchen table and sat down in the same chair Jackson had sat in. She looked up at him accusingly.

Will hurried to fill the empty air. "Remind me to find out why you keep coming around, if all you intend to do is insult me."

"Remind me to tell you when I want you to know," Bertie replied with a small, secretive smile.

JOEY AND TOMMY KARL PUT the filly out to pasture and stood watching Freedom's first few tentative steps. She looked back at the children, then suddenly bolted toward the other horses. Joey held Freedom's halter and lead rope in her hand. Her mom had been pleased with the half-hour workout and maybe next time she'd let Joey hold the longe line. Maybe not. The young horses weren't that easy to control, except for Moonshot. RugRat was the worst of the lot. Joey liked all the horses, but she didn't much care for Ruggie. He was a little too quick to whirl and kick. Though Mom said it was just high spirits, she'd cautioned Joey to keep her distance.

Tasting the dust on her lips, Joey knew the windy morning had left her "smelling like a horse" as her mother always said. Tommy Karl looked much the same, streaks of dust cutting across his forehead and clinging to tufts of corn-blond hair which stuck out below his baseball cap. Mom would make both of them take a shower before she drove them into town for a hamburger. She'd promised McDonald's for lunch and Mom always kept her promises.

All morning Tommy Karl had acted as if he wanted to say something. As they watched Freedom greet her friends, he shot a sideways glance her way, then blurted out, "I think my dad wants your mom to marry him so I can have a mother."

A surge of possessive anger made Joey's chest feel tight. "She's my mom, not yours. You can't get a mom by taking mine!"

Tommy Karl nodded, ducking his head and grinning shyly. "Yeah, I know, but if she marries my dad, then he'd be your dad, too. Wouldn't you like that?"

He had a waiting, hopeful look on his face that made Joey feel sorry for him. "Jackson didn't come over to our house today. Mom said he had to work on his father's farm. I wouldn't mind having Jackson for a daddy. He's fun." Reluctantly, she added, "I guess your daddy would be all right, too."

"I think you'd like my dad best. Jackson won't stay, my dad says. Where's your real dad, anyway?"

It wasn't the first time Tommy Karl had asked that question and it wasn't the first time she didn't know the answer. In the summer heat, Joey's dark hair stuck to the nape of her neck. She lifted it away from her damp skin. The breeze brought welcome cooling. Joey hated thinking about the father who had abandoned her and her mother. She hated Tommy Karl's question, but finally she said, "I told you before, I'm not sure where, exactly, but I know it's far away. He probably won't ever come back."

Tommy Karl's frown gave way to sympathy. "That sucks."

Joey didn't want T.K. to see how badly she wanted her own father, not his father and not even somebody really, really nice like Jackson. Her *own* father. Scuffing a boot through the pasture grass, she finally replied, "I don't care. I probably wouldn't like him anyway. I hate him for leaving me and Mom."

"That sucks," Tommy Karl said, again.

Like his father, Tommy Karl never said much. "Yep," Joey agreed. She huffed out a big breath.

"Maybe he'll come back," Tommy ventured.

His words increased her bitterness. "I'd hit him," she said, savagely.

Tommy Karl, bending to pick a small stone from the ground, stopped and stared at her. "How come?"

"'Cause he left."

Tommy Karl studied the stone carefully, examining its various planes, and decided its worth by casually tossing it aside. "What if he's really big?"

"I don't know." Joey swung the halter at a gaggle of golden daisies growing beside the path. Several bright flower heads snapped off, the petals scattering away from the chocolate hubs. The violence released her tension, but Joey knew Mom wouldn't like the thoughtless act. She looked over her shoulder, as if her mother might see her, even at this distance from the house, then glanced sideways at Tommy. A few flowers, more or less, didn't bother Tommy, but her temper did sometimes.

"What if he says he's sorry?" Tommy asked, probing her anger.

"I don't know." His questions were unanswerable. She didn't know, any more than Tommy Karl did. The halter's buckles jingled as she increased her pace.

Tommy's legs were considerably longer than hers. He didn't have to stretch them much to keep up. He made a point that must have been made to him fairly often. "Dad says you have to forgive somebody if they say they're sorry."

Joey answered without any consideration for a daddy

who might say he was sorry. "I won't! Never. He left me and Mommy. I hate him!"

EARLY THE NEXT MORNING, Jackson called Cat and told her he couldn't make it over because he had to help till the north field. Not a lie, because he did intend to help, but Buddy could have done it alone. Still, a backbreaking day in the sun, sitting atop a dusty tractor, would give him time to think. His father seemed surprised at his decision to stay home, but refrained from asking his son why, for which Jackson was grateful. Especially since he wasn't exactly sure why.

The next day, Jackson spent only a few hours at Cat's home, cutting, sawing and hammering a half-dozen boards to fill the hole in the wall where he'd knocked out burned wood. To all of Cat's overtures, he turned a deaf ear, pretending complete absorption in his task. He could hardly bear to look at Joey, yet found his gaze constantly drawn to her. Was the shy sprite his own child? The question haunted him each time he looked at her. When he could take it no more, he put away his tools, announced that he was needed at Gray's Way and would return the next day.

That night, Jackson lay in bed, unable to sleep. The humid night air blew gently past the bedroom curtains, but added little to his comfort. A sticky sheen of perspiration coated his bare chest and he'd long ago kicked off the tangled sheet. Finally, he got up, groped in the dark for his jeans and T-shirt and pulled them on. He felt around on the floor for his boots and found them shoved under the edge of the bed. He put them on, raised the window screen and crawled out. In the light of a bright, high moon, he started walking through the night to Cat's ranch.

He intended to confront her despite it being past midnight, no matter how angry his late arrival made her and regardless of how much he feared her answer.

After he crossed the empty field, he stood in the shadow of a tree for long moments, staring at the drab old ranch house. Moonlight splashed the raw, unpainted new wood, underscoring how it clashed with the old dark siding. His future with his past, he thought. If Joey was his child, it would chain him to Engerville for the rest of his life. If she wasn't, it would be as devastating, because the little girl had taken no more than a few weeks to find his heart. She drew him just as Cat did. Despite the fear trembling inside him, he couldn't stand not knowing.

At the side of the house, he stood beneath Cat's bedroom window, moonlight casting the night in shadows all around him. As he scratched at the new screen, trying to wake Cat without disturbing Joey, his own idiocy appalled him. Morning would have been soon enough. A sudden chilling thought cut through the night heat, propelling him backward into the shadows. If Cat kept a gun handy, he might find his hide full of buckshot.

A small, dim light flicked on. Her face appeared at the window, shadowed by the darkness, a pale wash of indistinct white behind the screen. "Jackson, is that you? What are you doing here? Do you know what time it is?"

He appreciated the night shadows, but his embarrassment wouldn't keep him from learning the truth. Tonight, not a day later, not even an hour more. He had to know. "I need to talk to you, Cat."

She frowned. "Well, come back in the morning."

Jackson refused to be put off. Tonight, he would know the truth, no matter if it damned him to hell, or to Engerville, which was pretty much the same thing. He clenched his fist, realized it, and straightened both hands. He'd be reasonable, but adamant. "No. Now. I need to talk to you."

Cat's reply had a trembling edge. "Can't this wait, Jackson?"

Something in her voice alerted him. She hid something, he knew. He wouldn't let her off the hook. "No, it can't."

A note of resignation crept into her voice. "A few hours isn't going to change anything."

She knew what he wanted to ask and he knew the answer. Now, he was certain. "Come on, Cat. Pull the screen up and I'll help you down."

"In my nightgown?"

Embarrassment gave way to anger. She stalled him as if that would change things. Tonight, they'd both face the truth and whatever pain it might bring. "What does it matter? Get dressed if you want to. I'll wait."

Cat stared down at the thin white nightgown she wore. No blessed way would she go out the bedroom window into Jackson Gray's arms wearing nothing but this thin bit of cloth. She hurriedly pulled on the jeans lying across the chair beside her bed. She started to tug on a T-shirt and changed her mind, choosing a baggy gray sweatshirt instead. As if it mattered, she raked her fingers through the tangled black strands of hair flying around her head, trying to tame the mess into submission.

She slid into his arms, the heat from his body offset by the coldness in his winter eyes. Her father always said that the best defense was a good offense. Cat attacked. "What's so damn urgent that you come scratching around my bedroom window at midnight?"

Shadows cast his face into hard, angular planes, washing away any color, leaving it pale and cold. He glared accusingly at her. "I think you know."

Right was on his side, but he wasn't the only one entitled to be angry. A gathering knot in her stomach stirred her defenses. "I'm in no mood to play guessing games, Jackson. Say what you want or hit the road. I need my sleep."

"Yeah." His gaze raked her bitterly. He clenched his hands into fists and parked them on his narrow hips. "I'll make it short. Who is Joey's father?"

Bitter emotion washed over Cat. In all her imaginings, she'd never once pictured Jackson and herself engaged in angry confrontation. Why hadn't she told him that first day when she drove him to Gray's Way? Why hadn't she told him when she first suspected she was pregnant? She twisted away, unable to face him. "I don't think that's any of your business."

He took her arm and turned her so she had to look at him. His gaze burned into her, his voice as low as the growling of a bear. "I think it is. Damn you, Cat, tell me!"

She saw the hard set to his mouth, the way the moonlight made his eyes glitter. Night camouflaged the lower half of his face, but there was no mistaking his mood. Cat suddenly despaired of making him understand. "You already know, don't you?"

Jackson let her arm go. "She's mine, isn't she? That night at Needlepoint Rock, I got you pregnant."

Waiting for him to discover her lies had been the worst part. Now he knew. The threat was reality. It couldn't be worse than her fear. Relief gave rise to caustic humor. "Well, you had a little help. Don't try to take all the credit."

The tall ex-Marine held a hand up in warning. "Don't make jokes about this, Cat."

It angered her. All the long, lonely days angered her. The turmoil of emotions brought about by the combination of fear, guilt, and relief threatened her control. Her voice rose. "Are you the only one allowed to hide behind a joke?"

"Why didn't you tell me?"

Jackson's question accused more than asked. She put up a defensive wall. "I had my reasons."

"Why, Cat? I had a right to know." His voice had an edge that hadn't been there before.

She slammed her own rage toward his tall figure. "You didn't have *any* rights! You left town, didn't you? You said you'd never come back, didn't you? You were the one who said you hated it here!" Cat crossed her arms in front of her, and braced herself for his reply.

"I did hate it here! I do. You know that. I told you. I still hate farming, Cat, but that doesn't excuse you. Why didn't you tell me?"

She relaxed. This answer, at least, she could articulate. "That's why, Jackson. If you stayed because I was pregnant, then you'd hate me for keeping you here. I didn't want that to happen."

The wind disappeared from his sails. He seemed to fold in on himself, as if his outrage was all that held him upright. His words were a whispered plea. "But you could have told me. I would have helped."

How many times had she wanted to pick up the phone and do just that? Too many times to count and doubt had stopped her each time. "Would you have helped? Or would you have wanted to know who else I was messing around with?"

Jackson scowled. "Cat, that's not fair."

Did she imagine the ruddiness of his cheeks or did he blush? It was difficult to tell. She hesitated, then replied, "Maybe not, but how was I to know? We were friends, one-time lovers, and I didn't know how you'd react. Do you?"

Jackson opened his mouth to say something, but must have reconsidered. He closed it without speaking and turned away from her. "I had a right to know," he whispered to the night.

His soft words touched her with guilt. "I would have told you, but I was afraid," she admitted. "As time passed, I thought I'd waited too long, that there was no point in telling you. You weren't coming back anyway. If it's any consolation, I know I was wrong to keep it from you. I'm sorry." She paused. "Jackson, are you okay?"

Only the slight movement of his shoulders betrayed him. "Jackson, don't. Please. I'm sorry."

He didn't turn around. "How could you hide this from me? I had a baby and I didn't even know! Damn you, Cat. I hate you for this!"

His words sounded as if they'd been criss-crossed with a chain saw, spoken from a throat ragged with pain. The force in his reply startled her. She'd expected the strength of his fury, but not this hard-edged bitterness. She spoke to the broad outline of his tall body. "I'm sorry, Jackson. I should have told you. I know that, but I was just a kid, too. You'd hate me for keeping you in Engerville and my father would have made you marry me. It was a tough time and I made what decisions I had to make, but I didn't make them to hurt you. I didn't! I was just trying to get through it as best I could."

He turned around. In the moonlight, his stark, cold face was stony. "I never knew I had a child! You had no right to keep me out of the decision-making. I'll never forgive you for this, Cat. You don't deserve to be forgiven.''

In her imagination, he'd always said he understood, but this was no imaginary daydream. Jackson Gray loomed over her as icy and unforgiving as her father had. How could she make him understand? How could she make the hurt go away? She held out a hand in silent plea. He ignored it. Defeated, Cat let it fall back to her side. ''Jackson, I did it for you. It wasn't some plan to keep you from seeing your child. I didn't want to hold you in Engerville.''

''Don't you think I deserved a choice?''

''You weren't here. What was I supposed to do? Have the sheriff haul you back to face my father's shotgun? Or your own father? How do you think he would have reacted if he'd known?''

Jackson's unrelenting glare went through her like a sharp knife. ''I know one thing for sure. He isn't going to be happy knowing he has a grandchild he was never allowed to love! Pop would have wanted to know, just like I would. Didn't you give any thought to our feelings?''

Overwhelming guilt choked her. She fought past the lump in her throat. ''I said I was sorry. Isn't that enough for you?''

A hollow, bitter laugh curled his lips. ''Would it be enough for you? How would you feel if you didn't get to see Joey for eight years? Eight of the most important years of her life. Do you know how many memories I don't have because of you? She might have been unplanned, but she wouldn't have been unwanted.''

Sharp tears stung her eyes. Jackson had a right to reproach her. Only her own doubts and fears had been important. Now her selfishness came home to her, settling like snow in the pit of her stomach. The hostility on his face went straight to her heart and she did something even her father hadn't been able to get her to do. She begged.

"Please try to understand, Jackson. Can't you see my side of it? I was scared. All I knew was that if I brought you back here, you'd hate me the rest of your life."

His low growl cut through the night. "You don't know that."

The moment of weakness disappeared. "Damn you, Jackson, you're asking me to be honest! The least you can do is to be honest, too. You shook the dust of North Dakota from your shoes when you left and you've only been back once. That one time you came and left without bothering to look me up to see if anything had changed." She paused. "Or even to say hello."

He sighed. "For my mother's funeral. Yeah, I know, but hell, Cat, if I'd known about Joey…"

The lost years stood before her like so many accusing, pointing fingers, but when did he give her a thought? He'd left and never looked back. "What would you have done differently?"

A long moment of silence stood between them before he spoke. "I don't know. I honestly don't know."

She nodded. "I just knew I didn't want a loveless marriage and a husband who hated me."

"I would have thought of something. We didn't have to live in Engerville. I could have got housing on base."

"And have Joey live like a gypsy? I don't think so, Jackson. That did cross my mind, but I wanted a better life for her. I grew up moving from town to town, state to state. I went to a dozen different schools before my aunt left this farm to my father. I never had any friends until we settled here. I hated not having a real home. I wouldn't—I *won't* let my child grow up that way."

"My child, too," he protested. "I should have had some say in it."

Sadly, she shook her head. "You left, Jackson."

INSIDE THE HOUSE, the rising sound of angry voices awakened Joey. She lay still in her bed for several minutes listening. She couldn't understand the words, but she recognized the voices. Why was her mom arguing with Jackson when it was dark outside?

Joey shoved the covers aside and slid off the bed. She stood for a moment in bare feet, her too-short nightgown twisted around her, knowing she shouldn't try to eavesdrop, but too curious not to. Tiptoeing over to the open window, she crouched down beside it and listened to the sounds of two adults arguing.

"So what happens now?" Jackson asked. "Are you going to hold it against me that I left when I didn't know you were going to have my child?"

"I never felt that way, Jackson. It was my fault."

"Does it matter whose fault it was? That's the past. Are you going to try to keep me from seeing Joey?"

"Oh God! Jackson, what do you know about me that makes you think I'd do that? Of course, you can see Joey. She likes you already."

"That's nice. She likes me. She ought to love me! I'm her father."

The nasty edge to Jackson's voice made his words perfectly distinct. Joey crouched lower, making herself very small.

Joey thought her mother sounded as if she were about to cry. It scared her. Mommy never cried. Hardly ever.

"How many times do you want me to say I'm sorry?"

"I'll let you know when you get there."

"Go home, Jackson. I'm not up for this tonight."

"Too bad, Cat. Neither am I. Pardon me if I don't feel a whole hell of a lot of sympathy for you, but the way I see it, you didn't even give me a chance to take responsibility. I have rights, too, and the faster you get around to understanding that, the better off we'll be. Tomorrow, my daughter better know who her father is."

"Don't threaten me, Jackson!"

"I mean it, Cat. You've kept me unaware of my child's existence and let her grow up thinking her father didn't want her. You've cheated me out of knowing her as a baby. I don't care what your reasons were! That wasn't right and you know it."

"Go home, Jackson!"

"I'm leaving, but I'll be back! You can bet your sweet ass on that!"

The soft sound of footsteps fading away were followed by choked sobs from her mother. Joey stayed by the window for a long time, trying to make sense out of what she'd overheard. Could Jackson Gray be her father? Was he the man who hadn't wanted her?

She'd liked him well enough before, but now he'd yelled at her mother. Rising resentment tore at her, filling her heart with righteous rage. If he was her father, then he was the one she hated, not some distant stranger whose face never quite came clear in her mind. Why had he not come back sooner?

A tear tracked down her face. Sadness engulfed her. Why had he made her mother cry? He could come back all he wanted to, but she'd never love him. Never! The thought did little to soothe her hurt. Why hadn't Mommy told her the truth when Jackson came to visit? Joey wasn't supposed to keep secrets and Mommy wasn't supposed to, either. It wasn't fair.

She crept back to her bed and pulled the sheet tight around her. Later, when her mother opened her door to check on her, she pretended to be asleep. After her mother's bedroom door closed, Joey let her resentment slide down her face in fat, salty tears.

CHAPTER NINE

CAT WATCHED her daughter fiddle with the spoon beside her plate. "You like Jackson, don't you, Joey?"

"I guess so."

Joey's sullen visage didn't bode well for the conversation Cat planned. Her daughter's normally sunny disposition hid behind a pouting lower lip and a refusal to meet her mother's gaze. Still, she pressed on. "I have something very important to tell you about him."

Joey pushed her plate of oatmeal and eggs away from her and stood up, a stubborn scowl on her face. "I have to go to the bathroom."

"Wait a minute, honey. I need to talk to you."

"I have to go really bad."

"Go ahead. We'll talk when you get back." Cat sighed heavily as her daughter almost ran out of the kitchen. For an hour, she'd been trying to get Joey to sit still long enough to hear the truth about Jackson. For some unexplained reason, Joey chose not to listen.

Jackson would be here any minute, expecting Joey to know he was her father, and Cat still hadn't told her. Uneasily, she stared at Joey's empty chair. What could Jackson say that he hadn't said last night? His harsh words had kept her awake until dawn. The anger, hurt and confusion cured her of idle dreams about things working out between her and Jackson. It wasn't going to happen.

Before Joey came back from the bathroom, the doorbell rang. For the first time since Jackson arrived in Engerville, she dreaded seeing him. Heart thudding madly, footsteps dragging, Cat went to the door. His scowl greeted her. Evidently, a good night's sleep hadn't improved his temper. Her own mood wasn't exactly at its peak. "Good morning, Jackson."

"That's your opinion," he growled.

His brooding gaze raked her. Despite the guilt she felt, Cat decided she had no good reason to put up with Jackson's manner. "I'm not going to be treated like a criminal, Jackson, so lose the attitude or take off! I'm past the point where I'll let anyone run my life or make me hang my head."

His glare didn't recede, but his tone softened slightly. "Does she know?"

A dozen excuses hovered on Cat's lips, but she refused to utter them. "Not yet."

He pushed past her, looking around the living room for the object of their discussion. "Then we'll tell her together."

"We can try. Maybe she'll sit still for you. I've been trying to corner her and give her the news all morning. She's antsy about something."

Skeptical, Jackson asked, "Are you sure you tried?"

"Don't question what I say, Jackson," she retorted. "You don't have the right." Cat turned away from him at the light patter of Joey's footsteps in the hall.

Jackson heard, too. "There she is now. Hey, there, Short Stuff! Are you going to be my main man today? I figured we could get the wall panels up, if you help me. Whaddaya say?"

Dressed in jeans and a faded red T-shirt, her daughter hesitated before coming into the room. Her dark hair swung loose around her shoulders. Usually, she tied it back in a ponytail or braids. Joey didn't look at Jackson, instead she kept her gaze on her mother. "I promised Tommy Karl I'd go fishing with him today. You said I could, Mom. Last week, remember?"

Cat thought hard, but could recall no mention of a planned fishing trip. "I don't remember, Joey. Are you sure it was today?"

Joey nodded her head. "Yep. I'm going to ride Moonshot over to his house. Tommy Karl said he'd bait my hook. He promised. Why don't you come with us, Mom?"

"But honey, we have work to do here."

"You promised!"

Cat didn't remember a promise to go fishing, but a lot had happened. Maybe she'd forgotten. "What about Jackson? He wants you to help him. You can go fishing another time."

Stubbornly, Joey shook her head. "I want to go today. I told Tommy Karl I'd go and you said to never break a promise." She gazed accusingly at Cat. "Didn't you?"

Joey knew exactly how to slip past her defenses. "Okay, you can go, but first, Jackson and I have something to tell you. Let's sit down for a minute in the kitchen."

Joey brushed past both of them, determinedly refusing to meet their gaze. "I have to get my tackle box and rod from the barn. You can tell me later."

Cat watched Joey's red shirt disappear around the corner of the house. "What did I tell you. She won't hold still for a minute."

Jackson frowned. "Funny. Yesterday she couldn't get close enough to me."

"Do you think she heard us arguing last night?"

He shook his head and his stern frown deepened. "I doubt it. She was asleep. I don't think we were that loud."

"I wasn't, but your voice could be heard in the next county. What were you thinking of? Coming over at midnight."

"You know what I was thinking about. I made that obvious. I was mad as hell." Jackson frowned. "Maybe I did get a little loud."

"And a little threatening. Don't forget that." Cat walked toward the kitchen. Coffee might remove the taste of a bitter, sleepless night from her mouth, though probably not from her soul. She needed some-thing…anything, to bridge this awkwardness. She heard Jackson's footsteps behind her.

"I probably shouldn't have rushed over here last night, but dammit, Cat, my whole life just blew up in my face!"

"I know. I'm sorry—" She broke off the sentence as it threatened to repeat words she'd already said too often.

Jackson pulled a chair back from the table, then stood beside it. "I'm the one who should be saying 'I'm sorry'. I screwed up and got us both in trouble." He sat down in the old wooden chair, his weight causing it to creak.

Cat set two coffee mugs on the table, one at each end. She looked at Jackson and firmly said, "I think I might have helped a little bit."

"Yeah, but as the man, I was supposed to protect you."

"Spilled milk, Jackson, besides being debatable. Let's not talk about it anymore."

"It won't go away. We need to talk. There's a lot we

have to clear up and hiding it, refusing to think or talk about it, won't solve anything.''

Cat brought the coffeepot to the table and filled their cups. "Let's let it rest for a bit, Jackson. We both need time to think."

"I don't know what to think anymore," he complained.

His words had a plaintive note. Cat raised her cup to her lips, and sipped cautiously at the hot, aromatic brew. "I've been thinking for a long time and I've had to throw all my conclusions away, so we're even there. Give it time. Maybe the answers will fall into place if we quit trying to force them."

Jackson gulped his coffee, wincing as it burned his tongue and throat. He placed the empty cup on the table in front of him and stared at it as if the secret solution to their joint problem lay in it. Interminable minutes passed. Finally, he stood. "Right. I'll get started on that wall."

"Are you sure you want to keep working over here?"

Bitterness settled on his face. "Why not?"

"There's a lot of anger and resentment built up between us, Jackson. Even though I made the decision not to tell you, I still went through times when I resented you for starting a baby with me and then taking off. I couldn't help feeling abandoned even if that wasn't the situation, exactly. I think I hated most the thought of you being in the Marines, footloose and fancy free, while I was tied down with a baby and dirty diapers."

"If you'd ever been in the Marines, you wouldn't think of it as footloose."

"You weren't stuck here with a father who wouldn't stop telling you that you'd go to hell for your sins. You didn't have to make do with two dozen diapers when it seemed like the baby used that many every day!''

He paused in the doorway, the cold glare fading, replaced by a troubled frown. ''If I'd known, I would have helped. I had no idea—''

She stood, too. ''It seemed like the right thing, at the time, not to tell you. I tried to make it on my own so you wouldn't have to pay for something that was basically my idea.''

Jackson's lips curled in a sarcastic half smile. ''I don't recall being bulldozed into it. So what happened is that you paid for something we both did.''

A lump crowded Cat's throat. She didn't want his sympathy. It threatened to unglue the hard knot of control she clung to. ''That's not right, either. You would have been with Rebeka if things had worked out for you two. I know you loved her.''

''If? Ifs and maybes…yes, and *if* a toad had wings, he wouldn't bump his tail so much.''

Cat couldn't hold back a reluctant smile of her own. ''That sounds like your father talking.''

''You're right. Corny country sayings are his forte and red hair isn't all he gave me.''

''No, it isn't,'' Cat agreed. ''You're a lot more like him than I think you realize. Would you like another cup of coffee before we start? You hardly tasted your first.''

He nodded. ''I don't think I slept two hours last night, so I'll probably need the caffeine to stay awake.''

''I'll fix another pot. We can have our second cup in the living room. Are you going to put up the paneling first?''

''I'll need to replace the insulation we ruined by throwing water on it. I'll put up the paneling last.''

They didn't sit down to have the second cup of coffee, but set to work, not entirely easy with each other. The talk helped, but a current of animosity still lay just beneath the surface of Jackson's mood. And despite their angry words, their mutual accusations, his nearness still caused Cat's body to alternate between heated arousal and cold resentment.

JOEY HAD DIFFICULTY getting the saddle on Moonshot's back, but the filly waited patiently and she managed after several minutes of struggling. Hours of riding had strengthened her arms and legs. She hadn't been able to lift the saddle to the mare's back at the beginning of spring. The bridle was no problem, of course, as Moonshot obediently dipped her head for Joey to slip the snaffle bit into her mouth and the leather over her ears.

Leading Moonshot out of the barn, Joey glanced at the house. Inside, the man she called Jackson had turned out to be the mysterious stranger she'd resented since she was old enough to realize he was missing. A tumble of emotions welled in her heart. One part of her wanted to go back to the house and be close to the tall man, to call him "Daddy" as she'd heard Tommy Karl do with his father. Another part wanted to scream her fury at him. He'd left her and Mommy all alone for years. Now he wanted to come back and yell at her mother like it was her fault. No, Joey decided, she wasn't going to love him. Ever.

Grandpa John had made a mounting block for her and Joey led the filly over to the square platform built of wood scraps. She really missed Grandpa John. Maybe if he were still alive, he'd beat up on Jackson. Joey remembered hearing him say once that if he ever figured out who her daddy was, he'd kick the man's tail into the next county. Of course, he hadn't known Joey listened to his words.

Mom was going to be really mad when she found out Joey had left without even coming in for a goodbye kiss. Half of Joey wanted to go back to the house. The other half didn't want to be around Jackson for even a minute. The anger won out.

Trotting the filly most of the way, it only took about twenty minutes to get to Tommy Karl's house. A bit of luck came Joey's way when she heard the faint roar of a tractor engine in a distant field. She wouldn't have to explain her sudden appearance to Mr. Anderson.

As she rode up to the barn, Tommy Karl, dressed in well-worn, wrinkled jeans and a purple Minnesota Vikings T-shirt, came out carrying an armload of harness. He looked surprised when he saw her.

"Hi, Joey." His straight blond hair kept falling forward. With both hands involved in carrying the harness, he had to toss his head to flip the hair out of his eyes.

"Hi."

"I didn't know you were coming to visit."

"I'm not visiting, exactly."

"But you're here," he pointed out.

Joey's hands tightened on the reins. Moonshot responded by sidestepping. Joey relaxed her grip and Moonshot stood still. She frowned at her friend. "Yeah, I know, but I'm not visiting. I'm running away."

"From here?"

Tommy Karl didn't understand. "From home."

"How come?"

He looked puzzled. She didn't want to get into the "why" of it with him. She wasn't sure she completely understood it herself. "Do you want to come with me?"

He shook his head firmly. "I have to clean this harness. Dad wants it to look really nice for the fair."

Her lower lip curled out in protest. "Well, I won't be going to the fair."

"Why not? You always said you liked it."

Sometimes boys could be really slow. "Because I'm running away! I can't go to the fair if I run away."

Finally, alarm showed in Tommy Karl's stoic Norwegian face. Alarm and disbelief. "Aren't you coming back? Ever?"

Joey shook her head impatiently. Her best friend certainly appeared as slow as any other boy today. Hadn't he heard her? "Nope. No matter what."

"But how come?"

"Promise you won't tell anybody. Promise? You hafta promise or I won't tell." At his nod, she told him. "Jackson is my dad."

Tommy Karl looked upset, and more than a little put out. "Oh. Did your mom marry him?"

"I mean he's really my dad! My *real* dad." Joey exclaimed with frustration.

Tommy Karl shook his head as if not quite sure his ears were to be believed. "Not your stepdad?"

"Nope." And even when he understood, he didn't.

"I thought you liked Jackson."

Joey tossed her head high, like one of the young horses fighting the bit. "I *never* liked him! I just *pretended* to like him. He doesn't want to be my father, anyway. He was arguing with Mommy about it and blaming her."

"I thought you liked him."

"Well, I don't," she declared. "Are you going to come with me or not?" Her voice had taken on a cross note that Mommy wouldn't like, but she wasn't here and even if she were, Joey didn't want to talk to her. Mommy had kept a secret from her and she'd always said Joey shouldn't keep secrets. Didn't mommies have to go by the rules, too?

Tommy Karl frowned. "Dad would skin me if I ran away."

"Well, fine! If you don't want to come, then I'll go by myself." She tugged on the reins and Moonshot turned with the pull.

"Where are you going?"

She turned to look at Tommy Karl over her shoulder. "I don't know yet. Somewhere far away. He'll be really sorry."

"What about your mom?"

Joey pulled back on the reins and leaned forward on Moonshot's neck. She stretched to reach the hank of mane twisted under the bridle. She straightened it and then finally answered. "She likes him, so I don't care. I don't like him. I gotta go. If your dad sees me, he probably won't let me leave."

Tommy Karl's face reflected a look of adult worry. "I don't think you should run away, Joey. Your mom's going to be really sad."

"I have to," Joey announced. Scared, but instinctively sure she shouldn't let Tommy Karl know, she nudged Moonshot with her heels. The filly started walking away.

Tommy Karl dropped the harness he was carrying and trotted alongside the filly, reaching for the bridle with one hand and brushing his hair out of his eyes with the other. "Don't go, Joey! Please."

Joey tugged on the reins and Moonshot halted. She looked down at Tommy. "I wish you'd go with me, but that's okay, if you're scared."

Tommy Karl's shoulders straightened. "I'm not

afraid. Dad won't like it if I leave, though, and besides, I don't want to run away.''

Joey heaved an exasperated sigh. "Then don't!"

Tommy Karl considered. "I better go with you, or Dad'll be mad I didn't take care of you.''

"Stay here if you're scared. I don't care. I don't need nobody to take care of me! Me and Moonshot will be all right by ourselves.''

"Okay, okay! I know that, but Dad will still yell at me for letting you go. Wait a minute. I'll have to saddle my horse.''

JACKSON STEPPED BACK, looking around the living room with unmistakable pride. A lump formed in Cat's throat. Working with Jackson to repair the fire damage had been a mixed bag, sometimes sweet, other times upsetting. But today had been a kind of silent communion between the two of them. They'd talked little, but seemed to intuit what each other needed. She had handed paneling nails to Jackson as he held each panel in position, then reached out without looking to accept the nails she held for him.

He glanced sideways at her. "We do good work.''

She nodded. "The light color really makes the room look bigger, doesn't it?''

Jackson laid the hammer on the floor. He looked around. "I was unsure about your choice, but now, that little bit of green running through the white is picked up by the drapes. It looks classy. I think we did an outstanding job.''

"Now for lunch.'' Cat glanced at the wall clock Jackson had rehung. "Goodness, it's almost two o'clock. You must be starving.''

A reluctant grin crossed his face. "I could eat.''

"I'll fix us something."

"You don't have to. You're tired, too. I'll get lunch back at the farm."

A sudden desire to keep him close prompted her to protest. "Oh, no. You've worked too hard for me to send you away hungry."

He looked at his watch. "What time will Joey be back?"

The mention of their daughter immediately slammed tension into their conversation. Cat walked over to the window and pulled the drapes back. She peered through the gauzy undercurtains toward the barn. "I didn't get a chance to ask her. She left without coming back in to say goodbye."

"Should she have done that?"

Jackson's question pulled her attention back to him. "That's an iffy question. It's a little unusual for her, but I think she heard us arguing. She may be upset with both of us."

"Why don't you call Luke and ask him." Jackson stood, his tall frame seeming to fill the room.

"If they're still fishing, there won't be anybody to answer the phone."

His disappointment was obvious. "I guess so. I'd hoped to have a little time with Joey today. I want to explain to her why I wasn't around."

"I'll tell her it was my fault. It's the truth, after all. I'm sure you wouldn't have abandoned us. I wish I'd been a little more sensible when I was eighteen."

"It goes with the age, I suppose." He dropped his gaze to the bare wood floor and scuffed the toe of his boot across the surface. "It was as much my fault. I didn't take care of business the way I should have."

"We were young and dumb. I didn't think about getting pregnant."

His grin spoke volumes. "As I remember it, I wasn't doing much thinking at all."

Cat remembered. "You wanted to stop. I dared you."

He shrugged, his shoulders tightly outlined by his white T-shirt. "There's no point in trying to decide who's to blame. It happened, Cat. We can't change the past."

A startling truth escaped from her. "I wouldn't want to."

Surprised, he asked, "You wouldn't?"

Cat smiled, her thoughts returning for a moment to an image of her baby daughter kicking vigorously as she bathed her. A wave of love washed through her. "Except for the part about telling you. I'd change that, but I can't imagine a life without Joey."

"Yeah, there's that. She's a cute little squirt."

Cat threw a glance toward Jackson before going over to the window and looking out for some sign of her daughter. "Headstrong, too."

"She is my child, after all." He grinned with obvious pride.

"And mine. We shouldn't expect her to be any different."

"Come on, I'll help you throw together something for lunch, and then we can clean up the sawdust and scraps of paneling. After that, I'd better get back to the farm. Pop wants me to spray the soybeans. We're getting some bugs in there."

"And you'll be exhausted before you start. You're a good person, Jackson Gray. Thank you."

A tinge of red buffed his cheeks. "My pleasure. I

mean that. It helps a bit with the guilt for not knowing about Joey.''

"How can you feel guilty for not knowing?''

"I never said I was logical, did I?''

This time his smile caressed her. A pool of warmth in Cat's stomach threatened her composure. She stooped to pick up a piece of paneling, letting her hair swing forward to hide her awareness of him.

CHAPTER TEN

ALTHOUGH HOT, exhausted and so thirsty her throat felt scratchy, Joey vetoed turning back with such vehemence Tommy Karl decided not to mention it again. Neither had ever led the way on one of their frequent fishing expeditions. They didn't usually go by horseback. His father had always driven them in his pickup, so it was no surprise to Tommy when they got lost. He spotted Indian Creek first, long hours after they should have reached it. It was noon or a little past, judging by the sun's position in the sky.

Tommy Karl wished he'd had the good sense to tell his dad instead of taking off with Joey. Of course, if he'd done that, Joey would have run away long before he reached his father in the cornfield, so she might have gotten lost anyway. All things considered, he'd done the best he could and he really hoped his dad agreed. He tried to think of everything, but it seemed impossible. For the hundredth time, he wished his father had come along.

"There are no fish here," Joey complained. "It's too shallow."

"I think we're higher up the creek than Dad usually takes us," Tommy explained. "We can just follow the creek until it gets deeper, but first we need to water the horses and let them rest."

"Yeah, Moonshot is tired. I can tell by the way she

walks. Maybe I should have brought one of the older horses.''

''They're not as fast as Moonshot.''

''She's awfully tired.'' A look of intense guilt swept over her face as Joey leaned forward to pat Moonshot's neck.

Tommy hastened to console her. ''So is Wizard. Aren't you, boy?'' He dismounted and let his horse crop the meager grass as he looked up at Joey. ''We can rest here.''

Joey swiped a dirty hand across her forehead, pushing back her messy hair. ''Then what do we do?''

Tommy Karl's answer was sharpened by his own confusion. ''How would I know? This was your idea!'' At her crestfallen look, he backtracked. ''As soon as we get to the deep part, we'll try to catch some fish for lunch.''

Joey's eyes widened. ''I'm not eating raw fish!''

''I have some matches, dummy!'' Tommy Karl retorted angrily. ''We can cook them on a stick like Dad showed us.''

''How was I supposed to know that? You didn't say anything about cooking the fish!'' Joey tossed her head. She grasped the reins with one hand and pushed flyaway strands back with the other, peering sideways at Tommy Karl as Moonshot fidgeted and turned away.

Just like a girl. As if *he* wanted to eat raw fish! Tommy Karl knew his voice reflected his irritation, but for once, he didn't care. ''Never mind. Go ahead and get off Moonshot.''

''How will I get back on? I can't reach the stirrups from the ground.''

She looked at him helplessly. It chased the gathering irritation to the back of his mind, to be replaced by worry. She was awfully little. He should have managed to keep her at the ranch until Dad came in from the fields. His father would remind him that he was older and should have known better. Too late, now. "Don't worry. I can give you a hand up."

"Won't I be too heavy?"

"I'm really strong. You'll see."

Joey slid down the filly's side. Moonshot stood quietly, too tired to sidle and prance as she usually did.

Tommy Karl watched Joey. She looked as tired as Moonshot. Dust coated her face and clothes. Sadness seemed to weigh her down. A peculiar feeling rose in him. He'd always liked Joey. They got along well and enjoyed the same things, like horses and *Star Wars* and computer games, but this was the first time he'd wanted to protect her, to take her pain and fatigue on to himself. It was a very grown-up feeling and he wasn't at all sure how to handle it. He slipped Wizard's reins over a tree branch and went over to Joey and took Moonshot's reins from her. In a very kind voice, he said, "You go wash up in the creek. I'll put halters on the horses and let them eat some grass. It'll be okay, Joey. I'll take care of you."

CAT BECAME MORE UNEASY as she and Jackson made a luncheon of turkey sandwiches and a can of Campbell's potato soup. Afterward, they went back to the living room and while Cat swept sawdust and shavings from the floor, Jackson toted debris outside. Finally, she could stand it no longer.

"I'm going to call Luke," she announced with no prelude to her thoughts.

Jackson sat back on his heels and watched her. She dialed the number and waited, but the phone rang again and again with no answer on the other end. "They're probably still gone," she said, trying to reassure herself.

"Do they usually stay out this long?"

"Sometimes, but I'm with them or Luke is. I'm sure it's okay. Luke will take good care of Joey."

A tiny muscle in Jackson's jaw began to twitch. "If you're sure she's okay, why is your face so pale?"

"I just have this feeling that something is wrong. I can't explain it." A knot formed in her stomach. "Don't laugh at me, Jackson." Saying the words, giving voice to her suspicion, made the possibility more likely.

Jackson said, "I wouldn't dream of it. Mother's intuition?"

She nodded. "I suppose. Or something I ate. Am I being silly?"

Jackson began picking up his tools. "I don't know, but if you are, you're entitled. Want me to drive over to Luke's and see if I can find out anything?"

His thoughtfulness warmed her. "Oh, I'm sure that's not necessary, and besides, you have to get back to the farm, don't you?"

Jackson shook his head. "Pop will understand. I can't leave you alone when you're worried about Joey."

There was no way to explain it, but his sharing her worry made her stronger. "Maybe we should wait a little longer. I don't want to raise an alarm if nothing is wrong."

Jackson stood up, decisively. "Dithering won't help, either. Waiting won't set your mind at ease. I'll take the truck over to Luke's and see what's going on."

"Are you sure? I like your father and I know he's easygoing, but you came home to help him, not me." She didn't want him to change his mind. She wanted him to take charge. The realization was unsettling.

"Pop will be okay." Jackson looked down at her and made a tentative move in her direction.

She thought he might kiss her, but he didn't, though he'd been so close he could have. Probably her imagination. "Should I go with you?"

"No. You stick around here. If we both left, that would be the exact moment Joey would pick to come home. She'd be upset at finding you gone. You stay here and wait. I won't be long."

He touched a finger to her cheek, turned and left before she could react. She touched the spot he'd touched and quieted the tingle.

Time's passage poked along so Jackson's absence seemed like an eternity to Cat. She paced from room to room, making no pretense at all that she did anything more than wait. Finally, a bare twenty minutes later, she heard his truck pull up in the yard. She raced to the door and saw Luke's new red pickup pulling in right behind Jackson. Only Luke. Neither of the children. A terrifying premonition of Joey's danger raced over her. Cat had trouble breathing. The sense of foreboding took over her body, squeezing out all other sensation.

The two men were shoulder to shoulder as they hurried to the door where Cat stood frozen in fear. She didn't give either of them a chance to say hello. "Luke, where are the kids?"

Luke's worry flashed for a minute, before he hid it behind a calmer air. "Cat, they've just gone out riding. They'll be back. Jackson says Joey claimed we were supposed to go fishing. That's not true, of course. Tommy Karl's horse is gone, so it's obvious he went with her."

"Where could they have gone? Just riding or fishing by themselves?"

Luke's reassuringly familiar face tightened. "Maybe the real question is why. Tommy Karl doesn't do this sort of thing on his own. He's never left the ranch without permission."

Jackson shouldered between Luke and Cat, a fierce look on his face. "The real question is *not* why. The only question is where! We've got to find those kids before either one of them is hurt. They're way too young to be running around on their own. Think, Cat. Where would they have gone?"

Cat's concern swelled. Ice in the pit of her stomach caused her to tremble. Chill bumps appeared on her arms. She crossed them in front of her and reached deep for control, but found none. "I don't know why they left! How can I guess where they went?"

"Tommy Karl sure didn't have a problem at breakfast this morning," Luke interjected. "He talked about going into town and renting a video for tonight. I promised him he could get a movie as a reward for being so much help this week. He's a good kid and doesn't get into trouble. Was Joey upset about anything?"

"We don't know it was Joey's idea. Maybe Tommy put her up to it," Jackson said, thrusting his words between Cat and Luke as he had moved to protect her earlier.

"I'm not trying to place blame," Luke defended. He shot a cold look at Jackson, then returned his gaze to Cat. "Has she been upset about anything, Cat? Anything at all?"

Cat hesitated. Remembering the quarrel she'd engaged in with Jackson, she had a good idea of what had upset Joey. Her daughter must have overheard their argument. What interpretation had her childish mind put upon their confrontation? She chose her words carefully. "Luke, you have a right to know, since your own child is caught up in this, too. She might have overheard an argument Jackson and I had last night.''

Luke leaned forward, blond head bent attentively toward Cat. ''Last night? What about?''

For the third time, Jackson moved to intercept Luke's words to Cat. ''Cat, you don't need to go into all that. It's not any of your business, Luke,'' Jackson said, addressing the tall rancher directly.

Cat shot an irritated glance at Jackson. ''Yes, it is,'' she contradicted, and decided there'd been enough lies in her life. If ever there was a time for truth, this was it. ''Tommy Karl is with Joey, so Luke has a right to know.'' She swung her nervous gaze to Luke. ''Jackson just figured out that he's Joey's father. We were... discussing things.''

Luke tipped his hat back and shot a scornful glance at Jackson. ''You mean just yesterday? This week? Slow learner, isn't he? What took him so long?''

Jackson looked at Cat unbelievingly. ''You mean Luke knew? You told him, but you couldn't be bothered to write me a letter? Who else knew while you were keeping it such a damn big secret from me? The whole freaking town or all of Traill County, too?''

''Did you think nobody would notice when I gained so much weight? Of course the whole town knows I had a baby, for pete's sake! Luke is the only one who knows you're Joey's father. He's been a good friend to me.'' Cat's voice rose as she reacted to the accusation.

''I'll bet. I'll just bet he's been a *very* good friend.'' Jackson turned his back on both of them and went over to the window. He lifted the curtain and looked out for a moment before dropping it and turning back to glare accusingly at Cat.

Get FREE BOOKS and a FREE GIFT when you play the...

LAS VEGAS

GAME

Just scratch off
the gold box with a coin.
Then check below to see
the gifts you get!

YES! I have scratched off the gold Box. Please send
me my **2 FREE BOOKS** and **gift for which I qualify.** I understand
that I am under no obligation to purchase any books as
explained on the back of this card.

336 HDL DUYL   135 HDL DUY2

FIRST NAME   LAST NAME

ADDRESS

APT.#   CITY

(H-SR-03/03)

STATE/PROV.   ZIP/POSTAL CODE

7	7	7	Worth TWO FREE BOOKS plus a BONUS Mystery Gift!
🍒	🍒	🍒	Worth TWO FREE BOOKS!
🔔	🔔	♣	TRY AGAIN!

Visit us online at
www.eHarlequin.com

BUSINESS REPLY MAIL
FIRST-CLASS MAIL   PERMIT NO. 717-003   BUFFALO, NY

POSTAGE WILL BE PAID BY ADDRESSEE

HARLEQUIN READER SERVICE
3010 WALDEN AVE
PO BOX 1867
BUFFALO NY 14240-9952

NO POSTAGE
NECESSARY
IF MAILED
IN THE
UNITED STATES

"Oh, I give up, Jackson! Think what you want to. I'm only interested in finding Joey and Tommy Karl. Where do you think they might've gone, Luke?"

"Toss a coin. Pick a direction. Kids like that roaming around this country could get in real trouble—gopher holes, snakes, the creek, even Goose River if they head south. Farms are too big and too far apart, though there aren't any predators to worry about."

Jackson rejoined Cat and Luke. "Joey mentioned fishing. Is it possible they went to wherever you two usually took them?" Jackson addressed his question to Cat, turning a cold shoulder to Luke.

Luke answered him, speaking to Jackson's shoulder as if it weren't deliberately turned away. "That's the only thing we have to go on. I'm not sure they could find the place on horseback, though. We usually took the pickup and parked on the side of the road, then walked to the creek. It's a lot longer by horseback."

Jackson thought about it, then said, "Indian Creek gets pretty deep in some parts, though it's mostly shallow. Do the kids know how to swim?"

"Tommy Karl does. We were going to teach Joey this summer," Luke said.

If any color had been left in Cat's face, it disappeared with stunning suddenness, leaving her barely able to stand. "Oh, no. Please don't say that!"

"Calm down, Cat. Nobody mentioned what you're thinking. With the drought we're having, the creek will be pretty shallow, most places. They're smart kids. They know how dangerous the creek can be and Tommy Karl won't let anything happen to Joey. He's a smart, very responsible kid."

Jackson stepped away from them, paced angrily to the window, looked out, then again turned his attention to the rancher. "I wish I had your confidence, Luke. He's just a kid, himself. What can he do?"

Cat gathered her strength. The light coming through the window emphasized the hard line of Jackson's jaw. He was intensely concerned about his daughter and ready to take his anger out on her and Luke. Not that she blamed him one little bit. If she'd done the right thing years ago, her daughter wouldn't be in danger today. The knot in her stomach curled tighter as she hurried to reassure him. "He's right, Jackson. Tommy Karl is very sensible for his age. He'll do what he can to protect Joey."

Luke growled, "I'll give him an A for effort, but right now I'm pretty damn mad at him for taking off with her. He'd better have a good story cooked up."

Cat turned on him, her face warm with anger. "Luke, how can you talk about punishing your son when you don't even know if he's okay?"

"He's just fine," Luke retorted.

His words seemed more an effort to reassure himself than firm conviction, Cat thought. Her gaze turned to Jackson. Beneath his newly acquired tan, ashen skin made his grim eyes seem even harder. Had he just found his daughter to lose her so quickly? That mustn't happen. Cat's heart thudded dangerously. Joey had to be okay. "Let's go look for them," she said.

Both men nodded grimly.

JOEY AWOKE TO THE insistent call of Tommy Karl's voice. "What'cha want, T.K.," she muttered sleepily.

"You've been resting a long time, Joey. I think we should get going. It's getting late and we should find some fish soon. I'm awfully hungry."

Joey rubbed her eyes. Her clothes were stained with

the grass she'd slept on and her hair had tangled badly. She'd never be able to get a brush through it. Then she remembered she hadn't brought a brush. All her things were at home. She sat up, her empty stomach choosing that moment to rumble loudly. "I'm hungry, too. Didn't you bring anything to eat?"

"No. I didn't think about that. You were in such a hurry."

His words accused. Joey hastened to defend herself. "Me? You were afraid your father would come in from the field."

"No, I wasn't! I wish he had."

Joey's eyes welled with tears. Nobody loved her. Nobody. Not her Mommy and not Jackson, for sure. Not even Tommy Karl. Her chin trembled. "I thought you wanted to go with me."

Tommy Karl backtracked with desperate swiftness. "Aw, Joey, don't cry. I wanted to come, but I'm not sure we should have."

"I'm not going back," Joey announced stubbornly. Tears spilled over and streaked her cheeks through the layers of dust.

"We don't hafta, Joey. Don't cry. Please don't cry. Come on, let's see if we can find the deep part of the creek. You'll see, the fish will taste really good. Betcha I can catch a dozen sunnies. They're easy."

"Will we cook them over the campfire like we did with Mom and your dad last time? We don't have a pan."

"Dad showed me how to wrap the fish in leaves. Or we can put them on a stick. Don't worry. I'll take care of everything."

She felt a lot better and Tommy Karl must like her or he wouldn't have offered to take care of things. It made up a little bit for the way her mommy had lied. And for Jackson, although Joey wasn't at all sure why she had this hollow ache in her stomach when she thought about him. She didn't care about Jackson. Really. That was good, because from now on, she'd be alone, except for Tommy Karl. She took a deep breath and let it out in a troubled sigh. "I like you, Tommy Karl. You're my best friend."

"Yeah, I know. Come on, now. Get up."

Joey scrambled to her feet and looked around for the horses. They were standing in the shade of a nearby tree, head to tail, casually flicking flies from their hides.

Tommy tightened the saddle girths and replaced the halters with bridles. True to his word, he cupped Joey's foot in his hand and with hardly any effort, shoved her up far enough so she could scramble into the saddle.

Joey looked around. She couldn't see any houses and this place didn't look like where they had gone fishing. It looked like a long ways from nowhere. Fear rippled through her. She wished her mommy was here, but when she ran away from home, she'd left her mom and Jackson behind. Doubt entered her mind. Mommy was going to be really mad at her when she found them.

A cold, uneasy shiver went through her, like taking a shower in winter. No matter how far she and Tommy Karl ran, it wouldn't be far enough. There was no doubt in Joey's mind that her mother would find them and when she did, Joey knew her mother was going to be *very* angry with her. A part of her feared her mother's anger. A larger part cheered at the thought of her mother kissing her cheek and telling her it would be all right.

GETTING TO THE FISHING HOLE took only a few minutes. Luke cut the engine after he threw the gear into park.

Cat sat between him and Jackson. All in all, it seemed the wisest choice. The two men acted like a couple of strange wolves who'd just met. They kept circling each other, heads high, tails stiff, looking for an opening to strike. Men, she thought. Always acting like testoster-one-poisoned teenagers when you needed them to be adults. Wisely, she decided not to mention her observation. Time enough for that after they found the kids.

Both men stood beside their open door and motioned for her to get out. Scowling at Luke, she shuffled across the seat to slide out the passenger door Jackson held for her. The slightly smug look he threw at Luke came close to changing her mind. Worried, irritated and scared, she set off down the narrow path to the creek and left the men to sort out who would follow close behind her, and who would have to come second.

The path ended at a grassy bank next to two huge willow trees. Below the trees, a wide bend in the creek formed a small pond. The kids were nowhere in sight. Despair blossomed in Cat's chest. Hopelessly, she raised her hands to her mouth and called out, "Joey, Joey! It's Mom, honey. Joey!"

Beside her, Luke's deep bellow joined hers. "Tommy Karl! Tommy! Are you here?"

Silence greeted their calls. Jackson stood helplessly by. "What now?" he asked.

"I'm not sure. Cat? Got any ideas?"

"I can't think. Maybe they didn't come here at all."

Jackson looked around at the willow trees, the knee-high grass and the still water. A mosquito buzzed near his face. He swatted it away. "Maybe they headed for here and got lost."

Luke grunted dubiously. "I don't know about that. Tommy knows how to find his way around."

Jackson nodded. "I've seen grown men get lost, let alone a little boy. Do you know if he had a compass with him?"

Luke shook his head. "I taught him how to find his way by looking at the sun or stars."

"Did you leave him out in the woods by himself to see if he got lost?"

"Jackson, that's not fair!"

"No, wait, Cat. He's right. There's a big difference between theory and practice. You're right about that, Jackson. I didn't leave him in the woods by himself. Not on purpose, anyway. However, two years ago, he and his dog got separated from me and Jae for several hours. He beat us home."

"So who led the way? Tommy or the dog?"

Luke flushed. "He didn't follow the dog. He told me he found the way by facing the setting sun, knowing that was west and therefore, the direction the farm lay in. I believed him. Honestly, Cat, I think they're okay. They're just too stubborn to come home."

"I think it's more likely that they've lost their way," Cat said.

"Are you saying it's my Tommy's fault?"

Cat covered her face with her hands. The creek started to spin around her in a lazy circle. Frantically, she opened her eyes. The spinning stopped. She had no time for hysterics and fainting or for arguing with either of the two men. "No, Luke. Joey's always been the leader when those two got together. Tommy Karl would do anything she asked him to do."

Luke threw an arm over Cat's shoulders and hugged her. "Don't worry, Cat. We'll find them."

Jackson eyed the two with animosity. "I'm not much concerned about pride right now. I want to find my little girl. I say Davy Crockett got lost. If they found the creek at all, it wasn't here. There's no sign anybody's been around here for days, maybe weeks. If you're right, Luke, and Tommy knows what direction to go in, then he either got to the creek farther upstream, or downstream. What's your best guess?''

The tall, blond rancher turned, hands to his eyes, shading them from the setting sun, as he scanned in all directions. He thought for a moment, then announced decisively, ''Downstream.''

''Can we take the truck?''

''No, this is the only spot along the creek that the road is close to. We'll have to walk. Cat, maybe you should wait here. It's going to be rough plowing through that bramble, not to mention snakes and gopher holes.''

She shuddered, then resolutely stared at Luke. No one was going to make her stay behind. ''I'm not waiting anywhere. I'm going with you.''

Luke nodded. Jackson turned away and started downstream, his silent figure ahead of Cat. He didn't look back to see how she was doing. *If anything happens to Joey, he'll hate me forever,* Cat thought. *No problem there. I'll hate me forever, too.*

CHAPTER ELEVEN

EVEN THE LANDSCAPE SEEMED bent on adding to Cat's misery. Briars grabbed her ankles. Scruffy, half-grown trees deliberately slapped her with low-hanging branches. Gopher holes tripped her up. Loose stones rolled under her shoes, but the bugs were the worst. She brushed away a mosquito from her neck too late to prevent his drinking her blood like a thirsty vampire. After the sun set, the voracious insects came out in droves.

It took forever to trudge several miles along the winding creek bed. There were spots where the creek channel narrowed so much they could step across. Other places, where the silent, dark water scared the hell out of her. It was too easy to picture Joey lying on the bottom, pale and lifeless.

When the sun set, full darkness descended rapidly. The moon and stars compensated very little for not having brought a flashlight, though it was easy to distinguish each figure against the horizon. Details were missing in the tangle of sometimes waist-high weeds growing in wild abandon on this uncultivated stretch of prairie. Cat began hanging onto Jackson's belt with one hand, since he seemed to have the best night-sight. He rarely stumbled and didn't seem to mind her holding on to him, though he never reached back to help her. There was seldom room enough for the three to walk abreast.

Finally, Jackson stopped. He grabbed Cat when she

stumbled into him. "I'm not sure this is the right way," he said. "Maybe we should go back and call the police. They have the equipment to conduct a night search. We don't."

Cat had an unreasoning urge to scream Joey's name into the blackness. Calling the police meant it was no longer a childish prank, but deadly serious. She pushed down the panic. Instinctively, she turned to her dear friend and neighbor. "What do you think, Luke? Jackson might be right. If it means finding Joey and Tommy Karl faster, I'm willing, but I don't want to call out a posse when we might find them any minute. Do you think we should go back?"

A match flared as Luke peered at his watch. In its short-lived light his face reflected her own anxiety. "I'm for going on ahead. It's ten o'clock. It would take too long to go back to the car, then drive to a phone. We'd have to wait for the police to get here from town. I think we'd be better off searching on our own. If we don't find them in another half hour or so, we head back and call the police."

"How about splitting up?" Jackson asked. "You and Cat could go back to the truck and call for help. I'll continue on."

"No!" Luke and Cat said the word in unison, though Luke's angry voice overrode hers.

In the night shadows, Jackson's tall silhouette stood out against the starry sky. "Marching through these weeds is rough on all of us, Luke. I can keep this pace all night, but I still think splitting up might be best. It's time to bring in the police."

"Then, I'd suggest you take Cat back and I'll keep going. Get the police involved, if you want to. I'm not leaving until we find them."

Jackson's voice lowered to a whispered plea. "Cat, don't you think it would be better if you two went back? They might not even be out here. What if they returned home after we left?"

"That would be great," Cat answered. "They might be a little scared, but they're safe if they're at home. Jackson, Luke is right. It's not a good idea to split up. It's especially not a good idea to leave you alone out here. You could fall, maybe break a leg, or trip and go head-first into the creek. Same goes for the one who heads back. Luke won't quit as long as Tommy Karl is lost and I'm not going back, either, so this discussion is closed."

Jackson slapped the side of his leg in obvious frustration. "Okay, then. Okay." He looked around, then expelled a noisy sigh. "You win. We'll keep going. Cat, hold on to me. I don't want you falling in the damn creek!"

"I'll be fine." At least he cared that much. Little enough for a broken heart to hang on to. If only Joey and Tommy Karl were all right, nothing else mattered, not broken hearts or broken dreams.

"Finding the kids is most important now, not anything else," Jackson echoed her thoughts.

"Hold still," Luke said. "I think I hear something."

All three held their breaths for a long moment.

"I guess it was an animal. Sorry."

They skirted a narrow bend in the creek where a tree lay across their path. When they emerged on the other side, a half mile ahead of them they could see a small campfire and two indistinct figures huddled close to it. "It's them," Cat said and started a headlong flight toward her daughter.

Jackson grabbed her arm, pulling her back to his side.

''Turn me loose!'' she hissed.

''Slow down, Cat. You can still fall. Do you want to be carried out of here on a stretcher?''

''We don't want to scare them to death,'' Luke added.

''Oh, no?'' Jackson retorted. ''Speak for yourself.''

''They're just kids, Jackson. Don't be too harsh.''

''Do you know how many mosquito bites I have?''

''Is that the Marine way?'' Luke taunted.

''Nobody is going to do anything to those kids,'' Cat declared. ''If we let our relief at finding them turn into a way to vent our own frustration, we'll all wind up hating ourselves tomorrow. They'll be scared to death, tired and hungry. I think that's punishment enough.''

''Hell, Cat, I'm scared to death, tired and hungry and I didn't run away from home,'' Jackson said.

A wash of euphoria spilled over Cat. She giggled. ''Oh, no? You just didn't get caught so quickly.''

''We ought to sneak up on those brats and give them a good scare,'' Luke suggested.

Cat shook her head. ''Not my baby,'' she warned. ''I'll shoot the first one of you who speaks a harsh word to her. Or Tommy Karl.''

The kids saw them when they drew a little closer. Manfully, Tommy Karl stood up to face them. Joey huddled under a horse blanket, looking frightened and unwilling to raise her gaze from the fire. Cat couldn't keep from running the last few yards. Slowly, Joey stood up to meet her. Cat choked back a sob and breathed a silent prayer of thanks as she swept Joey's thin, tense figure into her arms.

Luke's rough growl made Tommy stand up straighter, a look of fear in his eyes. ''Boy, what the hell are you doing out here? Do you know what time it is?''

Tommy Karl quickly glanced at Joey and stuttered, "I—I think it's about nine o'clock."

Luke roared, "I don't care what time it is! What are you doing out here after dark? Are you out of your mind?"

Cat reached out a hand to Luke. "Let's wait until we get back to the house, Luke. Please?"

Luke grumbled something, swore under his breath, then nodded. When he spoke again, his voice no longer resonated his anger though his words were clipped short. "Where are the horses? Never mind, I see them over there. Come on, son. Help me saddle them."

Cat saw Luke put an arm across Tommy Karl's shoulders and pull him closer. He might roar a little bit, but he never could stay mad at Tommy Karl for long. They returned in a few minutes leading the two horses. Joey refused to look at anyone. She kept her face buried in Cat's side.

Luke touched her on the shoulder. "You kids get on the horses. We'll have to lead you out. It's too dark to see much, even with the moonlight."

Jackson said, "Cat, you ride Joey's horse. I'll carry my daughter."

"I don't want you to," Joey yelled suddenly. "You're *not* my father! I hate you!"

Jackson gave her a cool, impersonal look. "Hate me tomorrow, kid. You've caused enough trouble for one night."

"I can walk," Cat protested.

"There's no reason for you to walk when we've got the horses. You can lead both horses, can't you, Luke?"

"Sure, and I agree with you. It's been a long trek."

Joey pleaded, "Mommy, I don't want him to carry me. You carry me. Please, Mommy? Please?"

Jackson's firm voice interrupted. "Joey, I know you're mad at me, but you're not the one making decisions around here. I'll carry you and your mother will ride the horse. Get used to the idea."

Cat groaned. Joey's sullen, tear-stained face grabbed her right square in the heart. "Take it easy, Jackson. She's not a Marine, you know. She's just a little girl who's very tired, very hungry and very upset. Don't make it worse."

Jackson threw his hands up. "I know, I know! Have you got a better plan?"

Cat bit her lip. Jackson might be justified in being firm. Certainly he had the right. "Okay, then, but remember she's a child, not a Marine on a forced march."

Jackson shot an angry glance in her direction. "I'm not a drill sergeant, either, Cat, so quit worrying. It's not going to hurt her to know she's not in control right now."

He took Joey from Cat. Joey pushed away from him, her body stiff, screaming at the top of her lungs, "I don't want to! I don't want to, Mommy. Make him put me down!"

For hours, Cat had pushed her body and her emotions. Like a spring that suddenly snapped, Cat reached the limits of her tolerance. "Joey, if you say one more word, you're going to be grounded for a month and that means no riding, too! You're acting like a spoiled brat! You've got some explaining to do when we get home. For right now, if you're smart, young lady, you'll keep quiet and do as you're told."

No riding. The threat hung heavy in the air. Joey closed her mouth quickly. Obviously, she preferred dire corporal punishment to the loss of her riding privileges. She whimpered and snuffled in Jackson's arms, but it had been a long day for her, too. Within a few minutes, she relaxed against his shoulder. Shortly thereafter, her eyes drooped shut and she fell asleep.

Cat watched her daughter from her comfortable perch aboard Moonshot. The high moon glowed softly, showing her daughter's relaxed face. The bittersweet pleasure of seeing Joey in her father's arms surged through her. Her eyes filled with tears. Jackson looked so strong and caring, with his child tucked up high against his neck. Why couldn't things be like this forever? Was that so much to ask?

JACKSON DIDN'T GET HOME until after midnight. He lay in bed, wide-awake, thinking about what had happened. Joey had slept through the long walk back to the truck, and her warm weight in Jackson's arms stirred conflicting feelings. He cherished the burden, and didn't know why. By all rights, he shouldn't have any feelings for her. He'd heard comments from other guys about fathering a baby and never seeing or supporting the child. They'd had no regrets. At least, none they admitted. Most seemed to be of the opinion that if they weren't married to the mother, then the kid meant nothing to them.

Yet, from the moment he'd seen Joey, he'd felt a connection. At first, he'd thought it was because of the fascination Cat Darnell held for him. Later, he realized that he just plain liked the little girl. He enjoyed the way she came running every time he appeared at the ranch. It wasn't just her obvious hero worship, either. She was a sweet, giggling little tease. He should have known he was her father when she reminded him of Cassidy at the same age.

One night of lovemaking had resulted in a child. It

shouldn't have happened and yet he couldn't find it in himself to regret Joey. She'd become too precious to him, too quickly. Did it mean, though, that he had to give up his dreams? Did he have to live in this damn hick town forever, because one moment of carelessness resulted in a lifetime of responsibility? No matter how much he loved Joey, he felt the tight jaws of a trap snap shut.

At last, total exhaustion resulted in sleep. He awakened late, but Pop hadn't left the house. Jackson could hear him rattling around in the kitchen. Time to get up and face the music. He didn't look forward to telling his father he'd left a baby behind when he ran off to join the Marines. Pop would be sure to throw a fit. If there was one thing Will Gray despised, it was a man who neglected his responsibilities.

The jaws of the trap tightened. Jackson struggled against the inevitable conclusion. There had to be a way out. Some way he could go to Seattle and still take care of Joey. And Cat. He made a decision. Later, he'd tell Pop about Joey. He needed to straighten things out with Cat first.

His father sat at the kitchen table, a cup of coffee and a plate of buttered toast in front of him. His face was still too pale from his long recovery, but beginning to get more color now that he spent most of his day outdoors. Did the skin around his eyes have more lines or was it just the harshness of the morning sun shining through the kitchen window? His red hair had so much gray mixed in. It gave Jackson an uneasy feeling. His father seemed frail this morning.

"You got in awful late last night."

Jackson hurried to conceal his concern with annoyance. "I didn't know you had a curfew here."

His father's cold gaze raked him from head to foot. "Common respect ought to tell you that I need to know when you're going to be home. I thought maybe there'd been an accident. Must I remind you that you're still my son? I worry about you now, the same as I did when you were a kid."

Jackson remembered his own whirlwind of worry, anger, grief when he realized Joey had run away from him. Now he knew with unrelenting certainty what his own absence must have done to his father. His voice softened. "I'm sorry, Pop. There was trouble at Cat's. Joey and Tommy Karl took off on their horses without telling anybody. When they didn't come home, I helped Luke and Cat look for them. I should have called."

Pop's face paled with frightening suddenness. "Is everything okay? They weren't hurt, were they?"

"Everything's fine. I have a feeling Luke is going to ground Tommy Karl for the rest of his life and I know Cat is going to give Joey a stern lecture. She's not into the spanking thing and, anyway, Joey is too little to spank. I don't think they'll be running off like that again."

"Good." Pop straightened in the chair, shook his head for no apparent reason and appeared to dismiss the matter. "I expected you to spray that field yesterday. When you didn't come back, I had Buddy do it. Big job for one man, son. Never mind that now. He's going to check the cows over this morning. He'll need some help. I'm concerned they may not be getting enough grass. It's been too dry for good growth lately. We might need to feed them some hay. There's not that much left in the barn, so somebody's going to have to call around and see who's got some they don't need."

Jackson got himself a mug of coffee and snagged a

piece of the untouched toast from his father's plate. He looked out the window, towards the barn. Buddy came out, carrying a red, five-gallon gas can. The weight of the can pulled the short man a bit sideways. Jackson hesitated, then said, "I planned on going back to Cat's place this morning. I still have a lot to do on her living room."

"Suit yourself. You're not much help lately." The old man stood up and left the room, his face cold, his shoulders stiff.

Dammit! Pop didn't know how important this was. Or he just wanted to order his son around again. Disgusted, Jackson stood up. He'd done his share around here. More than his share. He intended to see Cat today and nothing his father said would change his mind. He'd tell Pop about Joey soon. Once he explained things, Pop would be more understanding. He didn't want to hurt Pop again, but this was important. Like the-rest-of-his-life important.

CAT FIXED PANCAKES for Joey's breakfast. She knew preparing Joey's favorite food would comfort both of them. Running water and splashing sounds came from the bathroom. The doorbell rang. Cat knew who it was before she looked up and saw the truck outside.

She fixed a firm smile on her face, then opened the door. One look at Jackson wiped it off. His eyes had dark smudges below them, as if he hadn't slept. His jaw seemed set with concrete, his blue eyes gray with fatigue. His brilliant bronze hair contributed the only color to his face. "Good morning," she said. "You don't look like you slept too well."

He nodded, a barely civil gesture, and ignored her comment. "How's Joey?"

"She's okay. Totally unaware that she worried everybody to death yesterday. I haven't talked to her much. We haven't had breakfast. Would you join us?"

He looked as if he might refuse, then changed his mind. "Thanks. But how's Joey going to feel about that? She was pretty definite last night." He shot an accusing glare at her.

Cat's defenses reared up. "You're blaming me for her attitude, aren't you?"

"Cat, I don't want to start that again this morning. Frankly, I'm too tired. I just want to talk to Joey and explain why I wasn't around for her."

He looked like ice. Colder. No sun would melt that frozen blue glare. He followed her into the kitchen. Joey had finished brushing her teeth and sat at her usual place, wearing a pair of too-small pink pajamas fringed with a wide band of white lace around the shirt bottom. She looked like an angry elf. Cat shot an anxious glance at Jackson, but his cold eyes warmed the minute he saw Joey.

"Good morning, Short Stuff. I missed saying goodnight to you last night. You were fast asleep when we tucked you in."

Joey's lower lip puffed out. She cast a beseeching look at Cat.

"Aren't you going to talk to me, Joey? I carried you a long ways last night."

Cat interjected, "At least you can thank Jackson for carrying you home, Joey. Where are your manners?"

Staring down at her plate, Joey muttered a barely heard response that marginally resembled "Thank you."

Jackson tried to give the impression he hadn't noticed Joey's sullen pout. "No problem, Cat. Joey needs to know why I wasn't here when she was a baby. She isn't going to get over being mad until we tell her."

Cat knew he was right. That didn't make it any easier. In a hesitant voice, she began. She tried to explain without going into the physical details Joey wouldn't understand. At least, she fervently hoped Joey wouldn't understand. Kids grew up so fast nowadays. Afterward, Joey looked from one parent to the other. Her darkly lashed eyes accused Jackson and pleaded with Cat.

"I don't love you, Jackson. Mommy, I don't have to love him, do I?"

Cat looked at the tall Marine, sitting almost at attention, his hands on his knees, fingers knotted into fists. "This is going to be harder than we imagined."

His jaw tightened. "If you had told the truth, we wouldn't be having this particular problem."

Only now did Cat realize the full extent of the damage her lies caused. She wanted to defend herself, but the truth was the truth. "Yes, I should have, but it's too late for 'should haves.' I can't change the past. Neither can you. With time, Joey will get used to it." She looked at Joey. "Honey, I think it would be a good idea for you and Jackson to take a little walk and get to know each other."

Joey's large eyes brimmed with tears. "I already know him and I don't want to walk."

"Would you do it for me?" Cat put all her love into that question. Maybe, maybe, Joey would recognize it and give her a second chance.

Joey shot an angry glance at Jackson, one only slightly less angry at her, and sighed plaintively. "I guess so, if I hafta."

Jackson ate the last bit of toast on his plate and stood up. He rubbed the paper napkin over his lips for longer than it really took to wipe a few crumbs, trying to formulate a reply. "I'm not a bad person, Joey. I'm your father and I love you. One day, I hope you'll love me. We can get beyond the anger and accusations, if you'll give me a chance. What do you say? Shall we try?"

Joey stood up. She gave Cat one last appealing glance, then nodded. "I'm not going to love you, but if Mommy says I have to walk with you, I will."

She went to her bedroom to get dressed. Jackson drank the last of his coffee standing beside the kitchen sink. Cat thought he looked worried. He should be. He was about to find out little girls were different from adults and very different from Marines. Overwhelming guilt prompted her next words. "I'll go along, if you think it will help."

Jackson braced both hands on the counter behind him and studied the worn linoleum floor. He didn't look up to meet Cat's gaze. "No. This needs to be between me and my daughter."

CHAPTER TWELVE

WORRYING HOW TO BEGIN, Jackson walked beside Joey, clad now in blue jeans, a white blouse dotted with periwinkles, blue socks, and wrinkled, dirt-stained tennis shoes. It was one thing to insist on his right to speak with her, quite another to figure out what to say.

He stopped at the corral and leaned against the fence, resting his forearms on the top rail. Focusing his gaze on the pasture, instead of her, he said, "I know you don't understand what's been happening between your mother and me. It gets pretty complicated, even for adults and sometimes I don't understand it myself. I know you're very upset. Heck, I am, too, but I want you to know I love you and always will. Just trust me for a little bit, okay? I want us to work through past mistakes and become friends. Will you give me a chance to explain?"

Joey turned her back to him. Her stiff shoulders answered him, even before she replied. Her little voice remained calm and as clear as the morning air. "I hate you."

He studied her stubborn form. Rising heat flushed his cheeks. He hadn't been this awkward since the first time he'd asked a girl for a date. Again, he tried. "No, you don't. You're just mad."

"Do, too."

He took his gaze off her and directed it to a wild stretch of rough pasture. "Aren't you going to let me explain? I promise I'll tell you the truth. I'll keep that promise, Joey, if you'll give me the chance.''

She kicked at the dust with her scuffed shoes. ''Nothing to 'splain.''

He sneaked a hurried look at his daughter. ''Aren't you going to let me tell you how sorry I am that I missed seeing you born? I would have been here if I'd known.''

She pushed dust over the toe of her left shoe, using her right shoe as a scoop. ''Don't care.''

Jackson straightened. He sighed. ''I can't fight that. I guess I'll leave then.''

She looked over her stiff little shoulders at him, a sullen pout on her face. ''I knew you didn't love me.''

A spark of hope flickered, then blazed in Jackson's heart. ''Don't you want me to leave?'' he asked, cautiously.

Joey moved away from him another few inches, very casually. ''Never said that.''

He blew out a puff of air, exaggerating the whistling air sound. ''This is getting nowhere. We're talking in circles. What do you want, Short Stuff?''

''I don't know.'' Carefully, Joey traced her name in the dust with the toe of her shoe. She got as far as the left wing of the ''y'' before scrubbing the whole name away with an angry foot.

Windjammer and one of the fillies raced toward them from the pasture, shearing off as they approached the corral. They ran along the fence line for a few moments before stopping. Jackson watched as they began to crop the short grass, then nodded to himself. ''Maybe I should just eat grass.''

He'd thought she might smile at his feeble joke, but her face remained closed. ''We can't settle anything if you won't talk to me, honey. Do you want me to tell you why I left Engerville?''

"I don't care. You can if you want to."

Jackson stared out across the pasture. She had no enthusiasm for listening to his excuses and he had a feeling this might be the last chance he'd have with Joey. He had to get it right and had to say it in such a way that she'd listen. How do you talk to an eight-year-old who doesn't want to listen, when it's the most important thing in the world for her to *hear?* He had no practice in dealing with kids, so likely he'd screw this up, too, but the ache in his chest pushed him. "I wasn't very old then. Only eighteen, and I wanted to know what it would be like to live in another place, to see other towns, other countries."

Rage burst from the small figure. She stared up at him with a hot, anger-filled gaze. "But what about me?"

She was listening, though she might not understand. He picked his words as carefully as if he were treading his way through a minefield. "You weren't even born then, Short Stuff."

"Mommy was born! And you left her, too."

No arguing with that one. "I know. I wish I hadn't, but you see, I didn't know I loved her."

"I know I love her. How can you not know when you love somebody?"

"Love is different for adults. Or maybe it isn't different and we just think it is. Anyway, we'd dated only once. Usually, it takes more times than that to fall in love. I thought about her a lot after I left. I didn't know about you."

"Didn't Mommy tell you?"

Jackson knew the ground he trod with this question could open up and swallow him. He didn't dare make

Cat the villain in this soap opera, but if he took all the blame on himself, Joey might never forgive him. He wet his lips and tried to swallow. They really did need rain to settle the dust. "Honey, your mommy thought I wouldn't be happy to stay in Engerville, so she didn't tell me."

Joey stared accusingly up at him. "Is it her fault? You said it was her fault."

No way could he tell this stubborn elf that her mother betrayed them both. Even if a gnarly spot in his guts believed that. "We were young, but that's not a very good excuse. I don't blame you for being upset. I just wish you'd forgive me."

Joey said nothing.

"Well, maybe you'll let me get to know you and tell you about myself. I guess you have to know somebody before you can forgive them. Right?"

"Where were you?" Her voice cracked on the question that was almost a plea.

It made him want to pick her up and hold her so tightly she'd never wander away again. Jackson's heart squeezed. His hand started to move and he yanked it back before it could smooth Joey's dark curls. "I joined the Marines. I spent some time in South Carolina, then went to Japan. After that, a tour at an embassy in Africa, and then I was stationed at Quantico, Virginia. That's where I've been for the last three years."

"What's Quantico?"

"It's a base where they train officers to lead soldiers in case we get into a war."

"Do you have any little girls there?"

"No. No, I don't."

"Maybe you have some more that you don't know about."

The look on Joey's face seemed compounded of fear, jealousy and sullen anger. The jealousy part heartened him. "Well, darling, I think it's a terribly wrong thing to make a baby unless you stick around to take care of that baby. I'm pretty sure you're the only little girl I have."

"You didn't want me."

Jackson's head spun. "We're doing the circle thing again, Joey. I would have wanted you, if I'd known. I didn't know. Isn't that good enough for now?"

Her cat-green eyes filled with a diamond glint of moisture. "I want my mommy!"

He gave up. "Okay, fine. We'll talk more later."

She took off, running on fairy feet across the grass, back to the only home she knew. Back to the one person of whose love she was very sure. A lump formed in Jackson's throat. He couldn't talk her into loving him. It was supposed to happen naturally, not like this.

It was too late. Way too late. Damn him for being an inconsiderate idiot! Why hadn't he ever called Cat to see how she was doing? He'd only thought of getting out of town and away from his father. Did he really believe Cat would regret their lovemaking once the glitter of prom night faded? Or was that just his excuse?

If he dug a little deeper into his soul, would he find, buried beneath his callow excuses, a fear that Cat would put a claim on him, force him back to Engerville? Was he a coldhearted bastard who'd let her suffer rather than come back? The thought gained credence.

He should leave her alone, bottle up the desires that had surfaced as soon as he saw her again. He had no right to want her. No right to dream about the emerald fire in her eyes. No right to want to put his hands where they'd been before.

Would Joey allow him any closeness? Could he blame her if she didn't? Did his guilt over Cat demand that he lose Joey to make up for his teenage mistake?

He *couldn't* lose her. He wouldn't.

A pall of depression and undirected anger settled on him. On his way back to the house, he stopped at the pump and splashed cold water on his face.

Cat had been watching the brief exchange from the kitchen window. She didn't have a lot of hope vested in Jackson quickly winning over Joey. Her stubborn daughter didn't give in easily. No doubt it was a trait she inherited from her father.

When she saw Joey start running toward the house, she knew the encounter had ended. A blast of guilt caused her to mentally cringe. She was the one Joey should blame. Too late for regrets, Cat thought. Too late.

Joey burst into the kitchen, slamming the screen door behind her. "Mommy, I don't want to talk to him anymore. Do I have to?"

Cat knelt and gathered Joey's slender form to herself. Holding her tight, she rocked the small girl in her arms. "Honey, he just wants you to understand, to give him a chance. Can't you try?"

"I don't want to," Joey said, and salty tears tracked down her cheeks.

Cat smoothed back the dark hair, kissed away the moisture and held Joey a bit away from her. "Hush, now, darling. Don't cry. He'll wait until you want to talk to him." She looked up. Jackson stood in the doorway, holding the screen door open behind him. Accusing grief glared out from burning blue eyes.

"Go to your room for a few minutes, Joey. Jackson and I need to talk."

Joey nodded mutely and crept silently from the

kitchen. Glad to go, Cat thought. Glad to leave the confusion, the anger, and her father behind. She stood. "She's all mixed up. You'll have to give her time."

His voice as rough as his sandpaper beard, Jackson retorted, "I don't have much time, Cat."

"You're leaving?" Though she knew the answer to the question before she voiced it, her heart swelled with anguish.

He nodded, his gaze boring into her. "I have to be in Seattle by the first of September. You knew I wasn't staying here. I can't."

"A month, then. I know. I've always known you'd leave. You're not a farmer."

"She's pretty upset, which is no surprise. I couldn't get her to listen to me. How do I get through to her?"

"I wish I knew. She's hurt, too. I'll talk to her and try to get past the anger, make her understand it was my fault, not yours. That's all I can do, Jackson."

"Not very much, is it?"

"What do you want me to say, Jackson? I've already said I'm sorry."

His eyes turned as hard and cold as a backlit glacier. "I *want* you to go back in time to when you knew you were pregnant. I *want* you to call me and tell me I have a child on the way. That's what I want. What do you suppose the chances are that I'll get it?"

"You know I can't change the past!"

Jackson spun on his heel. "Neither can I!" he yelled over his shoulder, slamming the door as he left.

Cat stood silently in the old kitchen, staring out the warped screen door at the stiff back and long legs rapidly retreating. An angry child in the bedroom, she thought, and Jackson running away from her as fast as he could go, just as angry and terribly unforgiving. A heavy weight settled on her heart, the weight of guilt accumulated over long, lonely years multiplied by a love she couldn't declare and the pain she'd caused to the two people she loved most.

THE SUN SANK ALMOST to full dark before Jackson straightened his aching back and grinned at Buddy Sutherland. "Try it now. I think I've got it."

Buddy nodded. "I hope so. This corn won't make a peck an acre without water. It's been too dry."

"Flip the switch."

Buddy frowned at Jackson. A dour, reticent man at the best of times, today's long labor had soured an already acid disposition. He turned to the pump and touched the switch. Streams of water fountained from the holes in the pipe. The wheels that carried those pipes in a continuous migration over the fields began turning.

Jackson grunted with satisfaction. He had an affinity for motors, though he'd almost despaired of repairing the worn-out irrigation equipment. It was past time Pop replaced it, but the stubborn old man wouldn't listen to him.

"Let's call it a day, Buddy," he suggested.

"That's fine by me," the little man agreed. "Wife will be wondering where I am. It's passing late."

Jackson's own fatigue shot home with Buddy's remarks. His shoulders ached. Dust covered his face and clothes. Water from the pipes had mixed with the dust to form a mortar-hard layer on his hands. At least for a while, he'd managed to quit thinking about Joey.

And Cat. His bitter disappointment that Joey refused to have anything to do with him kept prompting accusations toward Cat, adding fuel to his own guilt. As if it weren't enough that Cat had borne his child without his support and raised her alone, now he accused her of responsibility for his child's hostility.

It wasn't fair. He knew that, but he ached every time he thought of Joey—every time he imagined her as an infant, saying her first word, taking her first step—and he'd missed it all. Now it looked like the rest of her life would be lost to him, too. He could think of no way to get close to a child who wanted to shut him out.

In the backyard, the bandy-legged farmhand climbed into his beat-up truck and barely waved a hand in parting. When Jackson entered the house, Bertie and Pop were sitting at the kitchen table, shelling new peas, their heads close together, as if they were conspiring. Pop looked up at him quizzically.

"How'd it go? Did you manage to get the water flowing?"

"It's working now. Anything left for my supper?"

"There's corn and tomatoes and a couple of pork chops. I'll get you a plate," Bertie offered.

"You don't need to wait on the boy," Will pointed out.

"I'll help myself. Thank you, Bertie." Jackson ignored his father.

Pop wasn't going to be ignored, though. "Have you noticed the worms are getting bad in the south cornfield? The one alongside the road? I figured we could take care of that in the morning. I'm pretty near well, now, so I'll go along with you and Buddy."

Jackson grabbed a plate from the cabinet and forked a pork chop from the pan on the stove onto it. He spooned a handful of corn to the side, a couple slices of tomatoes near that, then tore off a hunk of brown-crusted cornbread and parked himself at the end of the table. "It's going to be too hot tomorrow. You better stick around here. Besides, I'm going over to Cat's in the morning. I'll do the cornfield tomorrow afternoon. Okay?''

''Oh.''

Jackson pushed his plate away. ''I knew you'd say that.''

''I just said 'oh.' What are you reading into that?''

He picked up his fork and looked at it as if he weren't sure what purpose it served, then glanced at his father. ''You're angry with me for not doing more around here.''

Will snorted. ''Hah! You're doing that mind-reading thing again. Did you ever consider getting a job with the Psychic Friends Network?''

''Come on, Pop. You know you're mad because I have a life of my own.''

''You think you can read people's minds, do you? Maybe you should start your own psychic hotline. You could call it Psychic Farmers' Network.''

Jackson glared at the family comedian. Pop's jokes were occasionally funny. Not this time. ''Wasn't that what you were thinking? That I'm not much help?''

''Now that you mention it…''

''Oh, hell. If you're feeling so much better, maybe I should get out of your hair.''

Will Gray leaned back in his chair and stared at his son. ''Now, I wonder why that doesn't surprise me?''

Jackson quietly laid his fork down on the plate. ''Pop, I don't need this.''

An alert look brightened his father's eyes. ''Well, son, why don't you tell me what you do need?''

All the anger Jackson couldn't direct at Cat and Joey threatened to pour onto his father. He fought his temper and barely won. With great effort, he maintained silence.

Pop leaned forward, jutting his jaw toward his son. "Jackson, I'm listening. Do you want me to read *your* mind? I'm afraid I have no talent in that direction. If you want to say something to me, now's your chance. Do it or quit complaining."

"Pop, I'm trying very hard not to argue with you, but you're making it damn near impossible! All my life, every time I had something planned that I really wanted to do, you'd manage to guess and I'd get stuck shoveling manure or picking corn worms off the new plants or shoeing Cass's pony or *something*. You always had six things that just had to be done so I couldn't go with my friends."

His father's eyebrows lifted in amazement. "Is that what all this is about? You grew up on a farm and had to help out with chores?"

Jackson splayed his palms on the kitchen table, grinding them into the smooth cherry wood top. "Dammit, no! I knew I had to do my share. That's what being part of a family means. I just wanted to be able to do something *else,* occasionally."

Pop leaned back in his chair and replied in a caustic voice. "If you want to go somewhere, go! I'm not stopping you. You've been hanging out after Cat Darnell ever since you came home. Piddling little bit of help you've been! Why don't you just pack your bags and stay over there?"

Jackson went cold with rage. He'd busted his ass in the six weeks he'd been here. Even counting the time he spent at Cat's, he'd more than done the work of *two* hired hands. Pop had no right— "Maybe I will!"

His father snorted and turned his head so he didn't have to look at Jackson. "Go ahead. For once, do something, 'stead of just threatening to do it."

Bertie's soft voice interjected a protest. "Now, Will, you're being a little harsh with Jackson."

His father paid her no more mind than he did his only son. "He deserves it, Bertie. Don't you fret about *Jackson!* He just *loves* to complain!"

Looking at him hopefully, Bertie suggested, "Jackson, I'm sure if you apologize, your father will, too."

Bertie had been the soul of Christian charity, helping to care for his father. Not a bit like her reputation for being so crabby, the warmhearted inhabitants of this piece-of-shit town had named her that. Jackson forced the harshness from his voice. "Bertie, this is between Pop and me. Don't take this the wrong way, but I'd be pleased if you'd have the kindness to stay out of it."

His father's gaze jerked away from Bertie. His ice-blue eyes shot a baleful glare at his son. "Don't you talk to her like that! Show the respect you were raised to have toward women."

Jackson stood and calmly laid his unused napkin atop his plate. He carried it to the kitchen sink, disposed of the napkin and scraped his uneaten dinner into the garbage pail. Quietly, he laid the plate in the sink. Having regained control of his temper, he turned to face Pop. "Okay, that's it. I'm outta here. You don't need me around, Pop! Just hire yourself another stable boy."

His father spoke not a word as he stomped out of the kitchen.

It only took a minute to stow his gear in the duffel bag. A Marine got used to packing and leaving at a moment's notice. It was more than enough time to regret his hasty action and bitter words. Not enough time for him to get over his resentment at his father's abuse. Still, one glance at Pop's pale face as he stalked through the kitchen almost stopped him. He opened his mouth to say something apologetic, when Pop beat him to the punch.

"Go ahead and leave! You were never man enough to stay and fight."

That did it! He managed not to slam the door as he went out.

Bertie peered out the screen door, worry wrinkling her brow. "Don't you think you were a bit overbearing, Will?"

Will Gray gave a wry chuckle. He looked at his friend and shook his head with a slight smile curving his lips. "I knew it'd be hard to push him enough so's he'd leave. Jackson knows his duty. I had to make him mad enough to forget it."

Bertie looked bewildered. "You mean you weren't angry at him? You were just pretending?"

Will smiled. "Now, Bertie, when did you ever see me browbeat my kids the way I just did? Took every bit of the meanness I stored up for the last ten years right out of me. I love that boy. He's my own dear son."

She still looked doubtful. "What if he leaves Engerville?"

"He won't. Unless I miss my guess, that boy is walking over to Cat Darnell's ranch right now. If he's lucky, she'll sympathize with him for having such a mean old man. If *I'm* lucky, this will be how I make up for trying to stop him from leaving the first time." Will stood up and went over to the kitchen window. He pulled the gauzy curtains back and stared out at the empty landscape. No sign of his son.

"And if he's unlucky?"

Will let the curtain fall back to its limp, hanging position. A second of doubt shook him, but he refused to give in to it. "He won't be. He's my son. Us Grays are lucky in love." He winked at Bertie.

WHEN JACKSON STUMBLED out of the field on to Cat's land, he looked around at the night-shadowed outbuildings. He could go knock on her door and tell Cat his problem, or sit down and figure out the answer for himself. The lemon-yellow light spraying out in a hazy circle from the windows looked cozy. The closed door and the windows all pulled down was explained by the hum of the ancient air conditioner. In late July, the nights were often hot. Sitting in her cool kitchen, maybe having a beer and a sandwich, while he explained Pop's basic unfairness, tempted him beyond reason.

He thought about Joey, who'd probably still be up, listening to him bad-mouth his father. Reluctantly, he looked around and picked a tall pine tree to sit against, while he watched Cat's home, waiting for the lights to go out.

A half hour later, Jackson entered the barn, found an empty stall and tossed his duffel bag in the corner. He kicked together a stack of straw from the bedding someone, probably Cat, had scattered over the dirt floor. It would be a rough bed, but after two nights with very little sleep and a horribly long day under the hot sun, it didn't much matter. Within moments, he drifted into a light, restless sleep.

EARLY THE NEXT MORNING, Cat awakened to the soft burr of the alarm clock. No matter that she hadn't slept much. Farm chores awaited her. She understood Jackson's distaste for farm life and the never-ending ritual of chores, but there was no point in lingering in bed. Chores had to be done, animals fed and watered. *You shouldn't make the stock wait.* Her father had drummed that rule into her head. She decided to let Joey sleep another hour or two. Her daughter loved all the animals too much to need reminding of the rule.

A quick swipe of the toothbrush and a splash of cold water would do her until after she fed the animals. A few minutes later, having put on a clean pair of jeans and one of her father's old T-shirts, she emerged from the house.

She glanced at the sky. Already, it sported a blue so hard and intense that Cat knew it would be another miserably hot day. A few clouds wouldn't be unwelcome, she thought. Engerville corn needed rain.

She swung the barn door open and went inside. For a moment, she stood there as her eyes adjusted to the gloom. Then the hair rose on the back of her neck. A quick sweeping glance at the horses revealed nothing unusual. All waited quietly, eager for their morning oats. RugRat whickered softly. She looked down the other side of the narrow barn. One stall door stood open. She'd swept the runway and closed all the stall doors the night before. Unease raced over her.

Was there an intruder? Maybe she'd left the stall door ajar and its own weight caused it to swing open. Tentatively, she walked toward the stall, uneasiness slowing her steps.

CHAPTER THIRTEEN

CAUTIOUSLY, CAT PEEPED over the edge of the stall. She backed off hurriedly. Although he was curled on his side and she couldn't see his face, there was no mistaking the blaze of red hair against dun-colored straw. She leaned against the barn wall, the rough boards biting into her back, her legs weakened by the momentary glimpse of Jackson. She waited for her heart to stop pounding and her breathing to slow.

Why had Jackson slept on a pile of straw? Didn't he know he had only to knock at her door and she'd have given him a bed to sleep in, no matter what his reason? He knew, so he must still be angry. He'd never forgive her and he was right not to. What she'd cheated him out of deserved no forgiveness. The sting of tears burned her eyes. A pull she couldn't resist drew her back.

Again, she peered over the edge. Jackson, his face shiny with perspiration, had turned over on to his back. He lay sprawled on a bed of new straw, his duffel a few feet away. One arm was flung above his head, the other draped across his torso with his T-shirt pulled up so a two-inch band of heart-stopping skin showed between his blue jeans and shirt. The snap on his jeans gaped open. Her gaze drifted downward, then jerked up as she realized its direction. Cat stepped inside the stall. She knelt on the prickly straw and reached out a hand toward the still face. He looked so vulnerable in his unprotected sleep. Like Joey.

Unlike Joey, too.

Tracing a fearful line an inch from his skin, she followed the curve of his jaw to his full, sensual lips. Her fingers tingled with the ache to touch him. It had been so long ago, she hardly remembered what touching him felt like. Probably, after such a long time, it wouldn't be the same star-spangled magic. Regretfully, she drew back. For several moments, she remained still beside him, watching him sleep, mesmerized by the rise and fall of his chest. Her hand reached out again, to halt an inch from his lips. Jackson's breath, warm and damp, moistened her finger. It felt like wet lightning touching her skin. She shuddered.

Suddenly, like a striking snake, his hand shot out and grabbed her wrist, squeezing so hard her skin burned. Eyelids lifted to expose angry eyes. The contempt glaring out at her shocked her into a sudden realization of having violated his space in an indefensible way.

Voice low, he growled, "What's the matter, Cat? Want to make another baby?"

The brutal words struck her like a slap in the face. His fingers clamped on her wrist without mercy. She wrenched away, but his iron grip held fast.

"Let me go, damn you!"

The barn's shadows turned his blue eyes to harsh indigo. "You don't really want me to let you go, do you?"

"What are you doing here?" She twisted her arm, but he held her as easily as she controlled Joey.

"You didn't answer my question, Wild Cat." He ran a careless finger down her neck to the collar of her T-shirt and slipped under the thin material. For a moment, he hesitated, then pulled back. He tossed her wrist aside and sat up, casually flicking straw from his shirt. "I'd think it was pretty obvious what I'm doing. Or what I was doing, before you came in."

She gathered what wits she had left. "Dammit, Jackson, I know you're still angry with me, but don't play tough guy games. Why are you here?"

Jackson stared at her with cold unconcern. Elbows propped on his knees, hands dangling between his legs, he said, "Cat, darling, I'm here to see my daughter. I intend to get to know her."

He looked away from her, deliberately, she thought, to indicate just how little he regarded her wishes. She wanted to spit nails! "You think you can come into my home and take command? I have news for you, buster. It would take a lot more than one Marine to do the job, no matter how tough you think you are. You don't run things here, Jackson. I decide what happens with Joey!"

"Well, let's see," he drawled. "I've got a wad of cash burning a hole in my pocket." He looked up at the high ceiling, as if pondering a weighty question. "How much do you think a first-class lawyer would charge to get me custody of my little girl?"

For a few seconds his cold statement struck terror in her heart, then reason reasserted itself. Her anger dissipated. "Do you take me for a complete fool? I've known you since I moved to Engerville. You wouldn't do that to me or to her. Jackson, I do wish you'd try to see my side, but I also know the day you get bitter enough to separate me from Joey, you wouldn't be Jackson Gray. You have the softest heart of any man I know." She hesitated. "Even if I don't feel like I know you anymore."

Jackson shot a hot glare at her. "There's one thing you're right about. You don't know me."

She leaned away from him, a cold spot in her core that had been warm a moment ago. "You haven't changed so much. Threats from you can't scare me."

"You think you know everything, don't you? Don't push your luck," he warned.

She sat back on her heels, fixing him with an icy stare of her own. "Are you going to tell me what you're doing here? And why you're sleeping in my barn?"

He brushed straw from his shirt and raked a hand through his hair, sending bits of chaff flying. "Pop is pretty much okay now. He still can't do heavy work, but he has Buddy. I don't think he ever expected me to stay this long."

"Why have you?"

His cold gaze flicked over her, stinging like the touch of a whip. "Something of mine is here. Something very precious to me and I'm not leaving until I've made peace with Joey. Certainly not before you and I come to an understanding."

"I told you I wouldn't stop you from seeing Joey."

Jackson's jaw set in a straight, hard line. "There's more to it than that. I want a legal arrangement. I want my parental rights. What if you decide to get married? Your new husband might want to adopt Joey. Then where would I be? Out in the cold with no rights to my own child!"

"Married?" She tried to laugh. A strangled squeak came out. "I'm not getting married!"

"Ever? Come on, Cat, be reasonable! You won't stay single the rest of your life." He stared at her. "Why haven't you married? It can't be for lack of offers. Even including a child not their own, there have to be a dozen guys in Traill County eager to take you on. After all, they'd get the ranch as well as you and my daughter. A pretty good bargain, if you ask me.''

How many lonely nights were there in nine years? He didn't know the despair of a small farm in a North Dakota winter with only her dour father, Joey and the horses for company. And after Joey turned six, not even her daughter during the day. Just the harping complaints of a father who'd never forgive her. Though he loved Joey, he thought her birth the result of her mother's wild ways and seemed intent on making sure the mistake wasn't repeated.

Jackson didn't know, couldn't know, how much loneliness and pain she'd endured on this farm he thought might sweeten the bargain for a potential husband. She would never tell him. ''Your business is Joey. Whether or not I get married is up to me. I haven't tried to find out why you're still single, have I? If you want to make a legal arrangement, we can go see Allan Becker in town and get him to draw up papers. I'll agree to any equitable sharing of Joey. It's no more than what's right, and I trust her with you.''

Jackson looked disbelieving. ''That makes me feel special. Too bad you didn't think the same way eight years ago.''

Cat took a deep breath and clenched her hands into fists. ''I did, but I didn't know how you'd react. I even thought you might take her from me. You wouldn't…at least I know that when I'm thinking straight. I couldn't bear Joey being away from me, even for a few weeks and you'd never return to Engerville to live. You said as much and I believed you.''

Jackson sat for a moment in deep thought, one fist squeezing a handful of straw until the shafts broke and sifted through his hand. He tossed the leftover bits aside and wiped his hands on his shirt. "People change, Cat. Even if you were right back then, now is different. Maybe it'd be worth it."

"Worth it? You could come back to Engerville and even sacrifice your life to be near Joey, but how long before you turned bitter? How long before she knew she was the reason for your unhappiness? I watched my father try to lead the life my mother wanted and it nearly destroyed him. She left before the weight of his unhappiness could destroy her. Do you think I want that guilt dumped on Joey any more than I want it on me? No, Jackson, I don't think you want to go there."

"Damn." He'd whispered the word to the straw, not to her.

Jackson raised his head to gaze at her, his eyes full of heartache. "How did I screw up things so badly? I'm a fool. I've been one so long, I don't know if I can change, but I'm going to try. I'll think of a way. There has to be something we can do that won't hurt Joey. Maybe you and I deserve to be hurt. I don't know as much as I used to think I did, but there has to be a way, Cat. There has to." He hesitated, ducked his head, then finally looked back at her. Hesitantly, he asked, "In the meantime, I need a place to crash. Are you going to throw me out?"

A loud, restless neigh from RugRat punctuated his tentative statement. One of the other horses chimed in. "Jackson, this isn't doing any good. Don't you think I've tried to find a solution since the day she was born? I've failed. I know we made a huge mistake and we have to pay, but I don't want Joey caught up in our quarrel and I'm not sure it's such a good idea for you to stay here."

"You have to let me, Cat. It'll give me more time

with Joey. I've got a lot of time to make up, you know. Eight years' worth.''

Cat sat back on her heels and tried to meet his eyes, but found the pain in them too much to bear. Her fault again. She looked down to where her hand touched the matted bedding. "I hope you don't plan on sleeping on a bed of straw for—how long?''

"A month, almost. What about the tack room? I could put a cot in there.''

She searched for objections. "It would be too hot. There's no window in there, no air circulation.''

"I'll get a fan. How about it?''

"I don't know. There'd be talk.''

His voice softened. "Wasn't there before? It's a small town. Everybody knows everybody else. Bertha Gillis isn't the only one who gossips.''

She nodded. "Yes, but it was only for a while. People got used to it and pretty soon, they quit talking and accepted it. Your father helped.''

Jackson's brows lifted. "Pop? How?''

"He and your mother used to stop every Sunday and give me a ride to church. Dad never went and I probably would have dropped out entirely if it hadn't been for them. Your mom called me one Saturday night when Joey was about six weeks old and asked me if I felt well enough for church. I didn't want to. I was so possessive of Joey and so sensitive to what people were saying. She talked to me for ten minutes, trying to convince me, then your dad got on the phone and just said, 'We'll be by at nine-thirty. You need church and the church needs you.' He hung up the phone without giving me time to make excuses.''

"That sounds like Pop. Commandments from on high.''

"Oh no, Jackson! His voice, his tone radiated pure kindness. He's like you. Softhearted. He knew I'd have a hard time going back by myself. Anyway, your mom and dad picked me up every Sunday unless one of the four of us was sick. Right up until your mom had that stroke. I drive myself now, but Joey and I still sit with your father...or did, until he was hurt."

Jackson stared over her shoulder at nothing, then looked back at her. "I need a shower. Think Joey would be shocked if she wakes up and hears me?"

Cat hesitated. Nothing she said seemed likely to dissuade him. Jackson planned on staying and short of calling the sheriff to kick him out, she had no recourse. Maybe it would work. "It's the least I can do for you, I suppose. I think she'll get used to it. If you sleep out here, you'll still have to eat and wash up at the house."

He nodded as if the agreement had been made. "All right, that's settled. I'll shower, then run into town, if you'll let me borrow your truck. Where can I pick up a cot and a fan?"

Fighting Jackson's decision was useless. He intended to stay here. "Enger's Hardware might have camping stuff. Check there first. If not, you could drive into Fargo." She hesitated, then shrugged. In for a penny.... "Don't buy any blankets or pillows. I have plenty of those."

Jackson nodded. "What are you going to tell Joey?"

"The truth."

JACKSON CAME BACK from town with the pickup loaded with groceries, as well as the cot and fan. Cat eyed the bags and shook her head. "How long did you say you'd be staying?"

"A month at the most. I have to be in Seattle on September first."

She motioned toward the food. "You overbought. You've got enough to feed an army."

"Marines, Cat. Most of it's canned stuff. It'll keep."

The guilt factor, she thought. He's trying to make up for all the years he didn't provide food for his daughter. She studied his anxious face, the way he tried to appear casual, the gathering of hope in the rigid line of his jaw. The enormity of her love for him staggered her. Her heart might explode if she didn't look away. She shifted her gaze to a brown paper sack. Mist gathered in her eyes.

He grabbed the closest bag and said, "I'll carry everything into the kitchen, but you'll have to put it away. I don't know where you keep things. By the way, I'll do my share of cooking. I don't expect you to cook for me while I'm here."

"Can you cook?"

"Not much, but I won't poison you." His sly grin didn't inspire confidence.

"That's reassuring," Cat said. "I suppose you know that answer isn't going to get you much kitchen time?"

Jackson glanced around. "I'm counting on it. Where's Joey?"

She nodded toward his new home. "In the barn. I asked her to sweep out the tack room."

"She didn't object?"

Jackson so eagerly wanted to be friends with his daughter. It would take time Jackson didn't have. She knew he didn't want to hear a warning, but she had to try. "Joey likes you, but she doesn't want to forgive you for not being here. I think she'll come around. Give her time to get used to the idea."

He nodded grimly. "I hope a month is long enough. I don't want to leave here with her still mad at me."

By noon, the tack room had been converted into a bedroom with the addition of the cot, a fan and a small table radio-clock. Jackson hung his shirt on a nail driven into the wall opposite the cot and shoved his duffel underneath the bed.

He wore his thin white V neck T-shirt with no understanding whatsoever that it outlined his pectorals as if it had been painted on. Cat made a determined effort not to focus on the muscled chest beside her or the tangle of red-gold curls sprouting from the V. Instead she eyed the small space dubiously. "You won't have much room."

"It'll do. I'm only going to sleep here." He ushered her out of the room with a careless hand at the small of her back. "I'll sand the living room floor today and maybe get a coat of sealer on it. Are you sure you're happy with a bare floor?"

She nodded. "I think it will look good, and I can add rag rugs for warmth. I have a couple Aunt Johanna made that I packed away when she died."

"Okay, then. Let's check up on Joey." He led the way outside.

Cat wondered how long she'd be able to keep up this front of casual acceptance. Twenty-four hours a day of knowing Jackson was only a few feet away had her stomach in a turmoil. Fervently hoping her nervousness would go away, she followed him out.

In the corral, Joey put Moonshot through her paces. The young mare performed well. She walked, trotted and cantered to Joey's almost imperceptible commands. Joey worked her in a figure eight and Moonshot changed leads accurately. "She's a natural athlete," Cat said.

"Joey?"

"No… Well, I suppose she is, too, but I meant the filly. She's much further along than I'd expected. That's due to the extra attention Joey lavishes on her."

"Uh-huh."

Engrossed in watching Joey, Jackson seemed to have forgotten she stood beside him. An insidious thread of jealousy wormed its way through Cat. He'd never been that entranced with her.

"Is Moonshot for sale?" Jackson asked.

"That's the plan, but Joey is so attached to her that it's going to be tough to let go. I've tried to get her to spend equal time with Windjammer and Freedom, but although she's perfectly willing to ride any of the horses for training, the only one she wants to ride for herself is Moonshot."

"How much would you get for her?" Jackson settled his tall frame against the corral. His arms rested casually on the top rail as all his attention riveted on his daughter.

"She's not purebred and she'll never make a cow horse. Not big enough or strong enough. She might make a good barrel horse for a child. With Joey on her, she's greased lightning, but she's too small for a heavier rider."

"What's a woman who's raising horses for a living doing with a scrub horse? Isn't that a waste of your time?"

"We don't always know how they'll turn out. As a yearling, she looked pretty good, but she didn't get as big as Dad thought she would. His excuse was that he never actually bought her. RugRat's owner threw Moonshot in on the deal just to get rid of her or maybe as an added incentive for Dad to buy RugRat."

"How much?"

Cat did some mental arithmetic. "Two thousand would be a fair price. She's not full broke yet, though Joey has her eating out of her hand."

"I want her," Jackson stated firmly.

Cat laughed. "What would you do with a horse? Do you still ride? Even if you do, that little filly is too small for you. Better take a look at Windjammer. He's the big white colt. Runs the show in the pasture."

Jackson shook his head. "Not for me. I'll give her to Joey as a birthday present."

"Her birthday is not until February and I'm not about to sell her out from under Joey. You don't need to worry about that."

Jackson smiled, his gaze far away. "For the birthdays I missed and especially for her first one."

"If you insist then, but I won't take more than a thousand for her from you. And that's my final word."

"What a horse trader you are, Cat. Do you always skin your customers this badly?"

Cat nodded, but didn't answer. Jackson's aching need to make up for the years he'd missed filled her with remorse. She'd hurt her daughter and Jackson horribly. Could she ever make it up to them? Would they ever forgive her and could she forgive herself?

JACKSON GRAY IN a pair of tight blue jeans and minus anything at all above the waist was purely stunning, Cat thought. He'd discarded his shirt and the close-fitting jeans rode low around his lean hips as he trained Windjammer with a longe line in the corral. He was awkward, but strong. By the hesitant way he barked his commands, she could tell he was uneasy, which made it all the more remarkable that he agreed to take on the task.

He'd burned and peeled so many times since his return that his tan lacked any pretense of evenness. Across his shoulders the heavy muscles were darker, leaner than the lighter copper bands around his waist. Near his belt line, the flesh blended to a painful red fading to white as it dipped into his hips. The lack of symmetry emphasized careless strength.

Cat hadn't wanted to allow Jackson to work with the colts at first, but it was soon obvious he intended to earn his keep. He reminded her that his father kept horses while he was growing up and made sure he and Cassidy could ride to friends' homes so the distances between farms wouldn't seem so far. Though lacking her father's sure touch with a sulky colt, he handled the longe line well enough. He held a whip in his left hand to drive the colt, but he'd not bothered cracking it. Windjammer, eager to run, needed holding back, not urging.

Jackson's deep voice constantly wheedled the colt. "Easy now, fellow. Easy. Slow down, Jammer. This sun is just going to get hotter. Trot, now. Trot." Little by little, he gained confidence in himself and took control away from the white colt. He trotted Windjammer for a while, then let him canter until the horse's chest showed a darker gray where sweat dampened the white hairs. He halted the colt, ran the short metal chain through the snaps on the opposite side of the halter, and turned the young horse around. He clucked once to start Windjammer in the other direction. The direction change was necessary to ensure equal development of the colt's muscles, but she hadn't told Jackson. There were a lot of things he remembered.

He let Jammer run for a moment, then checked him with a word. "Trot, kiddo. Trot. Easy now." Within a few minutes, Windjammer acknowledged Jackson's mastery, bowed to his will and took his orders as if he too, had joined the Marines. Cat envied Jackson the obvious strength he had in those impressive biceps.

There was RugRat to consider, too. She could barely control the colt, and had refused to let Joey ride him. Could Jackson handle the pugnacious stud colt? RugRat was half thoroughbred, half quarterhorse. He combined strength and speed. He also had the size to be a hunter.

Jackson learned quickly. If he could stay ahead of RugRat, it might be the saving of the farm. If anything could bring Joey and Jackson together, horses might be the ticket. This, she knew, motivated Jackson. Though he liked the horses, he didn't have Joey's passion for them. Cat reminded herself, yet again, that nothing about a farm truly interested Jackson.

Joey stood beside her, feigning disinterest, but so absorbed in watching Jackson that she didn't even hear the truck pull into the yard. Cat glanced over her shoulder. Luke and Tommy Karl were dismounting from the pickup. Father and son strode side by side. Tommy Karl, a mirror image of his father's corn-yellow hair and lean, self-assured confidence, picked up his pace so he was a little ahead of Luke. Some link between the boy and her daughter caused Joey to look up. She grinned in delight, her dimples and wide smile totally entrancing.

"Hey, Tommy Karl," she said.

"Hey, yourself, Joey."

"Hi, Luke."

"Hello, Cat. How's it going?"

"Fine. How're you?"

Luke cast an irritated gaze toward Jackson and Windjammer. "Good enough. I see you've hired yourself a horse trainer. Is he any good?"

Joey piped up in a resentful voice, "He's not a horse trainer. He's Jackson and he's staying with us."

Luke raised an eyebrow. "Really?" He addressed the query to Cat.

Joey beat her mother's reply with a sullen response. "He gets to sleep in the barn with the horses."

Luke snickered. "Doesn't sound very comfortable to me."

"Bet they stink," Tommy Karl agreed.

"Joey, don't be a brat," Cat admonished her wayward daughter.

Joey hung her head for a second before smiling mischievously at Tommy Karl. "Let's go look for Freedom and Simba," she suggested. "I saw them down by the trees this morning. Want to?"

Tommy looked at his dad. "Can I?"

Luke clearly didn't want to agree to anything. His disgruntled attitude spoke as plain as a shout, but he gave in. "Don't be long. We have to get home."

Both kids giggled. Joey smacked Tommy on the arm and took off running, yelling over her shoulder, "Tag. You're it! Betcha can't catch me."

Tommy rolled his eyes at his father as if to say, "It isn't my idea." Then he took off after Joey, a broad grin on his face the minute he'd turned his back to Luke. Cat smiled. What a pair. Tommy Karl was so much like his father, it made her want to warn Joey what a stick he could turn into. Luke was a good friend, but far too serious. He really should try to lighten up once in a while.

The look on Luke's face spoke volumes. He was about to lecture her. Cat glanced at Jackson. She knew what Luke intended to say to her. Her lot in life seemed to be to sit quietly while someone lectured her. It really was getting to be an old song. She'd give anything not to hear it sung again.

CHAPTER FOURTEEN

LUKE LEANED CLOSE to her, his broad shoulder nearly touching hers, and lowered his voice. "Cat, I've always thought of you as practical and responsible, but it looks like you've gone off the deep end. I think you're making a huge mistake. Why are you allowing Jackson to live here?"

Cat resisted the urge to turn aside Luke's question. Being her good friend for many years earned him an answer, but how could she explain something she didn't understand herself? "Sometimes you have to go with your feelings, even if it means following those feelings out on a limb. We're good friends, you and I, and I've depended on your help a lot of times, but don't mistake me," she paused, hardening her tone. "What I do is *not* your business." There now. Maybe he'd leave her alone.

Luke's mouth twisted into a stern frown. "Of course it isn't. I'm not trying to run your life. You've done a good job of that…up to now. Hard work and responsibility have made a home out of this run-down ranch. I don't think your father would have made it out here, if you hadn't shared the load. You were always the sensible one in the family, except for a couple of years in high school. That's in the past, and I don't intend to bring it up today, even if I had the right. What I do have is concern for you. If I'm your friend, then I need to warn you if I see you doing something that could be harmful.''

''I know you mean it for the best, Luke, but I outgrew needing someone to tell me what to do years ago. You've been a true friend, always. I haven't forgotten that and I understand your concern, but it is my decision.'' He deserved a straightforward answer. ''Jackson is my friend, too, and he's staying here so he'll have more time with Joey. He'll be leaving in three or four weeks.''

Luke grunted in obvious disapproval. ''That long, huh? I'm surprised he's stuck it out as long as he has, but even a few weeks is enough time for the whole town to get the wrong idea about you two.''

Cat shook her head. ''The whole town isn't making this ranch a home. I am. And who knows, maybe they'll get the right idea.''

''If you're suggesting that people will realize Jackson is Joey's father, you're one hundred percent correct. It won't take a lot of brains to figure that one out. All it will take is the ladies sewing circle raking you over the coals.''

''They'll hear anyway.'' Without consciously thinking about it, she tipped her head so her long, thick hair swept forward. Aware that her voice sounded as sullen as Joey's, she said, ''Jackson wants Joey to have his name legally.''

Luke straightened and shifted his weight so he stood squarely on both feet. His face took on the same dark disapproval her father's face habitually had when he lectured her. ''I don't believe this! Are you seriously thinking about going along with that idea?''

''Why shouldn't I?'' Cat stood a little straighter.

''It seems unwise to give him control over Joey. Unwise may be an understatement. You said he was leaving. What if he wants to take Joey with him?''

Relieved, she laughed. ''Don't be silly, Luke. Jackson won't take Joey away from me.''

He frowned. ''You always see the best side of people, Cat. Think about reality, for a change, instead of fantasy. You don't know that. You're just hoping and hope is not a sure bet. Do you want to take chances with Joey's future?''

A certain peace settled over her. Luke couldn't know the way she did. He couldn't feel Jackson's quiet strength and goodness in the same way. ''Yes, I do. I really do know that Jackson will never try to separate me from my child. It's just not in him, Luke. You should know that, too. You've known him even longer than I have.''

Luke's face darkened with anger. ''Maybe he'll take both of you away.''

Startled, she glanced toward Jackson. The sun burst on his hair in a blaze of copper fire. His long, lean body moved in a graceful arc with the horse. For a second Cat allowed the vision to enthrall her, then shook herself free of the spell. She turned back to Luke. ''That can't happen. This is Joey's home. Jackson knows how I feel about living in Engerville.''

''And obviously, he doesn't want to stay here. Won't that be confusing to Joey?''

''It could be. Life is full of problems, Luke. Joey will deal with it.'' Cat wished she felt as confident as she tried to make her words sound.

His voice softened. ''It seems unfair to her. She's only eight.''

''It's unfair to everyone, but Jackson and I made the mistake a long time ago. Now we all have to pay the price. It's too bad that the one who'll pay the most didn't have anything to do with the mistake, but, as I pointed out, *life* is unfair.''

Luke nodded. ''I'm sorry, Cat. I really didn't come by here to argue. What you decide to do is your business, but if you left Engerville, I'd be very sorry. Damn sorry, and not just because Tommy Karl will miss Joey. I'll miss you, too.''

Cat smiled as she shook her head. ''Forget it, Luke. We aren't going anywhere. There's no need for anybody to miss us. I want to grow old in Engerville and someday I hope Joey has kids that ride horses around that corral, too. My roots are in Engerville so deep, they'll never come out.''

Luke's rueful smile answered hers. ''I hope so, for my own selfish reasons. You're a good friend.'' He touched her cheek gently. ''Hey, I almost forgot why we came over. I wanted to tell you that Rebeka and Burt will be in town in three days. She called last night. I told her about RugRat and she's anxious to see him.''

''Oh, wonderful! Tell her to come over anytime. I'm banking a lot of my hopes on her wanting to buy RugRat. He'll be an expensive investment, but I've not seen many colts that compare with him.''

Luke nodded. ''I'll tell her.''

They watched as Jackson led Windjammer to the far end of the corral and opened the gate into the pasture. After removing the halter, he slapped the white colt on the rump and Windjammer hurried through, then whirled, kicking out with his hind feet in sheer youthful exuberance. Jackson coiled the longe line as he walked toward Luke and Cat. He looked totally in command, she thought, as Luke stiffened beside her.

"Good workout, Jackson," Cat said. "You have Windjammer eating out of your hand."

"I'd hardly say that. He pulled me around like a rag doll on a rope, but he's a pussycat inside that tough exterior." Jackson's gaze lingered on her.

Self-conscious at his continued regard in front of Luke, Cat attempted a light chuckle. It almost worked.

Luke nodded toward Jackson. "You're not that bad with horses, Jackson. Are you thinking of becoming a trainer?"

Cat wondered how Jackson would respond to Luke's caustic tone. She didn't have to wait to find out.

He laughed. "I don't think so. Trucks are more my style."

"Yeah. You worked in the motor pool while you were in the Marines, didn't you?"

Jackson swiped the back of his arm across his sweaty forehead. He puffed out a gust of breath. "That sun is hot." He glanced at Cat, then back to Luke. "How did you know about the motor pool?"

"Will mentioned it. Have you thought about looking for work around here? I know you don't like farming, but if you want to drive a truck, there's places in Fargo and Grand Forks that you could try."

Cat wished Luke would quit trying to tell Jackson what to do. In a moment or two, Jackson would prove what redheads were famous for. She watched uneasily at the tightening of jaw muscles in Jackson's face and the edgy spark in Luke's eyes.

Jackson shook his head. "I've already got something lined up. I've got a job waiting for me in Seattle."

Luke grunted, then glanced at Cat. "Kinda far away from family, isn't it?"

Jackson's smile was no more than surface good manners. "Pop knows I'm going. We'll keep in touch."

"What about Joey? And Cat?"

Jackson's shoulders tightened. Cat knew he was angry. Lecturing Jackson was the last thing anyone ought to try with one of the Gray family. Their hereditary red hair came packaged with the legendary temper. She hastened to intervene. "We'll work things out, Luke. Don't worry about it."

"I can hardly help that, can I?" Luke retorted.

"Cat's right. We'll work things out. No need for you to worry yourself." Jackson's short smile showed his teeth.

Luke shifted his weight from one booted foot to the other. "I don't want to see Cat hurt. Or Joey."

The two men were much the same size, but Jackson's leaner build gave him a quickness that Luke's stocky rancher muscles couldn't match. She had no desire at all to see the two men try to prove which one had the most testosterone. Cat attempted a cheery response. "Really, Luke, you don't have to worry. Whatever we decide to do, we'll handle the consequences."

"As long as Jackson realizes that there *are* consequences…this time."

Jackson's hands clenched so tightly on the longe line that his knuckles whitened. "Stay out of my business, Luke. You have no say in this."

Again, Cat intervened. "Jackson's absolutely correct, Luke. Being friends doesn't give you the right to question me or what I decide to do. I know you're trying to help, but we'll handle this. Jackson won't do anything to hurt me."

Luke cast a pitying glance at her and a harsh glare at Jackson. "He already has."

THAT EVENING, Cat sat on the porch with Jackson and Joey. Her daughter had done her best all day to spoil any developing relationship between her mother and father. Cat made strawberry shortcake for dessert, but her daughter didn't allow it to sweeten her disposition.

"Tommy Karl says his daddy wants to marry you, Mommy. Why don't you? Then Tommy Karl and I could play together all the time."

Her daughter's challenging stare upset Cat more than her words. How deep did her anger run? "Joey, you're getting into hot water here. I've told you before that marrying without love is wrong. Luke and I don't love each other."

Jackson set his coffee cup on the porch step beside him. He had the same irritatingly demanding look on his face. "Maybe Luke loves you, Cat, and you don't know it."

"Joey, quit dragging your shoes that way. You'll scuff the toes. Don't be ridiculous, Jackson. I guess I'd know if a man loved me."

"Mmmh. Do you think so?"

"I know I would. I'm not a teenager anymore."

"Excuse me if I have my doubts…on both counts."

Cat glanced at her daughter. "I don't think Joey needs to hear this."

His face hardened. "Maybe you do."

"What are you trying to say?"

He stood, his legs spread apart in a defiant stance. "What's wrong with you and me getting married?"

Joey wiggled in the too-large lawn chair she sat in. She lifted her chin. "I don't want Mommy to marry you. She doesn't love you and I don't either."

Jackson rubbed his chin, and nailed his daughter with a tight stare. "Short Stuff, that could change. I think you'll like me when we get to know each other better. I already like you."

Joey snarled, "I don't care. I'm never going to like you. Can I watch TV, Mom?"

Cat's temper reached the boiling point. Joey had gone way over the top. "You can go to your room, Joey, and go to bed. Until you learn to be polite, your company is not very pleasant. Jackson is our guest and you'll treat him with courtesy or I'll know the reason why!"

Joey's face paled. Her childish voice sounded plaintive. "I told you why. I don't like him."

Despite his sinking heart, Jackson had to hide a smile. The kid was his, all right. A Gray to the end. Rightful granddaughter of stubborn Will Gray.

Joey left the porch with a sullen glare at her father. Jackson stared out at the field beyond the corral. Cat thought he looked troubled. He certainly had reason to be.

"She's not giving up her anger, Cat."

"I know. I thought she'd come around by now."

Jackson stirred restlessly. He paced the length of the small porch. "What did you tell her about me while she was growing up? Were you so bitter that you took your anger out on me?"

"No, of course not. I told her the truth."

"Your version?"

"It happens to be the only version she had a chance to hear. You were gone and not likely to come back to explain your absence." Cat thought he looked every inch the Marine at this moment. Tall, proud, but angry. A funny sensation, almost like sinking below choking waters, swept over her. A strong desire to flee from him became nearly impossible to resist.

Jackson sat back down on the porch step. "I had no reason to come back. I didn't know about Joey."

"You knew about me." The words were said before she had time to think.

Jackson growled, "That's what this is about, isn't it? You. It's never been about Joey! You're angry because I never came back to take care of you, aren't you?"

"That's not true, Jackson. I didn't say that. If I'd wanted you to come back, I'd have told you about Joey. I put you first—ahead of Joey, and ahead of me!"

Jackson turned away from her, facing the pastures where Simba and Windjammer stood quietly, switching their fly-swatting tails in alternating rhythm. For a long moment, he said nothing, then finally spoke. "You'd like to think that, wouldn't you?"

Cat's anger subsided. Quietly, she replied, "You have a right to question me, but I have a right to defend myself. Jackson, what do you know about me? We were friends as teenagers and we got carried away one night. That's all. I never wanted you to come back."

His glare blazed up at her. "You're lying!"

Her stomach flipped over. He couldn't care anything about her if he was so ready to accuse her of lying. "I'm no saint, Jackson, but I wouldn't lie to you."

He sneered. "You are! You're not adult enough to admit it, though." Jackson's tall length, framed against the porch light, threw a dark shadow over her. "Good night!"

She stood, too, reaching out a hand to grab his sleeve. "Don't you dare leave this porch! We're going to finish this discussion, Jackson Gray. For once in your life, stand still and talk about a problem instead of running out on it."

Jackson shook off her hand. "I can't talk to a liar,"

he retorted. He turned his back on her and marched down the porch steps toward the barn.

Cat stood for a moment, transfixed. What did he know about how much she'd wanted his help and support when Joey was born? She was the one who'd lain in a hospital bed, all alone, for fourteen torturous, pain-filled hours while Joey struggled to be born. What did he know? Nothing, dammit! Nothing but running away and leaving problems behind for someone else to solve.

She stepped down from the porch and followed him. "Wait a minute, Jackson. We need to talk."

"About what?"

"Us. You, me, Joey. Come on, Jackson, stand still for five minutes and face me."

He flipped an angry look over his shoulder and kept going. By the time they reached the barn, Cat's rage matched his. Jackson jerked the door open and stepped inside.

She hurried to enter behind him before the door could swing closed. The warm odor of horses and hay engulfed her. The scent of the wild roses she'd planted behind the barn drifted through the weathered, warped boards. One bulb burned at the end of the hallway between the two rows of stalls. Another from the open door of the tack room. Night gave spooky shadows to the spacious loft. It was a meager amount of light to illuminate the cavernous barn.

Jackson strode angrily to the tack room, ignoring Cat's presence.

When she stood in the doorway, he finally turned back to face her, half his shirt buttons undone and the tail hanging loose from his jeans. "Did you want to watch me undress?"

"Don't be crude, Jackson. I'm trying to get to the

bottom of our problem and all you want to do is run away.''

His eyes glittered in the raw light from the uncovered bulb in the middle of the ceiling, only a foot or two from his head. The three saddles perched on saddle trees and the half dozen bridles hanging from pegs gave the room an odor of well-used leather. The smell comforted Cat. This was her home. He didn't belong here. The thought had no more than passed through her head when he answered.

"I'm trying to keep the peace, Cat. That's all. Period. I'm not running away. I'm not refusing to talk. Simply put, I don't want to argue with you.'' He spread his hands outward. "What more do you want?''

Cat sighed. "Arguing is all we do. Maybe you should go back home.''

Jackson's jaw trembled from the force of his anger. He shot a dark look at her before turning his head away to break the impasse. "Is that what you want? Is that really what you want?'' His face hardened with implacable rage as he waited.

She hesitated, suddenly afraid of the almost-stranger so close to her. "I think so. Yes.''

He took a half step toward her and raised his hand, shaking the forefinger emphatically at her. "No, it isn't. Damn you, I know what you want!'' His gaze softened. He stepped nearer and bent close to her. "You know, too. Don't you?''

In the small room, his heady scent made her dizzy. She backed up a step. He came forward that distance and a bit more. His chest touched hers. He reached up and smoothed her hair with a tentative hand.

"Cat?'' he asked, his voice husky.

She trembled from the half-felt contact and struggled

to gain control of her will. She knew she should pull away, but couldn't. The desire to step closer was irresistible.

"You want me as much as I want you. You know you do." His hand cupped the back of her head and pulled her face close to his. From two inches away he stared deep into her eyes. His jaw muscles clenched hard against gathering passion. "This is your last chance, Cat. Are you going to leave me alone?"

She couldn't think and didn't want to. His words meant nothing. The sense of the sentence disappeared with the rising excitement that compressed her chest past thinking…past breathing. His breath on her lips held her as the bulb's bright light trapped the plain brown moth fluttering helplessly around it. She became lost in a whirlwind rise of emotions. His lips enacted a bitter campaign against hers, punishing her for the lost years, for Joey, for…what? She couldn't think. The rising heat of her own passion threatened to overwhelm her. Gasping, she raised both hands to his face, and pushed him away.

With their lips only millimeters apart, she uttered a muffled protest, "No, Jackson. Stop!"

He lowered his hands and stepped back, breathing heavily.

She couldn't help it. This was the only man she'd ever loved and even if it sentenced her to a lifetime of loneliness, she knew there'd never be another.

Their heated gazes met. She reached out to him. He stretched an arm above him, blindly, and pulled the cord that shut off the light. Liquid blackness enveloped them, hot and sweaty, as their bodies were. He pushed her back and she felt the edge of the cot against her legs. All her good resolutions were nothing against his desire and against her own.

He guided her on to the cot and covered her body with his. The suffocating weight took her breath away. As if they were one person and he knew her thoughts and needs, Jackson moved, lifted his body a bit to the side so he had one leg between hers and rested his elbows on either side of her shoulders. He pinned her with his torso, but took the brunt of his weight on his powerful forearms. Looking up into his face, able to make out only the dim outlines of his cheekbones and the glitter of his eyes, she tried to keep a clear mind, but as his lips descended onto hers again, she became caught in the moment.

His lips no longer punished, changing to a different tactic. Teasing, light, quick kisses that covered her face. Sweet touches of his lips on hers, on her cheek, on the smooth skin between eye and brow, against her ear, the moist touch sending hot waves of electricity to her core.

Impossible to think, impossible to resist. Cat turned her head to follow his teasing lips, seeking to capture them again. Mindless, sightless, helpless against the passion that surged in her body like a gathering storm. She moaned softly.

"Oh, my Catherine, my sweet, sweet Cat. You don't know how badly I've wanted to do this. To touch you, to kiss you, to hold you."

"Jackson, please..." She wasn't sure what she was begging for, but he seemed to know. He covered her lips with his, teased her mouth open and then plunged into her with his tongue, sweeping her mouth, tasting her.

Every inch of his body covered her. The raw scrape of his stubbled beard against her cheek and lips, the molded strength of his forearms pressing against the side of her breasts, the ridged muscles of his chest against her breasts. More than these sensations, the hard length of his erection against her focused her desire. Beyond thinking, beyond caring, Cat struggled against him, not to push him away, but to get closer. Closer. Past the thin, artificial barrier of clothing.

She called his name and then, her voice strained, whispered, "I don't recall your shirt having this many buttons before." A button popped off as she pushed his shirt up and inserted her hands into the warm cavity created between the shirt and his back. His skin against the palm of her hand glowed fever-hot with the same desire that pulsed in her. As if he sensed the inevitability of what must come next and struggled against it as she had, she felt him pull away.

"Cat, we can't. We can't. I want you so much I can't see straight, but we shouldn't do this." His breath came in hurried gasps as he whispered the warning against her lips.

"Do you know how many nights I've slept alone and dreamed about you? How many days I've spent wanting you? How many times I've cried myself to sleep because you weren't with me?"

"Are you sure this is what you want? Sweet love, I don't want you ever to be hurt by me again."

"I've hurt you far worse. Can you ever forgive me for what I denied you? A relationship with Joey that should have started the day she was born."

"I forgive you, Cat. I think I stopped blaming you pretty quickly, but I was so mad at myself that accusing you was the only way I could hide from my own guilt. I knew I'd hurt you terribly when I joined the Marines and didn't think twice about the consequences of that night at Needle Rock."

"Jackson, I love you. I always will. Do you know what will hurt me more than anything else?"

"What?"

"If I can't hold you, even if it's just for one night. I've loved you since I was fourteen. I think I'll still love you if I live to be a hundred and fourteen."

He kissed the corner of her mouth and his words slipped into her. "I love you, too. I always have, even when I didn't know it."

"I always knew."

"Cat, I don't deserve you. How can you want me after I hurt you?"

"It's the most right thing that's happened to me since...before."

Remorse roughened his voice. "Oh Cat, I'm sorry. I'm so sorry for leaving you."

She cradled his head in both hands. "Hush, Jackson. It was my fault."

"Mine."

She laughed, her lips close to his throat so she could feel each hurried heartbeat. "It was both our faults...or nobody's. Forget the past, Jackson. There's only now."

"I don't want to hurt you again. I have protection. Just a minute." He struggled out of her grasp and reached for his wallet.

Later, after he'd removed her clothes and his, he hesitated again, but she whispered the old taunt. "I dare you." He laughed and gave in. She pulled him closer, and in the small, narrow cot, time stopped, then reversed itself. Cat was eighteen again, on a spring-cool, moonlit night with a red-haired boy who excited her beyond caring. Wild roses and bright stars surrounded them. Moonlight danced in her memory and the heady rush of passion drowned her doubts.

CHAPTER FIFTEEN

CAT AND JACKSON LAY on the narrow cot, so closely entangled she wondered if he felt as she did—that it was impossible to get close enough. Maybe he did, for his whispered words soothed the hurt of the alone years.

"I hate myself for leaving you when you needed me most. I hate the years without you."

"Hush. It's over now. We're together."

His lips touched her ear as he whispered his regrets, sending tendrils of moist warmth from her ear to her chest, which seemed unable to hold so much happiness. It spilled over to the rest of her, leaving her warm and relaxed. Even so, an uneasy feeling that this interlude must end disturbed her mood. Jackson seemed completely unaware that anything could disrupt their pleasure.

"You worked so hard to give our daughter a home. I could see the worry in your face every time we met and never guessed all your problems were because of me. I wanted to help, but didn't know how."

She put a finger to his mouth, traced the compelling lip line. "Jackson, don't blame yourself."

He kissed the fingertip, then stroked her hip, his hand rough with new calluses. "Getting to you was difficult. You pushed me away so hard when I came home. That first day, when I saw you in town, taller than I remembered, too thin, staring at me, I felt as if I'd been hit by a truck. Your green eyes mesmerized me from across the street. I came racing over to you, eager to touch you again and you were as cool as a stranger.''

"I remember, too. You kept those feelings to yourself, you know. You didn't show much of anything except a reluctance to be back in Engerville.''

"I was hiding my emotions. I wouldn't even let myself know how I felt seeing you standing there. All along, you were the reason my heart did flip-flops. I thought my fear of facing Pop again caused that upside-down feeling.''

Cat's hand wandered over the broad, flat muscles of his chest, smoothing his bicep, trailing down his ribs and back to his shoulder, down his arm to his hand, twining her fingers with his. "I was afraid you'd find out about Joey. When you didn't come by, I was afraid you wouldn't find out about her. My feelings were all mixed up. I didn't want you around, because you might guess about Joey, but a part of me wanted you to know the truth. Knowing you were so close tortured me. I didn't want to be alone again after you left.'' She sighed.

Jackson touched his lips to the place where her neck joined the shoulder and nipped at the smooth skin, mumbling his words against her. "I fought your attraction as long as I could. I swear I did. I didn't want to hint that I'd stay just to get close to you, when all along I knew I'd leave. Then that first morning I walked over, I didn't even ask myself why, since, deep down, I knew. The answer scared me, but I couldn't stay away.''

The outside of Cat's stomach benefited from the warmth of Jackson's body. The inside shivered with apprehension. "Do you think your father knows?''

"About Joey or about us?''

"Joey, of course." In the darkness, she smiled against his throat. "I guess that includes us."

He shifted his weight so he was lying more on his side. "Not much room here, is there? Not that I'm complaining, my sweet Catherine." He kissed her lips, lingering over the taste. "I don't know, Cat. He's a sneaky old man. I thought maybe he knew something I didn't. The way he pushed me out…that isn't like him. Pop won't give an inch when he knows he's right, but he's always been fair. I wonder…."

"What?" She stroked the spiky softness of hair above his ear. It was heaven to be so close, to touch him without stopping to consider how much of her emotions she'd reveal. A part of her wondered how long this particular piece of heaven would last. How long before Jackson realized that nothing had changed? How long before he realized he was right back where he started from—wanting her, but hating Engerville.

He propped himself on one elbow, so he could look down at her, though the darkness hid all but a bare outline. "Maybe he did it on purpose, so we'd get together. Am I imagining things or is that possible?"

Cat hesitated, thinking about Will, picturing him in her mind's eye. Tall, like Jackson, but leaner, graying strands mixed in with the red curls. As compelling as Jackson in his own way. Shrewder? Maybe. "It's possible, I suppose. That would mean he knows."

"Yeah, that sneaky son of—" Jackson snorted, half amused, half angry. "He's a sharp one, Pop is."

Cat heard the reassuring sound of RugRat neighing softly. One of the fillies answered his inquiry and the colt settled down again. She trailed a finger along Jackson's arm, skin smooth and hot to her touch, then whispered, "Will used to bring Joey little things on those

Sundays when we went to church. You know, nothing big, just toys like Polly Pockets. You wouldn't expect him to think of those, but he did. Your mom did, too, only she almost always brought cute little-girl clothes while your dad would give Joey things to play with. I used to wonder if they'd guessed.''

"Why didn't you tell them?"

"Same reason I gave you before. I didn't want you pressured into coming back and living in Engerville. When your mom died, I went through agonies of guilt over not telling her. She never knew Joey was her grand-daughter.''

"I used to get a letter from her every couple of weeks. I miss her more than I ever thought possible." He shifted his weight, pulling her chin closer to his neck. "Strange she never mentioned you'd had a baby, but then she never mentioned too much beyond how she wanted me to make up with the old man. I wish I'd been a little smarter while she was alive. It would have meant a great deal to her to see me and Pop friends again. Second thoughts always come too late, don't they?"

"I hope she knew. Maybe you could ask your father. When you make up with him, I mean.''

"I will. He's going to give me a lecture about re-sponsibility, but for once, I agree with him.''

"I'm sorry.''

His voice dropped an octave with raw emotion. "Hush! Don't say you're sorry again. I love you and it was my fault you got pregnant.''

"Don't say that, Marine. I demand my fair share of the blame.''

"Cat, my Wild Cat who isn't very wild at all. You see, I do know you better than you think I do. You were never as daring as you pretended. I admired you for your courage. Most of our crowd didn't have sense enough to be scared at some of our escapades, but you did. Why did you hang with us?''

Amused, Cat let a giggle slip free. ''I might as well be truthful. I was trying to keep up with you. You were the daydreams of half the girls in the senior class, you know. Red hair and broad shoulders and that grin—you were always smiling. I used to wish Roy would find someone else. Rebeka, too. Heck, I even hoped they'd discover each other.''

He dipped his head and nibbled on her shoulder. ''I wish I'd known you liked me.''

His soft chuckle tickled her. ''What good would that have done? You were crazy about Rebeka's blond hair and googoo eyes.''

''Googoo eyes?''

Cat shoved at his chest, not too gently. ''Don't pretend you don't know what I'm talking about. Those big brown eyes of hers had you in a tailspin.''

He planted a moist kiss in her ear. ''That was then. This is now.''

''What does that mean?''

He raised up until he could stare down into her eyes. ''Do you know how many times I've dreamed about making love to you?''

''Tell me.''

''Almost every night since I've been home. A thousand times since I've been gone from Engerville.''

''Me, too. I missed you so much.''

''Sweet Cat, was there never anybody else?''

She hesitated, then shook her head. ''No. Just you. I ought to leave you wondering, but I'd rather you know the truth. I can't imagine me with anybody but you. I'll never lie to you again, Jackson.''

"I'll always believe you. I promise. I ought to be sorry that you were lonely, and instead, I'm glad nobody else ever knew you like this."

"I went out with Roy a few times, after Joey was born, but it was never the same as before. She always stood between us and he kept wanting to ask who the father was. I could practically see it on the tip of his tongue. 'Who, Cat? Who's the father? And why wasn't it me?' After a few dates, I started telling him I couldn't leave Joey with Dad anymore. I think he was glad. Sometimes I got the feeling he only called me out of pity."

"Poor Cat. I'm sorry, sweetheart."

"Don't be. I was happier than I'd ever been. I had my own little girl to love and I could see her resemblance to you from the start. In a crazy kind of way, it made up for losing you."

His arms tightened around her.

Her voice dropped to a whisper. "And you? There must have been others."

Jackson pulled her closer. "I'd like to change the past, but it can't be done. Not that often and not that many, but yes, there were other women."

A knot in her throat made her reply low and husky. "You're a Marine. I didn't expect you to remain celibate."

"Don't blame it on the Marines. I was young and foolish. Maybe not as much as some of the guys, but that's hardly a Good Conduct Award. One night affairs, most of them. Nothing promised or expected on either side. There was a female Marine I met at Quantico."

"Did you love her?"

"She was special. About as tall as you, with brown hair, brown eyes and a great smile. We talked about it, but neither of us really wanted marriage. She was a tough, independent person, an MP. She wanted to stay independent. I guess I did, too. We were together nearly a year, then she transferred to Washington, D.C.''

How could she expect him to remain alone for so long? I can't complain, she thought. I didn't tell him about Joey. He had no reason to be alone.

''What was she like? I want to know what kind of woman you loved.'' The one you loved while I was alone, she thought. A flicker of resentment resisted her efforts to subdue it.

''If Alisa and I had loved each other, we'd never have broken up. As it is, she left the Marines and went to work for the NSA. Later, I heard a senator had been assigned an ex-marine as a bodyguard. A female Marine. I knew that was Alisa.'' He sighed, touched her throat with a tentative hand and whispered, ''If you mean love with a capital L, there's only been one. You.''

''Can't you say the same about us? That if we'd really loved each other, we'd never have parted?''

''No, because neither of us knew what love was when it happened.''

''Is this love?''

''I swear to you, on my honor as a Marine and as Joey's father, that if this isn't love, there's no such thing. And I know love exists.''

''I love you,'' Cat whispered.

''I love you, too.'' His lips brushed hers. ''Can you ever forgive me?''

''Jackson, don't feel guilty. You wouldn't have abandoned me. I know that now.''

His grip on her tightened. ''I'll never leave you.''

''If you put your hand there again, you won't be able to leave. I won't let you.''

"Like this?"

"Oh, Jackson. I've wanted you so badly for so long."

"You have me now."

A horse stamped restlessly. Jackson shifted and pulled her on top of him. His restless hands swept down her back and over her hips. His mouth trailed tingling caresses across her shoulder. The feel of his lips tugging at her breast erased all thought. She whispered his name.

She'd thought the second time would be slower, calmer. It wasn't. Their fever flared like a brushfire in the spring. There was no containing the heat. It raced out of control. In a brief moment, a fierce climax claimed them both.

Afterward, she lay on his chest, her limbs so weak she could barely move. Finally, she gathered enough energy to whisper her most compelling need. "Water, please. I'm too weak to move."

He laughed, a deep, delicious sound that warmed her more than the close air in the tiny room.

"I have a six-pack of room-temperature Coke under the cot. Will that do?"

She blew out a breath of air. "I need the sugar. My energy level is very low."

Against her cheek, she felt his smile. "We can't have that. If you'll quit pinning me down, I'll get up and get you a Coke."

She wiggled. "I'm not sure I want it that badly."

"Come on, woman. You'll cripple me."

She raised her head and tried to see his face. "Is the tough Marine begging for mercy?"

"No way. Marines don't give up."

"Well, then."

"Sometimes we withdraw so we can attack again later. It's called a strategic retreat."

"A strategic retreat, huh? I'll have to remember that." She rolled into the meager space between his body and the wall.

He eased off the cot and stood. Under the narrow bed, he found a single can of Coke. "We'll have to share."

"Okay."

"It's stifling in here. I should have turned on the fan. Want to go outside for a walk?"

"Now?"

"Why not? There's a moon, so it'll be plenty light enough. And we can cool off."

"I don't want to go far from the house. Joey might wake up."

Jackson caressed her jawline. His touch lingered on her face. "We'll stay in sight of it. Want to go in and check on her?"

Cat sat up in the narrow bed, crossing her legs. "That's probably not a good idea. She wakes up easily."

"How about if we just stick our heads in the door and make sure everything looks okay?"

"That'll work, if we're quiet. It will make me feel better, too."

Jackson turned on the light and the two of them took turns stealing kisses while tugging on wrinkled clothing. Cat stared at her T-shirt with misgivings. "I could have hung our clothes. I wouldn't let Joey out of the house like this."

"I don't believe we were in a mood for hanging up clothes. Anyway, you'd look good in a ragged sheet. Or nothing at all. You look especially good in nothing at all."

"The light was off, silly. You couldn't see me."

"I turned the light on so we could find our clothes. Remember?"

"Jackson, you're embarrassing me."

"No, I'm not. I feel like you're the other half of me. How can you be embarrassed at showing a little skin to your other half?"

"Aren't you the least bit shy?"

"Honey, I showered with a hundred naked guys at Parris Island. You don't keep a lot of body modesty after boot camp."

"I'm not a Marine."

"Thank God! I wouldn't want you showering with a hundred naked guys!" He reached out and pulled her close, dropping a kiss on the curve of her neck. "Just one. Me."

She struggled free. "Jackson, don't. We'll never get out of here."

He grinned. "Is that so bad?"

"I thought you wanted to cool off. You're a little too warm."

"I can stand the heat. Can you?"

A dribble of electricity wandered past the exhaustion in her legs. "Mmmh-h-h. Quit teasing me, or your strategic retreat will be cut off at the pass. Come on. I think a cool breeze is what we both need."

"Whatever you say, darling."

"I could get used to that attitude. So uncommon, coming from you."

"Don't push your luck, Wild Cat."

Hand in hand, hips brushing, they left the barn. A quick stop at the house reassured Cat that Joey slept. They paced slowly toward Gray's Way on the gravel road that ran east and west in front of Cat's ranch. A gentle breeze whipped through their hair and dissipated the heat of their lovemaking. When they'd covered a half mile, Cat turned them around and started back. Jackson said little on the walk and she was content to say nothing, too.

High overhead, a full moon turned the roadbed white and made their way easily seen. When they reached the house, again they stood in the front yard, leaning against each other, both reluctant to part.

"You need some sleep, Cat."

"I know. It's just that I hate to leave you."

"Do you want me to come in?"

She looked up at him. "How would you feel about that?"

"Uneasy. I think we should be married first."

The breeze sent a cold chill wandering over her. "We haven't really talked about marriage."

"You will marry me, won't you?"

Cat hesitated. "I want to."

A note of fear crept into his voice. "That's not the same as saying yes."

"Jackson, nothing has changed except we know we love each other. You'll still be unhappy on a farm. I still want Joey to live here where she has a sense of place."

He hesitated only a second. "I'll stay here with you two and I won't regret it. I promise."

Saddened, she forced a smile. "That's your heart talking. Don't make promises until you've thought it out completely."

"What's to think about? I can't leave you now! I just found you."

His voice had risen with the force of his reply. Hastily, she raised a finger to her lips and nodded toward the house, then whispered, "I know. I know."

"Come over here." He tugged her hand and drew her to the willow tree, pushing aside its hanging branches.

"What are you doing, Jackson?"

"I want you to know how very much I love you. I want you to be as sure as I am."

Softly, she whispered, "You don't have to prove anything. I do know."

"You think you do." He sat on the grass and pulled her to his lap. Covering her face with kisses, he whispered, "My Catherine, I do love you so much."

The whip-thin hanging branches drooped to the ground. The full moon shone through the leaves, giving the natural enclosure a cool green, barely-lit semblance of privacy. Jackson removed his shirt and laid it on the grass, then gently persuaded Cat to lie back.

"Jackson, we're outdoors," she protested. "What if Joey wakes?"

"She won't. Trust me."

"I do." She relaxed against the cushioning grass.

Jackson pushed her shirt up and nibbled at her breasts. "Such a sweet body. So much sweetness."

The hot surge of desire came with the first touch of his lips. She struggled for control and tried to make light of his rising passion. "Behave, Jackson. We have to go in soon."

He slipped her shirt off and lay down beside her. Bare chest to bare breast they lay, gazing into each other's eyes. Then Jackson's hand wandered to her zipper. He stifled her protests with a deep, searching kiss. While she was lost in the delicious sensation of his tongue sweeping her mouth and nibbling her lips, she felt him tug her jeans off. It didn't matter. Nothing mattered except Jackson's fevered touch. The breeze couldn't cool her off now. Nothing could. She burned for the boy of her dreams, the man of her reality.

His lips tracked a path down her body to her breasts and tugged gently on her nipple, suckled, licked, kissed until the fevered heat reached new heights. He left her nipple and she moaned a soft protest. His palms engulfed her breasts as he kissed a straight line from her navel to her hips. Her muscles tensed, then jerked in electric reaction. She tried to pull away.

"Be still, Cat," he commanded.

"Jackson, I've never—"

"I know you haven't, Green Eyes. Don't you think I'd remember?"

"Jackson?"

"Hush."

He pushed her back when she tried to rise. She gave up. It was impossible to feel like this, she thought. Impossible. She whispered the word.

Afterward, he cradled her body on top of his, kissing her neck and shoulders as if he could never get enough of loving her. Finally, he asked, "Now do you believe I love you?"

"I believed you the first time you said it, Jackson."

"But now you know it," he said, smugly.

She smiled down at him, at the boyish grin curving his cheeks. "That was a very convincing demonstration, I'll admit. Didn't you mention something about sleep? We won't get much tonight, even if we go in right now."

"Some things, Green Eyes, are better than sleep."

Who was she to argue? Deliberately, Cat ignored a twinge of unease. They'd think of something. They had to. Maybe her outlook on life tended to be negative. If so, she'd change for Jackson. She'd do anything for him. Except leave Engerville.

CHAPTER SIXTEEN

JACKSON ENTERED THE BARN. With a little luck, he might get two hours' sleep before continuing the day with Cat. Being with her, looking at her, stealing kisses. It would be almost as good as making love to her. He stretched out on the cot without bothering to remove his wrinkled clothes. As soon as his head hit the pillow, or maybe even a second or two before, he expected to be asleep.

It didn't happen that way. Cat's sweet, rose-flavored scent permeated his room. Despite thinking he'd never indulged in such a prolonged spell of lovemaking and knowing to a certainty that he had nothing left, his flesh stirred. A satisfied smile tipped his lips as he lay there, waiting for sleep to claim him. Instead, a different odor disturbed him. The smell of the barn and the animals it housed reminded him that no matter what had taken place here earlier, it was still a barn. Still a farm.

But it was Cat's farm, not his father's. The disclaimer made no difference. He lay there, feeling the old discontent. Remembering his youth, he wondered if he could ever be happy here. With Cat and Joey, he insisted to that doubtful part of himself, it would be different. Not so, his argumentative half stated. His life would be bound by fences and crop rows, by horses and cows, maybe even by pigs, God forbid.

Every other four-legged animal on the face of the

planet produced that other thing he associated with farms. He'd been determined not to complain about his sleeping quarters, and truly, with the door closing off the tack room from the rest of the barn, it wasn't so bad, but the minute he stepped through that opening, he was assailed by the odor you couldn't get rid of when you lived on a farm.

A desperate sadness crept over him. He had to stay. He'd promised Cat he wouldn't leave and it didn't matter if the damn stuff squished under his boots with every step he took. It couldn't matter anymore, because he wouldn't leave her and Joey. Dear God in heaven, he'd let Cat chain him to a life he hated.

But he hadn't "let" Cat do the chaining. He'd done the deed himself, with a cheerful smile on his idiot face. Jackson groaned and sat up. He sunk his face into his hands.

He wouldn't be able to sleep with the beginnings of a nightmare headache stabbing at his temples. Might as well get moving. Outside the tack room, he paused, letting his restless gaze roam over the barn, from the high, nearly empty loft to the rows of stalls underneath it. The misery of being without Cat and Joey more than offset living here.

CAT SHED HER much-abused clothing and stepped into the hot spray. A shower, she thought, was just what she needed to clear her shocked brain. Every single thought she'd ever connected with Jackson-the-teenager and sex had disappeared after one stunning night with Jackson-the-man.

She let the healing water rinse away the sweat and soreness. Who would have guessed that the shy, clumsy lover of her youth would turn into a man so skilled he'd left her legs with half the strength of Jell-O? Jackson's love imprinted each of her sore, tired muscles.

A dab of shampoo in her hair, a swift sudsing, a quick rinse and she stepped from the shower feeling much more herself. She glanced into Joey's bedroom. Her single chick lay curled in a tight knot, a soft buzz issuing from her lips. Cat smiled and withdrew. She slipped into a nightgown in the cool darkness of her bedroom.

The silly smile stayed on her face as she lay on the bed, staring up at the ceiling. Maybe she could even have another baby. A brother or sister for Joey so the sprite wouldn't grow up thinking the world revolved around her. Cat allowed a moment of self-indulgence to hold its sway as she pictured a new baby sleeping in her arms, with Jackson on one side of her and Joey on the other.

The idyllic scene dissolved. She needed to be practical. When she found out she was pregnant with Joey, she'd allowed herself a day or two of regret, anger and desperation, then she'd sat down, thought out her options and made a plan for raising Joey by herself. It had worked, too. Her father had come around, despite his disapproval and learned to love his grandchild. Until Joey was six, Cat had worked at the pharmacy in Engerville, while her father baby-sat Joey and took care of his beloved horses.

Once the horse business began to bring in a sizable income, she'd quit her job. It had been heavenly staying home with Joey all day in the summertime and waiting for her to come home from school in the winter. Heaven had fallen apart when her father died. She could take care of the horses he'd already bought, but she knew she'd never be able to choose a fine horse from knobby-kneed colts. Her father's talents reappeared in Joey, but they'd skipped her. Once RugRat was sold and school began again, she'd have to look for another job.

Jackson wouldn't be here. He truly meant it when he said he'd stay with her and Joey, but Jackson hated farms, farming, and Engerville. He'd wither away if he stayed in North Dakota. A farmer's life would turn him bitter and angry, the way her father had been when he worked all those factory jobs. A higher power intended her father to work with horses, love them, train them, make his living from them. The same higher power gave Jackson Gray a different calling.

Jackson loved engines and the open road. The opportunity he'd been offered to drive a truck for two years in Seattle, then manage the terminal, must have been destined for him. He'd control a truck with more grace than he used in riding RugRat and with much more enjoyment.

Could Joey learn to be happy in Seattle? Could she? It didn't seem possible. The horses were everything to little Joey, just as they had been to her grandfather. As a teenager settling down for the first time in a real home, Engerville had brought a sense of permanence to Cat's life. She didn't want to lose that and go somewhere new, where she didn't know anyone.

If she lost the farm, she could get a job, maybe at the university or at a store in town, but she'd still live in Engerville. Joey could still have a small-town life with familiar childhood playmates and the horses she loved.

She couldn't hold Jackson here. She couldn't leave her home. That left nothing for the two of them, but the precarious link of an angry child. Someday, even that link would break, when Joey left home to make her own way. Even a passion as strong and precious as the one she shared with Jackson couldn't survive ten or fifteen years more of separation. Jackson would meet someone else, or she would, although Cat refused to believe in the possibility for herself.

She sat up in bed, crossed her feet at the ankles, and rested her elbows on her knees. Flopping her head forward, so her still-damp hair cascaded down like a waterfall, she pictured a life without Jackson.

The barn was shabby and old. The very home she lived in lost its allure. She studied her hands. Fresh from the shower, they should have been pink and soft. Instead, calluses and fresh blisters marred hands already burned brown from the sun. This harsh prairie farm might break her body, but next to that reality was a daughter running free in the fields with the friend she'd known since infancy. Her eyes filled with tears. For Joey, she'd endure anything. Even the heartbreak of losing Jackson.

The tears dripped down, splashing on her ankles. It wasn't fair! They'd already been apart for Joey's whole life. Was this brief interlude all they were ever going to have? Cat jammed a hand tightly over her mouth. She didn't want to wake Joey. How would she ever explain what she was crying about?

Later, she got up and splashed cold water on her face. Cat didn't want to give Joey another reason to resent her father. Jackson, already burdened with a past he deeply regretted, didn't deserve to see her like this, either.

FOR JACKSON, the day passed in a bewildering blur of fatigue and worry. He'd had longer days in the Marine Corps. Days when the company, carrying full field packs, marched for fourteen hours with only short breaks, then practiced digging foxholes. As if, he thought sarcastically, one had to practice digging a hole.

There was never a day in the Marines that compared

with this one. Cat put on a bright smile, but it didn't fool him. She was upset, too, and he could guess why. Both of them had allowed emotion and physical need to drive out reason. He could tell by the way her eyes looked—as if the light had gone out of them. She'd considered the consequences of their lovemaking.

He ached every time he looked at her and she looked away. He wanted to grab her and tell her he'd stay, he'd be true, this time, but Joey was always around. He needed privacy to convince Cat of his love. She needed to know all of them could be happy on this damn farm, not just her and Joey.

He made up his mind. He wouldn't tell her about his second thoughts, his reluctance. Hell, he did love her. He loved her so much his teeth ached. The thought of leaving her and the angry little elf behind while he trotted off to Seattle to have fun driving a truck made him sick. Even sicker than the thought of slopping hogs. Well, he'd put his foot down on that one. If he stayed— no—he'd definitely stay, but there sure as hell wouldn't be any pigs on any farm he lived on. And that was that.

Both of them settled for a stolen good-night kiss that evening. Cat was exhausted and he wasn't far behind. "Tomorrow," he whispered to her. "Tomorrow, we'll talk."

The next day dawned as hot and clear as every day had since he'd been home. You didn't have to be a farmer to wish for rain this summer. His skin itched from wind-driven dust, but the stock still had to be cared for and the colts worked. Especially RugRat. That took half the morning, but while Joey stayed out by the pasture watching the colts play, he cornered Cat in the barn.

He swiped a strand of her hair back from her face. The touch sent a shock wave through him. He really tried to ignore it. "You look a lot better than yesterday, Cat."

She pretended a frown. "Did I look so bad?"

"Not bad, just wiped out. I should have been more considerate."

She smiled shyly at him. "There you go taking all the blame again, Marine."

Her smile melted his insides. Helpless to resist, he pulled her into a tight embrace and kissed her like he'd been wanting to do all morning.

She tugged her head back, palms holding the sides of his face. "Jackson, we can't. Joey's just down at the fence."

He nudged her closer to the wall. "I can see through this itty-bitty crack, Cat. I just want to kiss you a little bit. Nothing else, I swear. I'll keep an eye out for Joey."

She gave in. Melted into his arms like hot chocolate, all sweet and delicious. He pulled her deeper into his body, his hands splayed across the back of her tight denim pants.

Cat moaned, a soft whimpering sound that caused his jeans to tighten up like a noose. He didn't start it. It was her hands that reached for his belt buckle, but he damn well finished it. With barely enough self-control to edge some protection out of his wallet before dropping it on the hard pine floor, he gave in to madness. Wrestling her jeans down just far enough and entering her in a rush. Hoisting her up and holding her sweet, slender body close, while he leaned against the wall. Awkward as hell, he thought, and as impossible to stop as a light-ning strike.

He bit his lip with the urgent need to hold back until she spasmed and her body jerked. Her movement fin-ished him. The whole episode took about three minutes.

Then he had to help her get herself together before Joey decided to come see what the big bad Daddy was doing to Mommy.

"Cat, I'm sorry. I didn't mean for that to happen. I swear to God I didn't."

She peeped at him from behind her curtain of black hair. "Honestly, you have a complex. You aren't responsible for everything that happens, you know?"

He shrugged, his knees still feeling as if she'd wiped them out with a sledgehammer. "You do things to me. I touch you and my brain goes into hibernation and my body revs up like an eighteen-wheeler. I owe you a hell of a lot more respect than I just showed."

She glared at him. "Jackson, you're going to make me angry. Respect had absolutely nothing to do with what just happened. It wasn't even about love. It was need, pure and simple. I needed you and you needed me. We were reckless messing around with Joey so close. We got away with it this time, and next time we'll be more careful. Nothing happened that I didn't want. Not today, not yesterday and certainly not nine years ago. I participated willingly. So knock off the guilty bit, okay?"

He pulled her back into his arms, pushing her head down against his chest, then just rocked her against him quietly for several minutes. Finally, he spoke. "You feel so damn good, Cat. Like you belong right here for all eternity."

She turned her head so her lips were against his chest. "I can't get enough of touching you. I feel like I've been on a diet for years. Now there's a feast in front of me and I can't help reaching out."

"Me, too. I love you more than it's possible to tell. I

wish I could make you understand exactly how much I want you.''

"I think I know that.''

"I don't mean physically. That, too, but that's not all of it.'' He threw his head back until he was staring at the high loft, then looked back to her, feeling the heat of her body against his, the shape of her breast against his arm, her hair where it touched the back of his hand as he cupped her neck. He sighed deeply. "I felt like a puzzle with a missing part until I came back here." He darted a quick kiss to her ear. "You were the missing part.''

She kissed his chest where the top two buttons had come undone. This time he decided he'd keep his animal instincts reined in. He couldn't go around jumping her bones every time she looked his way or touched him. Even if that's exactly what he wanted to do.

Instead he raised her face, dropped a tender kiss on her lips and said, "I figured we could get married this weekend, but why wait? Why don't me and you and Joey drive up to Fargo today and do the paperwork thing? Luke will feed the horses while we're gone, won't he? We can enjoy a few days of relaxation and get married as soon as possible. What's the waiting period? Three days?''

Cat pulled back. "Slow down, Marine! I never said I'd marry you.''

He couldn't help the sullen note that crept into his voice. "You're going to, so don't mess with my mind, Cat.''

"If you had a mind to mess with, I might try it. Now look at me. No, I mean it. I want to marry you—''

"Well, then, it's settled. If today is too soon for you, we'll—''

"Let me finish, please. I said I want to marry you, and I do. You don't love me a smidgen more than I love you. Trouble is, we can't. It won't work."

"We already settled that. I'm staying."

"I love you. I believe you love me, but we've got a problem and you know it as well as I do. Try to make me believe you haven't already had second thoughts. Go ahead. I'm listening."

Jackson slid his hands up her arms and let them rest on her shoulders. He looked straight into her eyes, considered lying, rejected that alternative and decided not to tell her the truth. Not to *lie*, just *not* tell the truth. He had to convince her. He had to. "Cat, I'm not leaving. Period. End of conversation."

A soft look stole over her face. A wanting touched her eyes for a moment, then vanished. "Jackson, you'll end up a bitter old man, knowing you lost your dream the very day you slipped a ring on my finger. I won't live with you in Engerville and I can't go to Seattle. That pretty much settles it."

He grabbed her and crushed her body against his. "Cat, don't say that! Please! I just want to love you and Joey. I can live with anything else."

She pushed against his chest, freeing a small space between them. "Jackson, I want you to stay here. I love you. I think I loved you the same day my dad and I came to live on this farm. Remember? You rode over on that scrubby-looking pinto pony, looking like the shining knight in one of my books. You had more freckles then, I think. Do you remember?"

"I remember. I wanted to find out what the new neighbors were like. You were all long legs and big green eyes. When I got home, I told Cassidy the new neighbors didn't have any boys for her, but there was a nice-looking girl who'd do for me."

"You didn't!"

He nodded. "I was only teasing Cassidy at the time, but those words were prophetic. You'll do for me."

"Thanks, Marine," she said, her misty eyes laughing at him.

He hugged her. "I won't let you go out of my life again. I mean it."

"We'll try, Jackson. I promise. We'll try."

LATER, CAT PREPARED a simple lunch of cold cheese sandwiches with a fresh garden salad and iced tea. Joey pushed her salad around, but ate the cheese sandwich with gusto. Jackson's glance kept going back to his daughter. Except for the hint of auburn in her hair and the two freckles on her nose, she looked nothing like him. Just as well, he thought. Red hair looked okay on Cassidy, but generally speaking, he preferred sea-green eyes and smoky, midnight hair.

"Joey, we've taken care of the horses. Let's you and me play hooky this afternoon. I'd like to take you deer hunting."

Cat interrupted. "I don't think that's a good idea, Jackson. It isn't even hunting season and Joey hates to see animals hurt."

"I wouldn't kill a deer," Joey said, scornfully. "That would be mean."

"I said deer hunting, not deer killing."

"Isn't it the same?" Joey asked.

"Doesn't have to be. Look at this." Jackson pulled a small disposable camera from his shirt pocket. "We'll bag our deer without putting a scratch on them."

Joey's eyes lit up. "Can I take the pictures?"

"Sure you can, Short Stuff. Is it okay, Cat?"

"Would it matter if I said no? Eat your salad, Joey, and you can go deer hunting with Jackson. It will give me a chance to sort those beads that arrived yesterday. I've been anxious for a chance to get at them."

"Something special?" Jackson asked.

"Uh-huh. I ordered a dozen blue Chinese porcelain beads for a necklace Werner Hawkins at Beads Are Grand in Fargo asked me to make. The beads are expensive, but they'll make a beautiful necklace and he can sell it for six times the amount I'll have invested. And I'll get half. Pretty good for a few hours' work."

"Show them to us when we get back. Okay?"

She nodded. "Sure."

His gaze fixed on her lips. He swallowed hard.

After lunch, Jackson and Joey headed through the open field across the road from the house. Jackson watched her run ahead of him with amusement. She was so like Cat, all eagerness and smiles when a new adventure lay ahead. Maybe the sprite would break down and forgive him soon. She'd seemed a bit friendlier today. He shrugged. She'd come around. She had to. He wouldn't be able to stand anything else.

"Hold up, Joey," he said, calling out to her. "We need to be quiet so the deer don't hear us coming."

"I'll be as quiet as a little mouse," Joey agreed, dropping back to walk by his side.

They tramped through the field, back along the path he'd taken that first evening when he couldn't wait to see Cat. Soon they approached the nesting area Jackson had spotted. He touched Joey's shoulder. "Now, we have to be really, really quiet," he warned. He dropped his voice to a whisper. "If they hear us, they'll run away too fast to get a picture."

Joey nodded, grasping the camera tightly.

"The film's already wound to the right spot, so when you see them, look through the window on top and push the button. Then wind it again quickly so you can get another shot."

"Okay," Joey whispered, tense excitement in her voice.

They crept silently to the small stand of trees where the deer had been. "Been and gone," Jackson said gloomily. "Sorry, Short Stuff. I'm afraid this is not our day."

Joey looked disappointed for a moment, but quickly clutched his arm. "Look, Jackson! In that tree. What kind of bird is that?"

"Looks like a red-tailed hawk. They're pretty common around here in the summer."

"Can I take a picture of it? Please?"

"I'm not sure we're close enough, but go ahead."

After taking the hawk's picture, Joey lost all interest in the missing deer. She happily looked around for more birds to shoot and carefully snapped the shutter on birds so far away they could hardly be seen with the naked eye. Jackson hoped she wouldn't be too disappointed when the developed film came back showing nothing but distant tree leaves.

Then they surprised a long-beaked bittern who froze at their approach, with its head stuck straight up in the air. Joey quickly raised the camera and snapped the bird's picture before it broke its pose and flew off.

"That one ought to be a keeper, Joey," Jackson said.

"I held my breath when I pushed the button, like you told me to. Wasn't it beautiful?"

"Almost as pretty as you," he answered.

Joey ignored the compliment. "There's the creek. Can I take pictures of some fishes?"

"Let's see how much film you have left." She handed him the camera and he checked the count. "You have three more shots. I don't know how many fish we'll find and I haven't got a clue how to lure them out on the bank to get their picture taken."

Her tone a touch scornful, she said, "We'll just look in the water, okay?"

He grinned. "Okay, we'll look in the water."

As luck would have it, near a large rock that edged out into the narrow creek, a small pool of still water showed a dozen darting minnows. Joey got as close as she could and aimed the little camera at the water's surface, snapping the three remaining shots within a minute.

Jackson sat down in an almost bare spot on the creek's edge. He watched his daughter dip her hands in the cool water trying to catch one of the silver streaks that darted too quickly for her grasp. She glanced back at him and he noted again that she had her mother's eyes, full of green mystery. How could he stand to leave her? How could he live knowing his daughter and the woman he loved remained in Engerville while he went on to Seattle?

"Where does this creek end?"

"It doesn't end, honey. It runs downhill until it meets a larger river and joins it."

"And it never ends?"

"No. Sooner or later the water going past you will reach the sea."

Joey stared at the water in complete fascination. "Really?"

"Yes, really." He grinned. "Every drop of water is a part of the sea and it always returns." A thought occurred to him. If...if things didn't work out so he could stay in Engerville, he'd have to think of a way to explain to Joey. Maybe this would work. "Think of it, Joey, as the way you're a part of me and a part of your mother. Even though you're a part of us, you're still yourself, the way each drop of water in that stream is part of the whole, but separate, too. Just as each drop of water goes on a journey to find the sea, someday you'll want to go your own way. You'll still be a part of me and Cat, but you'll be yourself, too, going your own way."

"I won't ever leave Mommy! When Tommy Karl and I get married, we'll live with her."

Jackson smiled. "That sounds like fun, but what I'm trying to say is that we'll always be a part of each other, no matter if we go our separate ways."

Joey's eyes flashed angrily. "Are you going somewhere?"

"We were talking about the creek, Short Stuff."

"*I'm* not going anywhere! I told you. I'll stay with Mommy always, but I think you're going away. Mommy cried yesterday. I heard her."

I cried, too, he wanted to say, but the words stuck in his throat.

CHAPTER SEVENTEEN

THE NEXT MORNING, Cat and Joey were in the barn grooming Freedom and Apache. Freedom acted like a first-class twit as Joey tried to clean out her hooves. The red filly, all legs and nerves, shied at every movement, threatening to rear at the least provocation. Cat gave up on brushing Apache and put the buckskin in his stall. She came back over to where Joey tried to calm Freedom.

"I'll hold her head, Joey. You give her a quick brushing. Don't bother with her feet. I'll have Jackson check them tonight."

"Okay, Mom. She sure is acting silly."

"Maybe it's the heat. I wish we'd get some rain."

"Me, too. There's too much dust. It gets in my mouth when I ride."

The phone shrilled a demanding ring. Freedom came close to dragging Cat off her feet as she tried to escape from the noise. "Dammit! Settle down, you ornery nag! I'll sell you to the glue factory! Joey, get the phone, would you? If I turn this featherhead loose, she's liable to strangle herself on the ties."

Joey tossed her brush into the tool box and walked over to the phone mounted just outside the tack room door.

"Hello… Oh, hi, Mr. Anderson. Yes, she's right over there holding on to Freedom. Yes, I'll tell her. Just a minute." Joey's bright eyes turned to her mother. "Mom, he says he's bringing Mr. and Mrs. Palmer over to look at Ruggie in an hour. Is that okay?"

Cat cast a despairing glance at the horse hair covering her jeans and T-shirt. She didn't have to sniff her armpit to know exactly what kind of body odor she sported. And her appearance was the least of her worries. "An hour? Oh-h-h," she hesitated, torn with the insane desire to say "No, it isn't all right." She dreaded seeing Jackson react to his former girlfriend. What if he still wanted her?

"Tell him okay, Joey." She reminded herself that he'd see Rebeka sooner or later and Jackson's feelings didn't flip-flop that easily. Despite being secure in Jackson's love, Cat still had an underlying thread of jealousy toward the woman who'd worn his football jacket draped over her teen model shoulders and his class ring on a chain between her perfect size 36C breasts.

Cat managed a two-minute shower and a quick change of clothes before she came out on the porch to join Jackson and Joey. Now, she and Jackson sat on the old metal chairs on the front porch while Joey perched on the top step. With mixed emotions, Cat awaited Luke's arrival with his sister and her husband. Out of the corner of her mouth, she muttered to Jackson, "I'm glad I had time to shower. I don't feel quite so much like Cinderella in rags waiting to see what new outfit the wicked stepsisters are wearing. I'll bet she buys everything that goes on her back in New York."

Jackson swiped a hand through his hair, longer now than when he'd arrived six weeks earlier, and looked at her quizzically. "That's something I don't understand."

"What?" Cat asked.

"How you ladies can tell where clothes are bought and why it matters anyway?"

"Well, for pete's sake, Jackson, just look at me!"

His voice lowered to a mock growl. "I've been trying not to."

She frowned. "Do I look that bad?"

"Sweetheart, that pink blouse is awesome. It looks like strawberry ice cream." He shot a cautious glance at Joey before continuing. "And you know how much I love strawberries." He dropped his left eyelid in a ridiculous slow-motion wink.

Cat laughed shakily as heat trickled down her stomach. "You're crazy, Jackson Gray. This top is two years old, and faded to boot, but thanks. If I start feeling too much like Cinderella, I'll think strawberries." She returned his wink, feeling better.

"Here they come," Joey announced, standing and moving to the edge of the porch, eagerly watching the dust haze rising in the distance.

Around the curve in the graveled road, a dirty brown column flowered out behind Luke's pickup. The dust rose toward the harsh cobalt sky, dissipating into a thin haze that remained suspended in the still air. "We really do need rain," Cat commented, unable to think of anything more appropriate as her apprehension increased beyond all reasonable proportion.

Jackson reached out and touched her shoulder, letting his fingers tangle briefly in her hair. He tugged gently. "She'll like RugRat," he promised.

"I hope so," she replied, her mind spinning with nervous worry. She feared Rebeka would bypass RugRat for the more captivating Jackson. She couldn't say that, of course. Not to Jackson who would be insulted, and not in front of Joey, who wouldn't understand. Glumly,

Cat propped her elbows on her knees, her chin in her hands and watched the truck slow to a stop in the yard.

Luke jumped out of the truck, followed quickly by Tommy Karl from the back seat. Burt Palmer untangled his long body and stood beside the door offering his wife a hand to step down. She ignored his gesture and got out of the truck with the same easy grace all the Andersons had. Rebeka's honey-blond hair swung in carefully combed elegance against a silk blouse almost the same color as her hair. A heavy gold chain belt lent sparkle to a carefully ordinary pair of tan jeans. Cat thought that on anyone else, the clothing might not be so special, but Rebeka looked like some high-powered supermodel slumming for the benefit of her country cousins.

Carefully, Cat pushed away from her own jealousy. She'd never be anything but what she was; a too-tall country girl with a passable face, a so-so figure and the saving grace of nice hair. Cat stood up to greet her guests, feeling the comforting warmth of Jackson's body between her and Joey.

"Rebeka, Burt...it's so nice to see you again. How was your trip?"

Burt's serious gaze turned her way. Brown hair, metal-rimmed amber sunglasses and a very ordinary face topped a lanky body a hair's breadth away from being too thin. Dressed casually in designer jeans, western boots and a light green short-sleeved shirt, he presented anything but an awesome figure. How, Cat wondered, had Rebeka managed to give up Jackson for Burt Palmer? Did Burt's money make up for losing the best-looking boy in Traill County?

"Great trip, Cat! We brought an empty two-horse

trailer, so I hope you can fill it for us. Luke tells me that new colt of yours is something special. Is that right?''

Cat tried to ignore the interest on Rebeka's face as her gaze slipped from Jackson to Joey. Maybe Luke told her, she thought. That's good, isn't it? An apprehensive chill went through her body as she watched Rebeka step forward eagerly and throw her arms around Jackson.

A full moment passed before she released him. Stepping back, she looked him over slowly, a faint smile on her lips. ''You crazy redhead! You finally came back to Engerville. That's wonderful! I've missed you. How long has it been? How's your father?''

Jackson's wide grin spilled over onto Burt and Luke, but its main force landed on his high school flame. ''Hi, Rebeka. You haven't changed a bit! Pop is much better, thanks. I'll tell him you asked after him.'' He glanced at the man who waited. ''Introduce me to your husband. I've never met him, although Cat's filled me in on everybody.''

Rebeka glanced at Cat, smiled briefly and nodded. She turned to her husband. ''Burt, this is Jackson Gray. Jackson, my husband, Burt Palmer.''

The two men shook hands. Obviously, Burt knew who Jackson was. Or who he used to be. Burt and Jackson eyed each other, Cat thought, like a couple of strange dogs. Truly idiotic. With that rather disjointed thought, she said, ''If you guys want to walk down to the corral, I'll bring out RugRat.''

''You go down to the corral with them, Cat. I'll get the horse,'' Jackson suggested.

''Okay. Thanks. Come on, everyone.'' She tried to inject enthusiasm into her voice. A lot depended on Rebeka and Burt liking RugRat. The farm, Joey's security and her own peace of mind. It made sense to pretend enjoyment at their visit.

The adults found perches on the top rail, while Joey and Tommy Karl waited to open the gate for Jackson. A few minutes later, he appeared, riding RugRat. Looking, Cat thought, better than any movie star cowboy she'd ever seen. She drew in a deep breath of dusty air, wondering if Jackson had the same effect on Rebeka. Carefully, she tried to avoid a telltale glance at the blonde, but her gaze flickered toward the other woman. Too quickly, Cat hoped, for her to notice.

Rebeka's dark sunglasses hid her eyes, but her attention never wavered from the redhead sitting comfortably atop RugRat, who chose to prance and paw as if he'd never heard of a saddle. The young horse sidestepped and sidled his way through a couple of circuits around the corral. Cat's heart sank. Why did RugRat have to pick today to misbehave?

Jackson brought RugRat back to where they sat and slid down from his back. In the short-sleeved royal blue shirt and tight jeans, with the sun turning his copper curls to light-blasted gold, he looked stunning.

Rebeka glanced quickly from Cat to Jackson. Luke frowned. Burt Palmer seemed totally oblivious to the byplay. He walked over to RugRat and took the colt's bridle from Jackson. Running one hand appreciatively down the bay's strong neck, he soothed the horse with a humming sound. RugRat quieted under his experienced touch.

''He's a smart-looking fella. Real strong hindquarters and beautiful legs. I can see why you think he'd make a hunter, Cat. What's the mix?''

''Half and half,'' Cat replied. ''He's out of Cleopatra, a quarter horse from South Dakota.''

Burt nodded. "I know of her. She's got good blood-lines by way of Dakota King. Who's his sire?"

"Raggedy Jack Spratt. He raced for a while at Canterbury Downs before being retired to stud. He's thrown some good-looking colts and Dad felt RugRat might be his best."

"He looks like a prospect, if he only had some manners," Burt said, his hand running down the colt's near leg, massaging the sinews and tendons. He turned, put one foot in the stirrup and mounted with a light spring. Guiding the young horse close to the rail, he put RugRat through his paces. First, he walked the horse, then trotted him several times around the ring. Finally, he pushed the colt to canter.

RugRat behaved much better under Burt's experienced hand than he had for Jackson, Cat realized. Her spirits rose. Burt's lean frame blended well with the young horse. After several circuits at a restrained canter, Burt put him through a series of figure eights and cloverleafs. When he brought RugRat back to the gate, the young horse's playfulness had disappeared. He stood quietly, with a sheen of perspiration wetting his shoulders and flanks. Burt dismounted and stood beside him, a thoughtful expression on his face.

"Not bad, Cat. Not bad at all. He's got great moves, very athletic."

"I like him. He's green, but he looks like a natural-born jumper," Rebeka agreed, her gaze finally having left Jackson and settled on the colt. "Can you see him at the Virginia Meet, Burt?"

"I'm not nearly as good a rider as you, Burt, but I'll be around to school him for a couple of weeks," Jackson offered. "He just needs someone to lay down the law to him and give him a few more hours under a saddle."

Burt nodded. "Any horse can act silly when they feel like it, so I won't judge him by today. If he's looking better in a couple weeks, we'll buy him and take him back to Virginia. I don't intend to green-break a horse, Cat. You know how I feel about that." He turned to Jackson. "A young half-trained stud nearly killed my wife. We'd been told the horse was ready to ride."

Jackson looked at Rebeka, shocked.

Rebeka's lips twisted in a sarcastic smile. "Not me, Jackson. His first wife."

Burt barely nodded. His long face reflected nothing, Cat noticed. Whatever he thought, he kept carefully hidden when he replied.

"Sorry, Beka. I should have said my ex-wife."

"That's right, honey. Your ex-wife. You do tend to forget."

You could slice the tension with a knife, Cat thought, and it didn't have to be very sharp. She hastened to break it up. "I have a nice three-year-old for you to look at, too, Burt. Windjammer's not the same quality as RugRat, but he's got some points of his own. He's not nearly the featherhead that RugRat can be, though he's younger."

Burt's interest shifted immediately. "Right. Let's do that. Coming, Luke?"

"Right behind you," Luke said. He shot a swift glance at Cat.

"Windjammer isn't far enough along for you to take him this time, but next year he's going to be a sweet buy for somebody."

Rebeka nodded. Her interest clearly lay on Jackson and the bay horse he led.

In the barn, Cat escorted the party down the narrow hallway, naming each horse as she came to its stall.

Windjammer, first, then Freedom, Apache and Simba. Moonshot had been put in the pasture earlier. Officially Joey's horse, now that Jackson had bought and paid for her, Joey had been quick to point out that she didn't want the Palmers to think her horse was on the sale block, too. Amused, Cat had agreed.

Rebeka loved the yearling, Simba, at first sight. "He's an absolute darling. Burt, look at those feet! He could pick his way through a field of daisies without crushing one."

"He'd eat most of them," Joey pointed out.

Everyone laughed.

Burt Palmer, his sunglasses in his hand, nodded in agreement. "RugRat's a maybe, Cat, if we can agree on a price, but Simba is a definite yes. I think we'll take a flyer on Windjammer, too. I know a certain overweight lady in Baltimore who would love to have a jumper strong enough to carry her. One who looks like Windjammer will be an easy sale. We'll take Windjammer with us. I'll get Robbie Stuart to finish him, but you'll have to hang on to Simba for us. Maybe next summer we can haul him back home, too. Rebeka, you'll have to find someone to train him. I won't have you on a green horse."

"He's not green. He's black," Tommy Karl contributed, knowing full well what the term meant.

Luke frowned. Everyone else smiled indulgently. Burt elbowed Luke. "Lighten up," he advised.

Rebeka turned to her husband. "Call that real estate agent again, Burt. I'm more anxious than ever to find a summer place around here. We wouldn't have to worry about where to keep the horses that aren't quite ready."

He nodded. "I'll give him a ring as soon as we get home. Maybe he'll have found something by now."

Did Rebeka want to move back to Engerville so she'd be closer to Jackson? The thought unsettled Cat, although she knew in her heart that Jackson wouldn't be here for long. Rebeka didn't know that. "Let's have a cup of coffee, Burt, and we can settle the paperwork," she suggested.

"You guys go ahead," Jackson said. "I'll give RugRat a quick rubdown and brush out the saddle marks."

"Go on and do your paperwork thing," Rebeka said to her husband. "I'll stay with Jackson for a few minutes and get caught up on old times."

Burt nodded. Cat felt her stomach tie itself into a knot. Despite telling herself not to be a total fool, she didn't want to leave Jackson alone in the barn with Rebeka.

Joey looked at her mother, then at Rebeka. A mutinous expression crossed her face before she stepped casually between Rebeka and Jackson. "Mom, can I stay here and help Daddy?" Joey asked.

"Daddy?" Rebeka echoed.

Burt looked startled and Luke's glare darkened. Jackson glanced at his daughter with the same surprise everyone else showed. Only Tommy Karl appeared indifferent to the pronouncement. He was engaged in holding a hand as close as possible to Simba's dark ears, so he could watch her twitch them away from his exploring fingers.

Naked jealousy motivated Joey's proprietary claim on her father. How like her daughter to pick now to give Jackson his proper title! Cat struggled to control the unguarded blush that warmed her cheeks.

Rebeka's confusion sounded as if it might be colored with anger when she asked, "Jackson, how did this happen? I thought I had you on a string our senior year."

Jackson's lips tipped up in a bare smile. "You were mistaken," he replied evenly. One hand settled on Joey's shoulder. He looked at Cat, warm pride in his steady blue eyes.

"Let's get that cup of coffee," Cat said, putting as much enthusiasm in her voice as she could manage. "You come, too, Joey. You can get the cups for me."

Joey's face twisted in a pout, but she didn't protest. As she joined her mother, however, she shot a dark look toward the woman who stayed behind.

Half an hour later, Cat had Burt, Luke and the two kids sitting on the front porch. The kids' empty glasses were pushed aside as they whispered and giggled. There was an air of indulgence about Burt and Luke. Burt enjoyed the haggling over horse prices and obviously felt he'd done well. Perfectly happy to allow him to feel that way, Cat mentally tallied her profits and figured she could keep the farm going another year if Burt also bought Ruggie.

The barn door opening caught her attention. What had taken them so long? Cat wondered, as she saw Jackson and Rebeka emerge from the barn, heads close together, talking intimately of…what? How could Jackson not prefer the perfect Rebeka over her? Rebeka and Jackson had always looked good together. They turned heads wherever they went and both had a sense of humor that drew people to them. Did Jackson wish he'd tried harder to keep Rebeka?

As they neared the porch, Rebeka asked, "All through with the paperwork, Burt? Cat?"

He nodded, smiling. "Cat drives a hard bargain, but I wore her down. We won't make a decision on RugRat right away, though. Give Jackson another couple of weeks to work with him and we'll see if he deserves the price Cat put on his head. That'll·take some doing, I'll tell you.''

''I definitely want him,'' Rebeka said, flashing a defiant smile at Cat.

Did she mean RugRat or Jackson? Cat forced a cheerful grin. ''Good. We'll work him hard, so the next time you look at him, he'll make a better impression.''

''Burt's way too conservative. I can handle him the way he is now, but if it will make my loving husband feel better, see what you can do with him.'' She turned to her husband. ''I want him, Burt,'' she warned. ''I mean it. I haven't been so impressed by a horse, since Miri Tatterson won the Virginia Meet on Candy Girl.''

Burt laughed, a harsh sound with no mirth. ''Trust you to drive up the price on me.''

''You can afford it,'' Rebeka answered, her voice high and tight.

Joey, no longer miffed at Jackson, hovered near him, shooting angry looks at Rebeka. Jackson, amused, kept a proprietary hand in hers, obviously enchanted with his daughter.

Burt stood up. ''Are you ready to go, Luke? Nice meeting you, Jackson. Hate to rush, folks, but we have reservations for dinner in Fargo. Coming, Rebeka?''

Rebeka turned to Cat. ''I'll run over in a few days, Cat, and we can catch up on all the news. You must tell me how Jackson managed to fool me into believing I broke his heart when Burt and I got engaged.''

For a moment, Cat could think of absolutely nothing to say. Finally, she shrugged. ''If there's any doubt about his heart, broken or otherwise, you'll have to ask Jackson, Rebeka. I wouldn't presume to answer for him.''

Rebeka laughed. A low musical chuckle that sounded

very high-society disdainful to Cat's heightened perception.

"I'll do that. Let's go, fellas." She marched toward the pickup, Luke, Burt and Tommy Karl trailing her like a string of baby ducklings.

Joey quit waving at the cloud of dust and announced that she was going to get Moonshot and put her in the barn.

Jackson waited until she left before he spoke. "I know you want to ask, Cat. Go ahead."

She knew what he meant and knew she didn't want to lie again, but it was still hard to put her insecurity in words. "I thought you and Rebeka took an awful long time in the barn."

"And you're wondering what we talked about?"

"No," she said, giving a short laugh. "If you two only talked, then there's nothing to wonder about."

"What then? Say it, Cat. Let's not leave anything between us that can be explained. I don't want you doubting me."

He stood close to her, but not touching. Hesitantly, she said, "I don't doubt you. Not really, but you loved her once."

He didn't evade the question. "Not like I love you. Not even close."

The words sounded so sincerely true and made so little difference. "She acted like she wanted to see if you still cared."

Jackson sighed. "Did I act like I still cared?"

"I don't know. I can't tell what you're thinking." I can tell, she thought. He does love me and whether or not he does, it can't matter.

"I can tell what I'm thinking and I can tell you this. I love *you*, Cat. Only you. Always."

She looked away. He hadn't given her any reason to doubt him. How could she explain that so many years of being alone left her with the firm belief that she'd always be alone. She wasn't going to marry him. She couldn't. And she wouldn't have anyone else. Jackson deserved a life away from Engerville. He'd left the farm behind when he was eighteen. He'd never be happy here, and she wouldn't watch him become depressed, made bitter by the life he led. Someday he'd look somewhere else for what she refused to give him. He had to or else her broken heart would never heal. "I know."

"No, you don't. You took too long to answer. If you can doubt me so easily, you can't know." He pulled her into his arms. "I love you. I want to marry you. You and Joey mean more to me than anyone else in the entire world. I wouldn't trade one of your kisses or one of Joey's hugs for a thousand Rebekas."

Cat pulled back so she could see his face. His promise was so sweetly said. "You mean that, don't you?"

Instead of answering, he bent and touched her lips with his, lightly. Like static electricity, his touch sparked a rush of desire. His kiss deepened. She pressed closer. Close enough to know the truth of his words.

As if he had all day and half the night to finish, his lips lingered on hers, caressing, teasing, daring her to doubt him. She let herself sink into the sensations he aroused. Everything but his arms and lips disappeared as he pulled her closer into his embrace. Cat lost all sense of the world around her, wanting only to love him.

"What are you guys doing?"

Cat turned to see Joey staring up at them from the grass beside the porch steps.

Jackson looked over her shoulder at his small daughter.

Cat was the first to speak. "Uh, nothing, Joey. Did you get Moonshot put back in the barn okay?"

"Yeah, but what are you guys doing? You're not supposed to kiss on the porch."

Jackson grinned, refusing to let Cat step back from his embrace. "This is an exception to the usual rule, sweetheart. Your mom needed a little convincing, that's all."

"About the rule."

"Yep. You got it."

Joey shrugged and climbed up the steps to the porch. She walked around them, opened the screen door and just before she went into the house, she spoke over her shoulder, "I think she knows now."

Jackson looked at Cat and grinned again. "Whaddaya say, Wild Cat? I have at least half an hour before it's time to feed the horses. Are you convinced yet?"

"I think you managed to do the job." Why was life so filled with hard decisions?

Jackson gave her a long, lingering look, then swatted her on the rump. "Don't forget again. I don't want to have to kiss you every time you have a few doubts."

Cat laughed as he turned and followed Joey into the house.

She sank back into her chair, legs weakened by Jackson's prolonged, very thorough kissing. She could trust him. She knew that. Then why did she feel as if the other shoe would drop at any minute? Overhead, the sky darkened, as gray clouds rushed in from the west. The rumble of distant thunder signaled a possible end to the long dry spell. Or, Cat thought, it might be just another empty promise.

CHAPTER EIGHTEEN

THAT NIGHT JACKSON LAY awake in his cot. Despite having lured Cat into his arms after Joey went to bed, his restless body denied sleep. Why couldn't he be happy in Engerville? Did he have to shudder every time he thought about buying a new tractor instead of a trucking business? Everything a man ought to want bloomed right here in Engerville, North Dakota.

Joey had been all sweet little girl tonight, climbing into his lap and cuddling close as if she'd never had a cross word for him. He'd kissed the top of her head, loving the smell of her, fresh from a noisy half-hour bath and gowned in a faded T-shirt that must have belonged to her grandfather at one time. Though as white as Cat could bleach it, the shirt still showed a few stains. The sleeve seams were worn and shabby.

He'd ached to get up right then and haul his butt into town to buy her something pretty and little-girl frilly. And new. Too many of Cat's clothes, and Joey's, too, showed their age. Cat had been through some hard years. She deserved to be taken care of, even if she wanted to take care of herself. How the hell was he ever going to convince her that his so-called spirit wouldn't be broken by being a farmer?

There were his partners to consider, too. He'd promised Juan and Marty he'd join them in the Seattle venture. The two men would have a tough time understanding why Jackson wanted to pull out.

He'd make them understand. Cat would have to learn to live with his decision. That's all there was to it. Jackson sighed heavily, wishing he felt better about staying. Being with Cat and Joey ought to be all he needed. It really ought to be, he thought.

Damn him for a selfish fool, but he still wanted the opportunity Seattle offered. He wanted it so bad he could taste it. So much it almost wiped out the lingering flavor of Cat's kisses. Almost, but not quite. He could live without the trucking business. He couldn't live without Cat, and the sooner she accepted that, the better for all of them. He turned on his side, facing the rough plank wall. One of the horses stamped restlessly. Jackson groaned and turned away from the noise. He closed his eyes and desperately tried to sleep.

Cat woke him, slipping into his tiny bedroom and sitting on the edge of the cot. He'd heard the door creak and without opening his eyes he could sort out her perfume from the rest of the smells in the barn. Over the bouquet of raw pine, old decaying wood, freshly soaped leather and straw generously laced with manure, her seductive rose scent brought a half smile to his lips.

"Hey, Marine, are you going to sleep all day?"

He opened his eyes. She was one good-looking female. A female he intended to brand with his name despite her objections. Her smoky hair brushed his lips as she leaned over him. He snaked a hand around her neck and pulled her closer, opening his mouth in anticipation of tasting her again. She allowed only a brief touching and a mischievous giggle behind her told him why.

He looked over her shoulder. Joey stood in the doorway, wearing the inevitable blue jeans, topped this

morning with a too-big yellow T-shirt. The faded Green
Bay Packers logo nearly covered the front of the hand-
me-down shirt. A merry grin accented the mischievous
twinkle in her eyes. Past the pride that tightened his
throat, a despairing need to take care of her roughened
his voice. "Hey, Short Stuff. What's up?"

"You're not," Joey said, giggling into one hand and
twisting the other through her hair. She came closer.
"Mommy and I have been up for ages! How come
you're still asleep?"

"I'm not still asleep. I'm talking to you, aren't I? I
couldn't do that if I was asleep."

"But you're still in bed," she protested.

"Leave Jackson alone, Joey. He worked very hard
yesterday. He's entitled to sleep in occasionally." Her
hand carefully hidden from her daughter, Cat stroked
Jackson's stomach.

"Better let me get dressed, sweetheart."

"I suppose I could," she mused, her other hand moving to his belly.

Jackson grabbed both of Cat's hands and held them.
She leaned closer. He groaned. "Have pity, woman!"

Concern brought a tiny frown to Joey's face.
"Mommy, are you hurting Jackson? I mean Daddy."

"No more than he deserves, Joey."

Joey came farther into the room. "You're holding his
hands. Are you holding them too tight?"

Cat grinned. "Maybe a little bit."

"I don't think you should hurt him, Mommy."

Jackson glanced at his daughter. A tender smile came
unbidden to his lips. "We're just playing, honey. Your
mommy likes to play."

"I do, too," Joey said, her eyes glinting as she sprang
onto the cot, landing between Jackson and the wall. She

clambered onto Jackson's stomach, one booted foot landing in the most tender part of his anatomy. He yelped.

Quick tears sprang to her lovely green eyes. "Did I hurt you? I'm sorry. I wanted to play, too."

An unrepentant chuckle escaped from Cat. "Don't worry, Joey. I think you might have kicked Daddy in a sensitive spot, but he'll recover."

Jackson picked Joey off his stomach and allowed her to dangle for a moment in the air, before lowering her just close enough for a quick kiss, then deposited her on the floor beside his cot. "Both of you wicked women get out of here and let me get dressed." He toughened his voice into a bad resemblance of Captain Richards's disgruntled snarl. "Move it!"

Cat winked at him and stood. "Come on, Joey. We'll give him five minutes. That's all, buster. Be sitting at the table in five minutes or no pancakes for you."

"I'll be there, now scram."

He watched them leave, grunting in appreciation of the little extra swing Cat threw into her hips for his benefit. He'd stay. She might as well get used to it. A wave of dejection settled over him like a heavy black storm cloud. And he'd get used to it, too. God help him.

Later, at the breakfast table, Cat slid a second stack of pancakes in front of Jackson. He raised a hand in protest, but she ignored it. "If you don't eat, I'll think you don't like my cooking."

"If you couldn't cook a lick, it wouldn't matter. You have other talents." He gave her another of his patented slow, deliberate winks.

A rush of desire caught her off guard. Her legs trembled and she quickly set the heavy frying pan back on the stove. She took another few seconds to compose herself before turning to face him. "Watch it, Marine. It's far too early in the day for this."

Jackson shifted his weight in the chair. "It's never too early, Cat."

"Well, then, it's too late. Joey will be out of the bathroom in about three minutes."

He exhaled a long woeful sigh. "I'll be good. I promise."

"You're always good. Eat your pancakes."

He stabbed the moist cake and raised a large bit of fluffy blueberry pancake to his lips, paused and studied her over the morsel. "So, have you made up your mind yet?"

"About what?"

"About what day we're going to get married."

Cat ached to tell him yes. The word burned her throat, but she fought the impulse. In a raspy half whisper she replied, "Jackson, please don't."

"Don't what? I just asked what day you'd chosen. I figure during the week would be best. We can ask Luke to feed the horses while we're gone. A couple of days away from this place would do you good."

Cat's happiness fled with Jackson's words. She didn't want to think about marriage and how it would change him. Quietly, she said, "See, that's what I mean. We think about this farm in two totally separate ways. You think it's great to get away from it, and I'm never happier than when I'm here."

He set his fork carefully across the edge of the plate. His voice had a raw edge to it as he said, "Okay, I understand. This is your home and you love it, but for crying out loud, don't you ever get the desire to see someplace else? Even for a few days?"

An awful lump crowded her throat. This was the crux

of their conflict and nothing he said, nothing she wanted would ever change it. "Jackson, I do love you. I don't want you to doubt that for a minute, but we can't make a go of marriage. We're too different in what we want out of life. I want a home and you want to roam. We're just different."

She could swear he had tears in his eyes as he stood and turned his back on her. Cat watched as he shoved tightly fisted hands into his pockets. It didn't work of course. He had to uncurl his hands before he could get them into his tight jeans. Not much room, she thought, as even at this depressing moment, she couldn't help admiring how the faded denim hugged his hips.

Without turning back to her, he asked, "Does that mean you won't marry me?"

A heavy weight settled in her chest. The room suddenly quieted so even the hum of the refrigerator was no longer audible. Only the ticking of the clock broke the oppressive silence. Cat drew in a deep, slow breath, then exhaled just as slowly. She firmed her voice. "I'm sorry, but yes. That's what it means." Despite her attempts at control, her voice cracked. "Oh, Jackson, I tried to tell you all along! You wouldn't listen."

His words sabotaged by throat-closing emotion, Jackson warned, "I won't give in, you know. I'll change your mind."

Cat shook her head, knowing he couldn't change anything. She'd made her decision too many years ago. Her heart ached and she wanted to weep for both of them. She wanted to scream out her defiance at all the fates who'd combined to make both of them miserable. "I love you, Jackson, but I can't marry you. Can't you just accept it? I have," she lied. He stood resolute before her, as stiff and straight as if he were one of the tall pine trees at Needlepoint Rock. She forced herself to continue. "I couldn't stand seeing your regret grow with the years. You'd end up hating me."

"I can't make you believe that won't happen, can I?"

"No."

"Well, then." He sighed deeply, a hugely mournful sound, and still with his back to her, whispered, "I'll be leaving next week then. Friday, I guess. That'll give me enough time with RugRat. I'll get him ready before I go."

Her heart shattered into a million tiny pieces. The light in the kitchen scattered over the pieces and obscured her vision. She couldn't see Jackson through the haze of tears trembling on her lashes. Grateful for that ounce of mercy, she said, "You don't have to. He just needs settling down a bit. He'll be okay."

"Let me," he said, his voice roughened into an emotion-laden plea.

She could see his need without seeing his face. His tightly set shoulders told her. She wanted to change her mind, to assure him that she would marry him and they could be happy, but all that came out was a strangled word. "Yes." She nodded, though with his back to her, he couldn't see that.

"Are you going to tell Joey or shall I?"

Joey would be devastated. Her sprite, who'd already missed a father in her first years of life, would have to grow up without Jackson. There'd be two broken hearts on this shabby farm, but if Jackson stayed, there'd be three miserable people. The same way her father's depression made her mother leave and left her bitterly aware that she was the only reason he continued to get up in the morning and go to a job he hated. Right up till Aunt Jo left them the farm, her father had been a man marking time. Just waiting for Cat to turn eighteen so he'd be free. He'd been happy only the last ten years of his life and that was something Cat could never forget.

"Joey's strong. She'll get over it."

"Joey won't get over shit!" His voice trailed off. "And neither will I." He sighed. "I need to explain to her. She'll think I abandoned her again. I couldn't stand that."

Jackson spoke the truth as he saw it. Her heart broke anew, but stubbornly, she insisted, "You're not leaving her forever, are you? You can call her on the phone, write letters and come back to see her as often as you can get away."

He nodded, started to reply, then shook his head and charged out the door. He didn't look back.

When he left the kitchen, Jackson stumbled forward without watching where he was going. What use to look, when he couldn't see. Trusting his feet to find the way, he set off across the open field.

He wanted to throw himself down on the ground and beat it with his fists like a spoiled child until the pain went away. Which would be never, he knew. He'd never have Cat beside him in their own bed. He'd never have Joey. He wanted them both with a ferocity that tore his heart. With a dull certainty, he knew his life would be empty without her and the child they'd made that long-ago night. He might as well give up now, though he knew Cat was wrong. So wrong.

He couldn't change her mind, though. Wild Cat Darnell didn't change her mind, once she'd decided. She'd doomed both of them—all three of them—to a life without the least bit of happiness in it. Damn her! Damn them both for screwing up their life together so badly.

He rubbed his burning eyes and looked around him at the weed-choked field. He was halfway home. Pop would tell him what to do. Pop would know. The heaviness in his chest eased. His stride lengthened until he was running.

WILL GRAY PACED from the bedroom through the hall to the kitchen, uneasy for no reason he could understand. Out in the barn, Buddy tried to get the old tractor started, while Will, alone in the empty house, fretted. Jackson could have fixed the tractor easily. Engine oil and machined parts were as much a way of life for his son as the green-growing beets dictated the order of Will's day. The thought drew him to the kitchen window. He looked out over the field toward Cat's farm. A couple hundred yards away, Will saw his tall son.

A moment's swift alarm drew his heart to his throat, then it settled back down. If it were trouble—the kind that meant spilled blood and coffins—Jackson would have phoned. No, something else had gone badly awry and he'd find out soon enough.

His son stopped at the edge of the field. He caught his breath before stepping into the yard. Even from here, Will could see the ravaged face, sweat and tear-streaked and his own heart began to pound. What had devastated Jackson? Intense love swept over Will. The boy had always been the apple of his eye, his tall, strong lookalike, the one he'd hoped would love the farm as much as he did. It had taken him many months to forgive Jackson for choosing another way of life. Years to know that Jackson looked like him, but didn't want the same things or think the same way. It had taken both of them too much time to forgive each other and start talking again.

Whatever troubled his son, and it was bound to have

something to do with his pretty little granddaughter, he'd brought it home for his father to sort out. Will did his best to look wise and sure of the answers to life as his son dragged the screen door open.

"Hi, Pop." Jackson ducked his head quickly in a nervous nod.

Will was too busy sorting through all the possible problems Jackson could have to do more than grunt. "Mmmh."

Jackson nodded again. "Yeah…I'm happy to see you, too."

Will went over to the coffeepot and righted two chipped white mugs that were upended, with three other cups, on the faded red kitchen towel next to the coffeepot. He poured strong black coffee into the mugs and handed one to Jackson. "You want to say something to me? You weren't much interested in talking when you left."

Jackson took the coffee cup with a hand that trembled. "You weren't exactly Sammy Sunshine yourself."

Will backed into a kitchen chair and sat down at the table. "Sit," he commanded. He waited until Jackson did so. "You'd try the patience of a saint, boy! I can see you've got something on your mind. Why don't you make an attempt to stay on the subject and tell me why you came over here."

His son stared into the coffee cup as if the answers might possibly be hiding there. "I've been staying over at Cat's place."

Will bit off a laugh. "That's a revelation!" He took a swallow of the coffee. Too damned hot for sure. The tip of his tongue felt raw. "The whole town knows about it."

Jackson looked defiant. "Does the whole town know Cat's little girl is my daughter?"

"Yep." Will totally enjoyed the startled look on his son's face at his own baldfaced lie.

"What?"

It would be a heck of a lot easier to get answers out of Jackson if he wasn't carefully considering every word he said. Jackson had his share of a redhead's temper. It didn't take much pushing. "You might be the only one who didn't know. Always thought you were a slow learner." He waited to see how the boy would reply to his blatant attempt to stir him up.

Jackson's blue eyes could have painted frost on the kitchen windows. They were that cold. "Well, dammit, why didn't you give me a clue?"

Will grunted. "Son, I've been trying to give you a clue since the day you were born. Didn't take too well. Like I said, you're a bit slow some days."

Jackson looked as if he'd like to take his temper out on his father, but settled, instead, for studying the black swirl in his cup. "So you knew?"

Will slowly shook his head. "Can't say I knew for sure, but I always thought Joey was the spit of Cass when she was little."

"Yeah, that's what finally tipped me off."

"She's a pretty little thing."

A reluctant smile lit Jackson's face. "Yeah. She is. Anyway, I wanted to tell you, but I guess I wasted my time."

Will pushed his chair back an inch or two from the table. The movement gave him a moment to decide how to answer. "No. I'm glad to see you, son. Don't let me scare you. I just get a little irritated at you sometimes. I love you, though. Always have. I love that little girl, too.''

"I wasn't scared,'' Jackson said, the lie as plain as daylight on his face.

Will chuckled, a dry raspy sound. "Sure you were. I never stopped being scared of my father until the day they put him in his grave. That's when I finally understood that it wasn't fear, but respect. I loved Daddy too much to be afraid of him, but I respected the hell out of him. Especially when I'd done something I shouldn't and had to tell him.''

Jackson met his eyes. "Well, maybe it's respect for you, but, I've been plain scared to come over here and tell you how badly I messed up.''

Will nodded. "Have you forgiven Cat for not telling you? Has Cat forgiven you?''

"Cat doesn't need my forgiveness. For what its worth, she has it, but I understand why she didn't tell me. She did what she thought best at the time. Second-guessing an eight-year-old decision won't get us anywhere. She forgave me, but I still haven't forgiven myself.''

"What are your plans now?''

"I want to marry Cat. That means settling down here in Engerville for good. I guess I can do that.''

Will stood. He walked over to the coffeepot and poured more of the hot black liquid into the dregs in his cup. He couldn't solve this problem for Jackson, but he hated watching his son make the biggest mistake of his life. He turned to look at him with pitying eyes. "Don't even try, son. You're not a slow learner. That was me pushing for real answers when I said you were, but you ought to think about this some more. Even if the woman you love and your child are there with you, you'll never be happy on a farm.''

"Cat said the same thing, but it's not true. I can't be happy anywhere else than with her."

"If Cat said the same, then maybe you ought to give it some thought, instead of charging ahead with no regard to how your feelings might change. That could do more harm to Cat and Joey than if you'd never come back."

"I know my own mind, Pop."

"You know how you feel now. You don't know how you'll feel ten years from now."

"I know how I'll feel a thousand years from now! This isn't a bad cold. I'm not going to get over it after a few weeks. I really, truly love her. Don't you understand?"

Will nodded. He set his cup down and went over to his son. He put his arms around him. Sometimes that was all a parent could do.

CHAPTER NINETEEN

THE NEXT WEEK PASSED in a blur. Time flew so quickly that Jackson felt as if he were on a carousel, circling past friends, the familiar Engerville farms, the town he grew up in, his father, Cat and Joey, not just once, but a thousand times. Each time he reached out, trying to catch them, the carousel moved faster. He'd be past them and looking back when they came around again. He'd never bring them on board the carousel and he couldn't get off.

Twice he begged Cat to let him stay, and each time his heart shattered when she refused. Green eyes, he thought, swollen from too many tears and so unhappy his begging words stuck in his throat, would be his defining memory of Engerville. Resisting the inevitable is futile, he thought, but I can't give up. I can't.

His last evening arrived with shocking suddenness. He sat on the front porch with a strangely silent Joey and Cat so restless he wanted to yell at her to, for God's sake, please let him stay. Knowing what her answer would be, he choked back his final desperate plea.

Cat had agreed to let him break the news to Joey. She nodded at him. "I'll get us another glass of Kool-Aid. Back in a minute." She paused at the screen door and cast him an uncertain look of entreaty. Her unspoken words were as plain as the setting sun. Don't break my daughter's heart.

"Short Stuff, I've got to tell you something important."

She stood up. "I'm going to the barn. You can tell me later."

Joey was so much like him. Running away instead of facing the truth. This time, he couldn't allow it. It was his last chance to explain to her. "No, Joey. Sit here a while longer. I won't get the chance to talk to you again."

His little daughter stood, her T-shirt stained where she'd spilled drops from her glass of grape Kool-Aid, her yellow shorts wrinkled from sitting on the porch steps. She cast him an angry glare, shook her head with a sudden, agitated motion and strode off toward the barn.

Jackson stood. His heart twisted with pain as he watched her determined back, as stiff and straight as his own, march toward the barn. An unhappy smile barely reached his lips. Maybe she thought her favorite horse would offer her more comfort than the adults in her life. Maybe she was right.

He expected to find her standing in front of Moonshot's stall, petting the filly, but when he opened the barn door, Joey was nowhere in sight. The single light bulb hanging from the rafter cast a raw glow down the concrete runway between the two rows of stalls. Where was she hiding? The tack room door stood slightly ajar. He couldn't think why she'd chosen that spot to hide, but when he opened the door, she was sitting on his bunk crying, her face a mirror of Cat's. Eyes blurred by tears, hair hanging like a curtain, shadowing the soft, little girl cheeks. Lips so sweetly curved he knew he'd remember her like this until the day he died. He'd already broken her heart. *Too late, Cat,* he thought.

"Don't cry, Joey. Please."

"You're going away." It was a statement, not a question.

He couldn't lie and the hardness of his reply choked him. "I have to."

"No, you don't. You don't love me."

He sat down beside her and draped an arm across her narrow shoulders. "I love you more than life itself, little girl. I don't want to leave, but I have to."

She glared through the tears. "You don't love me! I know you don't. If you really, really loved me, you'd stay here with Mommy and me."

"I can't. It's not that simple, Short Stuff."

Her lower lip stuck out in rebellion, she retorted, "I think it is. I think you hate me."

He pulled her trembling, resisting body into his side. Leaning down, he kissed the top of her head. "Hush, baby! Don't think it. Don't say it. I do love you and you know it. I don't love anybody in the whole world as much as I love you."

Suddenly, she thrust both her skinny arms around his waist and held on like a prickly burr. "Don't leave, Daddy! Please don't leave." Her shoulders heaved with her sobs.

He pulled her onto his lap and held her in the shelter of his arms, rocking her back and forth until the sobs quieted. "Don't doubt my love, Joey. I know you don't want me to go and I want to stay, but there are reasons I can't." *Your mother won't let me,* but he couldn't betray Cat with those accusing words.

"Can you take me with you? I want to go with you."

"And leave your mother? Do you want to do that?"

A miserable little face signaled a reluctant negative. "Will you come back?" She whispered her next question, then hurriedly burrowed into his chest without waiting for his answer.

Afraid, he thought. Too afraid of what she'll hear me say. His tough Marine's heart cracked wide open. How easily she penetrated his defenses. "As often as I can. And always on Christmas. I promise you, I'll never miss a Christmas with you, Short Stuff."

She turned her head left and right, wiping her runny nose on his T-shirt. "Promise?" she asked, her words muffled against his chest.

"I promise." She was such a warm little bundle in his arms. How could he leave her? How could he leave her mother? God, why are you doing this to me? I can't stand it.

BERTIE LOOKED unusually lovely tonight, Will Gray thought. Her blond hair had some gray mixed in. Not enough to matter, but enough to signal that life seemed bent on passing them both by. Maybe he should tell her what was on his mind. Helen had been gone long enough. It sure wouldn't disgrace her memory for him to love somebody else. She'd be the last person to want him to spend his life alone.

Cass was in Minneapolis and Jackson would be gone tomorrow. This place wasn't going to be much fun after Bertie left for Florida. Only four more months to enjoy her caustic essays on Engerville's inhabitants. His stomach flipped over and his throat tightened uncomfortably.

For a man who hated gossip, he sure did appreciate her acid asides about the misdeeds of her neighbors. He'd miss her, for sure. Will had just opened his mouth to tell her as much when his son's footsteps on the porch stopped him. Damn, he thought. That boy can be a regular pain.

He took his gaze off Bertie, standing at the stove, to glower at his son.

"Evening, Pop. Bertie."

"Isn't it a little late to come calling?"

"You cease to amaze me, Pop. I'm leaving on a Greyhound bus very early tomorrow morning. I thought you might want to say goodbye."

Will shrugged in resignation. "Of course, I do. I'm glad you stopped by. We'd both be disappointed if you hadn't. Right, Bertie?" She nodded. He continued, "Sit down, then. Bertie and I were just fixing to have a piece of her lemon cake. It's not more'n ten minutes out of the oven. Makes my mouth water just to think about it. There's a fresh jug of milk in the reefer. Why don't you pour us a glass to go with?"

"I'm not hungry," Jackson protested.

"Do it anyway," Will ordered. He could tell by his son's shadowed eyes that he was grieving over leaving. Life never seemed to get any easier for anybody.

Bertie sat down beside him and Jackson took the chair at the head of the table. Will forked a big piece of still-warm cake into his mouth. The flavor and sweetness mixed with the tart bits of lemon peel she had grated into it reminded him of her so much that, in a lightning-swift second of realization, he knew he'd have to figure out a way to convince her to stay in Engerville. He used to be a persuasive kind of guy with the ladies. He surely ought to be able to convince one sour old maid that love could be sweet again. Once more, his son interrupted his thoughts.

"Pop, do you think you could talk to Cat for me? She won't believe me when I tell her I can be happy here."

"Sounds like Cat is a bit brighter than you, boy. If

everybody was meant to be a farmer, the world wouldn't have so damn many used car salesmen.''

"I love her."

"If you really love her, then things will work out."

Jackson's eyes shot blue flames at his father. "*If* I love her? Cat and Joey are my whole life! I can't leave them. I just can't."

"You're not the first man who ever loved a woman he couldn't have." Will glanced at Bertie who kept her head down, watching her plate like she thought the lemon cake might get up and walk out the door. "Can't you talk her into going with you?"

"She won't leave Engerville," Jackson said, his words ragged as if torn from his throat. "She thinks...it would hurt Joey to uproot her from all her friends."

"That daddy of Cat's never settled down until he came to Engerville. I suppose that's why she hates moving so much. Never met anybody that loved horses the way he did. I can't think why he wasted so much of his life living in cities."

"I don't care about her father! I just care about Cat. And Joey."

Will thought for a long, depressing moment. "Son, you have to think about her father, because Cat is part of him. Her life before she came to Engerville probably explains why she won't leave. Just like your life on a farm explains why you have to leave."

"Pop, I can't stand it. I can't." Jackson's voice broke. "I have to have her! I never wanted anything in my entire life as much as this. You have all the answers. Tell me how I can make this work."

"Jackson...boy...if I knew how to solve all your problems, I would. I don't know as much as you do about how to fix this particular problem. You've got to do this one by yourself. I can't help you.''

"I know what he can do,'' Bertha spoke up, her low voice startling Will and Jackson.

They looked at her as if she'd suddenly grown two heads. Will cleared his throat. "Ah, you do? Well, now.'' He paused, then aware of the despair in his son's gaze, he murmured, doubtfully, "Go ahead, then, Bertha. Tell the boy.''

THE MOON LIT UP the night so much that after Cat closed the door behind her, she didn't bother to turn on her flashlight. She walked down to the corral, hoisted herself up to the top rail and leaned back against the old oak tree which didn't have more than a dozen good limbs left and should long ago have been cut down.

Nostalgic memories insinuated themselves into her head. Insistent pictures of herself at fourteen, climbing the tree and finding a perch on a lower limb so she could look over the fields toward Jackson Gray's home. One unforgettable vision of herself at eighteen, sitting under the tree late one evening and planning how she'd raise her child by herself. A happier picture of Joey at three, calling in a high, childish voice to "Go up, Mommy! Go up!''

She couldn't bring herself to cut the old tree down. Cat shook her head in bemusement. What silly memories sustained her. If it weren't so sad, she'd laugh at herself. Instead she looked at her wrist. The hands on her watch crawled with unbearable slowness toward midnight.

Tomorrow Jackson would leave and a day or two later, when Joey realized her father really wasn't coming back, the knowledge would devastate her. Cat didn't lie to herself. She was too practical for meaningless lies, especially to herself. Tonight might be her last chance to love Jackson, to make love to him. She wouldn't take a chance on his misguided chivalry. It might cause him to go to his bunk in the barn instead of into her arms. If tonight was to be their last night together, then she planned on storing up enough memories to last her through a lot of cold winters.

As the moon climbed higher in the sky, she thought about his lips on hers, his arms holding her close, the strength of his desire. A fearful, restless urging raced over her. What if he decided to spend the night with his father? That would be reasonable, considering the long rift in their relationship. It would be natural for Will Gray to keep his son close on his last night in Engerville. Please, God, not tonight, she whispered to the breeze. Give me this one memory. Then she saw the dark shadow moving across the field toward her.

Slipping down from the fence, she kept her gaze on the shadow slowly taking shape. Eagerly, she started toward him. He saw her at the same time and increased the length of his strides. A moment later she was in his arms.

"Aren't you up a little late?" he asked, brushing back a strand of hair from her face, his touch gentle.

His nearness caused her heart to pound. Her reply was nearly breathless. "I waited for you."

Jackson grinned. "You're sweet. I'm glad you did."

He held her close against the heat from his body. She nestled into the warmth. His arms tightened, then suddenly released her.

His face unusually solemn, he said, "I had a long talk with Pop."

"You did? I mean, of course you did. How is he?"

Jackson looked very relaxed, as if a weight had been

removed from his shoulders. "Great! Really good. I don't think he'll have any problems running the place now. That's one thing I won't have to worry about when I'm in Seattle."

"When you're in Seattle? That sounds so final."

"It's what you wanted. Isn't it?" he asked.

His words were unexpectedly cool. She stiffened her spine and forced out a reply that sounded like an excuse. "Not what I wanted, but the only answer for both of us."

He stepped away from her, although his hand lingered on her waist. "You'll be pleased to know Pop agrees with you. He said I was never cut out to be a farmer."

She nodded, although the bitter taste of his casual words lingered. "It's best this way."

His lips brushed her ear. "Darling Cat. You're practical, aren't you?"

Reluctantly, she nodded. "I've had to be."

He shrugged his shoulders as if dismissing the subject. "I won't pretend I'm happy about it, but I've accepted your decision. I can't fight you and my father."

Was this really what she wanted? And could she stand it when she got it? "You'll be back to see us. It's not forever."

"Oh sure," he said, squeezing her shoulder with a casual hand. "I'll write, too. We'll keep in touch."

"And telephone calls. We can talk on the telephone."

"Yes, but probably not as often. Long distance is expensive. I won't be making much money the first year or two. Say, do you have a computer?"

"No, I don't. Why do you ask?"

"We could e-mail. I used the one in the barracks a lot. Maybe you should think about getting an old computer. It doesn't have to be much to access the Internet."

He sounded almost cheerful, Cat thought, her heart sinking. "What a good idea," she agreed, without much enthusiasm.

"I'm glad I thought of that." He glanced at the night sky, where clouds were moving in from the west. "I'll bet it rains before morning. That'll be good, won't it? Dad was hoping for rain. Bertie, too." He smiled at her. "Morning isn't too far away, is it? You'd better get to bed. I'm sleepy, too." He stretched his mouth wide in an enormous, jaw-cracking yawn.

"I thought...nothing. You're right. It's late."

He bent down and kissed her softly on the lips. "Good night, Cat. Don't worry so much. You were right. Things will work out okay. Go on, now. I'll wait until you get inside before I head out to the barn."

He touched her lips with his finger, and grinned; a smoky shadow smile Cat didn't understand at all. Where were the tears he'd barely been able to suppress for the last week? How could he be so casual? This was their last night together. Didn't he understand that? Why did he act as if it meant nothing?

Maybe it didn't mean anything to him. The shocking thought seared through her. Jackson intended to walk away from her with a smile on his face. He didn't love her. Not the same way she loved him. He couldn't love her and be this casual about leaving. Practical Cat tightened her grip on her emotions. This was the memory that would sustain her in the lonely years ahead. Jackson, all too casual about going away, leaving her behind to live with a broken heart. Again. A lump the size of Needlepoint Rock lodged in her throat. Bleak misery seeped through her soul.

Cat walked away from Jackson Gray.

CHAPTER TWENTY

IT STARTED RAINING about three in the morning, a monotonous weeping punctuated by the crash of thunderbolts. Cat lay awake, her eyes as dry as the dust soaking up the raindrops. The hurt inside her swelled with each passing moment, until her entire body ached with pain.

She'd pretty much forgiven Jackson for leaving her the first time. They were both so young and he didn't know she loved him or that their tryst had resulted in a baby. This was different. It didn't matter that she'd made the choice for Jackson to go, or that her blaming him was irrational. She never doubted that he loved Joey, but his feelings toward her were as shallow as Indian Creek at the height of this summer's drought.

How else could he have smiled as he wished her a good night? Ha! What a laugh. A *good* night with a broken heart wasn't possible. She'd thought they could spend this time comforting each other, loving each other. How could she have misjudged him so badly?

Cat tossed restlessly from side to side. Her brain insisted on showing her a medley of pictures. Jackson's anger sparking his eyes to frosty blue when he found out she'd kept his daughter's birth a secret from him. Jackson carrying Joey back from Indian Creek, a look of unbearable tenderness on his face. The way his eyes glittered with passion when he made love to her under the willow tree, his hair darkened by shadows, his strong profile traced by moonlight. Flashing that "dare you" smile when he teased her into making love in the middle of the day. The mind-picture that gave her secret reassurance of his love; his jealous anger at Luke. And always with her, a still-sharp memory of the fourteen-year-old boy with hair so bright it looked as if the sun had woven its light through it…the prince who welcomed her to a fairy-tale permanent home in Engerville.

The lump in her throat threatened to dissolve in tears, but she held her emotions in check by sheer force of will. She'd cried all the tears she intended to shed for Jackson Gray on a long, lonely night years past. Why cry when no one was there to comfort you? The question brought back a memory she'd thought long forgotten. Her father picking up stakes and leaving a too-temporary home yet again. And Cat remembered huddling against blankets in the back seat of a rusty brown Maverick, the hum of tires on pavement gradually lulling her to a restless sleep.

For a long time, Cat lay awake, listening to the harsh roll of thunder and the persistent sad tapping of rain against the window, until finally, she drifted off.

"Mommy, are you awake?"

The hesitant question prodded at Cat's consciousness. As she always did when something happened to trouble her, Joey had crawled into Cat's bed, seeking her mother's comfort. This morning, Cat had no comfort to give. She cracked open a reluctant eyelid. Her daughter curled up beside her, looking lost in her pink cotton pajama shorts and matching top. Cat draped an arm around her kitten. "Hey, Joey. Are you awake already? What time is it?"

"Almost seven. Are you ready to get up yet?"

Cat rubbed her face sleepily. "Not really, but I have to get up anyway."

"Daddy is leaving today," Joey announced solemnly.

"I know, sweetheart."

"I don't want him to go. Make him stay, Mommy."

"Honey, Jackson likes different things than you and I do. He doesn't want to live on a farm. He wouldn't be happy here."

Joey's eyes glittered with unshed tears. She sighed, a very grown-up sound of resignation. "Will we ever see him again?"

"Of course, darling. He'll come back to visit. He promised."

"I still want him to stay."

Having no other words with which to comfort Joey, Cat wrapped her arms around her and brought the small, thin body into hers. The two clung together for a long moment, then Cat pushed her away. "Go brush your teeth and get dressed. We're going to drive Jackson into Engerville to catch the bus and we don't have a lot of time."

The trip into town was too long, and at the same time, too short. Jackson kept his arm across the back of the seat, his hand touching her shoulder, except when he dropped it down to caress Joey, who sat unmoving between them. Occasionally, he bent his head and brushed his lips across her hair. Joey's face remained pale with strain. She didn't return Jackson's touches, although she didn't shrink from them, either.

Cat thought the whole scene rather pathetic and decided, resentfully, that she wouldn't buy into it. She kept a determined smile on her face, which matched the very natural, casual smile that stayed on Jackson's sensual lips. It bothered her that he didn't seem at all upset to be leaving them, but she didn't intend to let him know it. Pride might be all she'd have left at the end of this day.

After he bought his ticket, Jackson came over to stand in front of her. For the first time, he seemed hesitant. He pulled an envelope from his pocket and handed it to her.

"What's this?" she asked.

"With this and what you got for the horses, it ought to be enough to cover your back mortgage payments and carry you through the winter. In a month or two, I'll be drawing a paycheck and I'll start sending you as much as I can."

"The money from the sale of the horses will pay the bank. You don't have to do this, Jackson. I never wanted to take money from you."

"For once, let me help. If you'd told me earlier...I would have."

"I never doubted you."

He leaned over and brushed her trembling lips with his own, stepped back and shrugged. "Past is past. No point in raking it over the coals. They're boarding my bus now. I have to go. I'll write."

He stooped down and picked up Joey, hugged her close for a long, breath-stopping moment, then set her down. "Take care of your mom, Short Stuff. I'm not going to forget you, so don't be sad. I'll be back."

Joey looked as if she wanted to throw a temper tantrum. Her lower lip stuck out a mile and her eyes were mutinous with suppressed anger. But when she spoke, her plea was little-girl heart-wrenching. "When? When are you coming back?"

"As soon as I can, Joey. Keep the faith, honey. I won't let you down. I promise."

He turned to leave, then whirled back, grabbed Cat

and crushed her body to his. His lips covered hers with devastating impact, as if this kiss was all he'd ever have of her. He made it last a full minute, his tongue tracing her lips until she opened for him, sweeping her mouth, teasing and taking her essence. Remember me, his kiss said. Remember this. When he released her, she felt faint. Her knees trembled, as he stared down at her, memorizing her, memorizing her lips. At last, he turned away and Cat, bereft, was left to watch his retreating figure.

Then, too quickly, he stepped aboard the Greyhound bus, and a moment later, it pulled away from the curb. Cat lowered the hand she couldn't stop from waving at the departing bus until it was out of sight. She looked down at Joey. Tears trickled down her daughter's cheeks. A weight in her chest threatened to crush her. Despair engulfed both of them. She couldn't let that happen. "Today, sweetheart, it's all right to cry. We're both sad. But tomorrow…tomorrow, we have to get on with our lives."

Joey, so like Cat, nodded sadly. She understood.

THE HOTEL ROOM WAS neither luxurious nor overly cheap. Adequate, Jackson thought. Certainly better than sleeping in a barn, wasn't it? It depressed him to realize his answer to that question was so ambiguous. He'd been in Seattle for two miserable days and it took all his willpower every moment of those days to keep from reaching out to pick up the phone. He'd give what remained of his stake to hear Cat's voice say hello. He'd give his life to hold her so tightly she'd never get away. Had Joey regained her anger at him? Would he ever be able to establish a normal father-daughter relationship with her? He glanced again at the phone beside his chair.

Determinedly, he kept his hands wrapped around the paper cup of too-strong coffee Juan had picked up in the kiosk next to the lobby. His friend had been speaking for several minutes, but Jackson's wandering mind couldn't focus on his words. For the third time, he asked, "What was that, Juan?"

His friend looked at him with deep pity. "I just asked how long you were staying in Seattle, my friend."

"I didn't say I was leaving."

"You didn't have to. Why did you come here anyway? You're totally miserable."

He swirled the dregs in the cup, then looked at Juan with a wry grin twisting his lips. "It's all part of my master plan. Did you think I didn't know what I was doing?"

"Red, my old buddy, you're so full of it, you stink. You no more have a plan than that disgusting wallpaper does." He waved a hand at the lime-striped pink wallpaper covering one wall. He leaned back against the olive-green bedspread, propping his head with the other hand.

"Well, I do," Jackson muttered, sounding unsure even to himself.

"What is it, then? Share your thoughts, Red."

"I've already talked to Marty. He's okay with it."

"Okay with what?" Juan asked, impatient.

"With my backing out of our agreement. I can't stay here, Juan. I can't. I left too much behind me in Engerville."

Juan sighed. "I figured as much. Your one chance to become a filthy rich capitalist and you blow it."

"Some things are more important than money, Juan. My family is my first priority."

"It's okay, Red." Juan's voice softened. "I wish I

had a family to sacrifice this opportunity for. I envy you.''

Jackson gulped the cold dregs left in his cup, avoiding a reply as long as he could. When he could put it off no longer, he looked at Juan and shrugged. ''I'm ready to go back and make a home in Engerville, but it's not a done deal yet. I still have to persuade Cat to let me stay with her and she's totally against it.''

''She loves you, doesn't she?''

''I think so. Yes, she does.''

''Then, it'll be okay.''

''That's what Bertie said.''

''Bertie?''

''My father's friend. She said the same thing.''

JOEY AGREED WITH Cat that they had to put Jackson's leaving behind them and go on with their lives. She agreed, but she didn't do it. Twice Cat caught her crying in her room. On the third day after Jackson's departure, she went to the barn in search of her daughter and found her standing next to Moonshot with a brush in hand, but its purpose forgotten. Her face buried in Moonshot's silky mane, shoulders heaving, the little girl poured out her grief to the one soul who wouldn't tell her not to cry.

Cat's eyes filled with sympathetic tears. She walked over to Joey and patted her on the shoulder. ''It's okay, Joey. I spend too much time bawling into my own pillow. Teddy Bear, I'm so sorry you miss him. I do, too.''

Joey left the horse and flung herself at her mother. As Cat held the tiny figure close, Joey sniffled in her ear.

''Please, Mommy, make him come back! Please.''

''I can't do that, Joey.''

''But you told him he couldn't stay. You said he

wouldn't be happy. I think he'd be happy. Please, Mommy?" Joey drew back, her anxious face pleading as hard as her words did.

Cat owed it to Jackson to tell his daughter the truth. "You're right, baby. I did say he couldn't stay. You know why. Jackson doesn't like living on a farm the way you and I do. He wouldn't be happy. Would you want him to be unhappy with us, or happy in Seattle where he can drive a truck?"

Another wash of tears welled in Joey's eyes. She blinked and they rolled down her face. "I want him to be happy, Mommy," she whispered.

"Me, too." She struggled with her answer, but finally replied. "Then we have to let him go."

"Can't we go with him? I'll be happy in Seattle, honest. I want my daddy!"

If Cat thought her heart couldn't ache any more, she was definitely wrong. She swallowed hard to get past the ache, so she could comfort her baby. "Oh, Joey, this is our home. We can't leave."

Joey glared. "I think home is where Daddy is. I want to be with him."

Cat stared at the defiant pose her daughter struck. Lower lip outthrust, green eyes glowing with tears, and small fists on nonexistent hips. "You'd have to leave the horses, Teddy Bear. And Tommy Karl. Could you be happy without them?"

Joey nodded vigorously. "Tommy Karl would understand. He knows I want a daddy. I'll come back and see him when I get bigger. Couldn't we take the horses with us?"

"No, honey. I'm sorry. Farms cost too much. This is the only place we'd be able to keep the horses."

''Then I'd rather have Daddy than the dumb old horses.''

A thrill of excitement shot through Cat. She pushed it down. ''Even Moonshot?''

Joey reached out to pat Moonshot's shoulder. Her face became a study in conflicting emotions, then she nodded. ''I love Daddy and I want to be with him. I'll miss Moonshot, but I miss Daddy more.''

Rising hope made Cat dizzy. She missed Jackson more than she would miss the farm, too. More than she'd ever thought she could. The shabby, old farm seemed empty without him. The weather-worn buildings were just buildings, not the stuff of dreams, not a child's fairy-tale home. Not her home.

Did Joey realize what she asked? Was she mature enough to make the decision to give up everything she'd known? ''You're only eight years old. Are you sure you won't be sorry?''

Practical Joey answered the way her mother would have, if she'd been eight. ''I might *want* to be sorry sometimes, because I'll miss Tommy Karl and the horses and the farm, but I really, really promise I won't be. Let's go to Seattle and find him, Mommy. Please?''

''Home is where Jackson is, huh? Maybe you're right, darling. I just wanted you to have a stable home. And I wanted it for me, too.'' She paused. ''Maybe I wanted it more for me than I did for you.'' She remembered the little girl in the rusty Ford Maverick. ''I only thought I was making the decision for you. Since Jackson left, this hasn't been much of a home for either of us. It's just empty buildings. Maybe we really should go to Seattle.''

Joey's lips formed a tentative, tear-streaked smile. ''Can we go? Really?''

In one moment of heart-stopping insight, Cat realized

she'd made a tragic mistake by sending Jackson away and thinking she could make Joey happy by herself. A home that stays put wasn't the most important thing in life. Home, for Joey, as well as herself, was in the heart. Joey's heart belonged with Jackson and her heart belonged with the tall Marine, too. "Never mind, baby. Finish brushing Moonshot. I'm going back to the house and call a couple of people I happen to know are looking for a farm to buy."

"Really, Mommy? Really? We can go to Seattle?"

"I think so." Cat's voice trembled. "Yes! Yes! We'll go to Seattle and find Jackson." If only she understood that last kiss. If only Jackson wanted them as badly as they wanted him.

THREE DAYS LATER, Cat stood beside a pile of mismatched suitcases, urging Joey to check her room one more time for any item she might have forgotten. Joey, wearing a new white dress trimmed with purple violets, looked excited and very happy. Cat fought to keep her own happiness contained. They still had to find Jackson and make him understand that they wouldn't regret leaving the farm. It might not be easy. She'd worked awfully hard to convince him it was the only place she *could* be happy.

Tonight they'd be in Seattle. With luck, they'd find Jackson tomorrow and nothing would part them again. Cat looked at her watch and called out, "Hurry, Joey. We don't want to miss the plane."

Joey ran back into the living room, holding out a necklace to her mother. "Look what you forgot, Mom!"

"Mother's jade necklace! Thanks, honey. Where did you find it?" Seeing the necklace brought back sad memories for Cat. Her mother had abandoned her husband and daughter, but maybe she'd just made the wrong decision and fate hadn't allowed her time to correct her mistake. With a little luck and a prayer or two, Car intended to correct her own mistake.

"On the bathroom counter. You'd be really sad to lose your necklace, Mom."

Cat laughed as she realized a sudden truth. "I'd be devastated, but not nearly as sad as I've been since Jackson left. Things aren't as important as people and we won't miss anything as much as we missed Jackson. I think we both set a record for gloom, Joey."

Joey giggled. "Not anymore. We're happy now, aren't we, Mom?"

The tinkling chimes of the doorbell interrupted their shared moment. "It's probably someone wanting to say goodbye."

She swung the door open. Will and Bertie stood on the small porch.

Will spoke before she could say hello. "I know we said our goodbyes when you called to tell me what you intended to do, but I couldn't let you leave without coming over."

Cat smiled. "Will, I'm so glad you did. And you, too, Bertie! Come in, both of you."

Joey smiled at the farmer. "Hi, Mr. Gray. We're going to Seattle!"

"I know, honey. That's why I came over, but don't call me 'Mr. Gray.' Call me 'Grandpa.'"

Joey looked at Cat. Cat nodded.

"Grandpa. You're really my grandpa, aren't you?"

Will struggled with his bad knee, but managed to kneel next to her. "Yes, I'm really your grandpa and I'm going to miss you like crazy."

"Why don't you come with us then? Mommy won't

mind. Will you, Mommy?'' Joey looked entreatingly at her mother.

"I wouldn't mind in the least. I love you, Will. I wish you could come, too.''

"Now, we can't all leave North Dakota, can we, Bertie?''

"Somebody has to look after the sugar beets, Joey. But Grandpa Will and I have already decided to come out and visit you soon.''

Startled, Cat looked at the older couple. Bertie stood just behind Will, with one hand on his shoulder. Her question must have been evident on her face, for Will nodded.

"Oh, boy!'' Joey threw her arms around Will Gray and hugged him tightly.

Will's arms enfolded his granddaughter. Moisture blurred Cat's vision. She swiped at her eyes. "I wish I didn't have to break this up, but Joey and I have to go.''

Before Will could answer, the doorbell rang again.

"Now who could that be? If we don't leave in the next few minutes, Joey, we're going to miss our plane.''

Joey turned loose from her newfound grandpa. "Tell them, Mommy. Just tell them they have to go away.''

Cat turned, her voice very firm. "I certainly will, darling.''

She opened the door.

Jackson stood on the porch. Through the lattice, the morning sun cast diamond-patterned shapes of broken light and shadow on his hair. Wearing a chocolate sport coat, with matching tie and a cream-colored shirt, he looked as pale and hopeful as Joey had when she'd pleaded to go after him.

Behind her, Cat heard Will's muttered aside to Bertie.

"That was a good idea of yours to come over and make sure they didn't leave before Jackson got here."

And Bertie's quiet answer. "Wherever she went, he would have followed."

Later, Cat thought, she'd have to think about that snippet of conversation and figure out what it meant. Right now, she was way too busy. Her heart soared to the skies. A tremulous smile came unbidden. "Jackson?"

He nodded. "Yes. It's me."

At any other time, Cat would have thought their exchange of the obvious nonsensical. "You came back?"

"I owe Bertie for the idea, because I was too upset to think of anything I could do to make you believe I really wanted to stay. She said she'd made the wrong decision, years ago, when her boyfriend wanted her to go away with him and she'd regretted it all her life. She always wished she'd had a second chance to give the right answer. She told me to wait two weeks, so you'd know your own heart, but I couldn't stand it another day. I hope this is long enough, because there's no way I could stand another minute without you. Is Bertie right?"

"She's right, but none of that matters now. We're going to Seattle with you."

Over her shoulder, he saw the suitcases, his father and Bertie. Cat knew the instant he realized the house had an abandoned air that gave those suitcases an unmistakable meaning. He shook his head in negation. "I had to come back. We're all staying in Engerville. Unpack your bags, Cat. Joey will always have a home here. Please say you'll let me stay and help make this home for her."

Suddenly, a small ball of fury pushed between the two adults. *"No!"* Joey screamed. "We're going to Seattle to be with you! Mommy says you won't be happy here and I want you to be happy!''

Jackson wrapped his daughter in his arms. His lips brushed her hair as he said, ''Oh, sweetheart, I want you to have a good steady home, the way your mom wants.''

Cat interrupted, the words bursting joyously from her. ''Jackson, our home with you will be steady! Nothing could be more stable than the place we have in your heart. I know that now. I should have known it from the beginning, but I needed my daughter to point out the obvious for me.''

Jackson stood, though his hand remained on Joey, holding her close. He reached out and pulled Cat to him. ''Are you sure, Wild Cat? Are you really sure?''

Cat leaned back so she could see his face. His eyes were diamond-bright with tears. Or were those her own tears? ''I'm sure, Jackson. We can both have our dream. This place has been empty without you. It's not been a home at all. Home is where you are. I know that now.''

Jackson reached down and lifted Joey up to rest against his shoulder. ''Dreams are important, but I would have given up mine for you and Joey and been delighted to do it. Believe me, Cat, because it's important. I want both of you so badly nothing else counts. Nothing! I'll stay here if you want me to, or we'll go to Seattle. The place doesn't matter. You do. And Joey does.''

Cat brushed his cheek with her left hand and traced his lips with the other. Her smile felt as if it spanned her entire face. She nodded, unable to speak.

''I'll see that both of you have your dreams. I promise. I'll make you a home so rock solid it will last a lifetime, sweetheart. And Joey,'' he kissed his daughter's cheek, ''if your mom really means it when she says she wants to go to Seattle, I'll find a place where you can keep

Moonshot. We're not leaving that pretty little filly behind.''

Joey's eyes lit up with disbelieving delight. "Honest? Mommy said the horses couldn't come with us."

Jackson grinned. "Not all of them, honey, but Moonshot is special. We'll find a home for her, too." He leaned toward Cat as if pulled by a magnet and brushed her lips tenderly. "We started out wrong, Cat, but I'll make it up to both of you."

Cat whispered her reply. "We started out right, Jackson. We got lost along the way, but we'll keep that beginning for the rest of our lives."

He hugged her so tightly she couldn't breathe, but it didn't matter. Nothing mattered but Jackson Gray and the daughter who clung happily to both of them.

Behind them, Will Gray swallowed hard. He reached out to Bertie and pulled her into his arms. "There's an awful lot of hugging going on here. I better make sure you get your share."

Her sweet voice replied softly. "I knew you'd get around to me, if I waited."

Witchcraft, deceit and more... all FREE from

HARLEQUIN®

INTRIGUE®

in October!

This exclusive offer is valid only in October,
only from the Harlequin Intrigue series!
To receive your **TWO FREE BOOKS** by bestselling romantic
suspense authors **Jayne Ann Krentz** and **Jasmine Cresswell**, send
us 3 proofs of purchase from any 3 Harlequin Intrigue®
books sold during the month of October.

*Proofs of purchase can be found in all
October 2003 Harlequin Intrigue books.*

Must be postmarked no later than November 30, 2003.

Visit us at www.tryintrigue.com

HIPOPOC03

✂

Your opinion is important to us! Please take a few moments to share your thoughts with us about your experiences with Harlequin and Silhouette books. Your comments will be very useful in ensuring that we deliver books you love to read.
Please take a few minutes to complete the questionnaire, then send it to us at the address below.

Send your completed questionnaires to:
Harlequin/Silhouette Reader Survey, P.O. Box 9046, Buffalo, NY 14269-9046

---

1. As you may know, there are many different lines under the Harlequin and Silhouette brands. Each of the lines is listed below. Please check the box that most represents your reading habit for each line.

Line	Currently read this line	Do not read this line	Not sure if I read this line
Harlequin American Romance	❑	❑	❑
Harlequin Duets	❑	❑	❑
Harlequin Romance	❑	❑	❑
Harlequin Historicals	❑	❑	❑
Harlequin Superromance	❑	❑	❑
Harlequin Intrigue	❑	❑	❑
Harlequin Presents	❑	❑	❑
Harlequin Temptation	❑	❑	❑
Harlequin Blaze	❑	❑	❑
Silhouette Special Edition	❑	❑	❑
Silhouette Romance	❑	❑	❑
Silhouette Intimate Moments	❑	❑	❑
Silhouette Desire	❑	❑	❑

2. Which of the following best describes why you bought *this book?* One answer only, please.

the picture on the cover	❑	the title	❑
the author	❑	the line is one I read often	❑
part of a miniseries	❑	saw an ad in another book	❑
saw an ad in a magazine/newsletter	❑	a friend told me about it	❑
I borrowed/was given this book	❑	other: _____	❑

3. Where did you buy *this book?* One answer only, please.

at Barnes & Noble	❑	at a grocery store	❑
at Waldenbooks	❑	at a drugstore	❑
at Borders	❑	on eHarlequin.com Web site	❑
at another bookstore	❑	from another Web site	❑
at Wal-Mart	❑	Harlequin/Silhouette Reader	❑
at Target	❑	Service/through the mail	
at Kmart	❑	used books from anywhere	❑
at another department store or mass merchandiser	❑	I borrowed/was given this book	❑

4. On average, how many Harlequin and Silhouette books do you buy at one time?

I buy _____ books at one time	❑
I rarely buy a book	❑

MRQ403HSR-1A

5. How many times per month do you shop for any *Harlequin and/or Silhouette* books?
   One answer only, please.

1 or more times a week	❏	a few times per year	❏
1 to 3 times per month	❏	less often than once a year	❏
1 to 2 times every 3 months	❏	never	❏

6. When you think of your ideal heroine, which *one* statement describes her the best?
   One answer only, please.

She's a woman who is strong-willed		She's a desirable woman	❏
She's a woman who is needed by others		She's a powerful woman	❏
She's a woman who is taken care of		She's a passionate woman	❏
She's an adventurous woman		She's a sensitive woman	❏

7. The following statements describe types or genres of books that you may be
   interested in reading. Pick *up to 2 types* of books that you are most interested in.

I like to read about truly romantic relationships	❏
I like to read stories that are sexy romances	❏
I like to read romantic comedies	❏
I like to read a romantic mystery/suspense	❏
I like to read about romantic adventures	❏
I like to read romance stories that involve family	❏
I like to read about a romance in times or places that I have never seen	❏
Other: _____	❏

*The following questions help us to group your answers with those readers who are
similar to you. Your answers will remain confidential.*

8. Please record your year of birth below.

   19 _____

9. What is your marital status?

   single ❏   married ❏   common-law ❏   widowed ❏
   divorced/separated ❏

10. Do you have children 18 years of age or younger currently living at home?

    yes ❏   no ❏

11. Which of the following best describes your employment status?

    employed full-time or part-time ❏   homemaker ❏   student ❏
    retired ❏   unemployed ❏

12. Do you have access to the Internet from either home or work?

    yes ❏   no ❏

13. Have you ever visited eHarlequin.com?

    yes ❏   no ❏

14. What state do you live in?

    _____

15. Are you a member of Harlequin/Silhouette Reader Service?

    yes ❏   Account # _____   no ❏   MRQ403HSR-1B

HARLEQUIN *Super*ROMANCE

What if you discovered that all you ever wanted were the things you left behind?

GOING BACK

The House on Creek Road
by Caron Todd
(Harlequin Superromance #1159)

When Elizabeth Robb left Three Creeks, she never expected to return. Even after all these years, she's not ready to face her painful past, and only a request from her elderly grandmother could bring her back to town. She hopes her arrival will escape notice, but she doesn't really expect that to happen—especially once she meets her grandmother's neighbor, a mysterious newcomer named Jack McKinnon.

On sale October 2003

In January 2004 look for...

Past, Present and a Future
by Janice Carter
(Harlequin Superromance #1178)

Available wherever Harlequin Superromance books are sold.

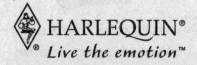

HARLEQUIN®
Live the emotion™